WAKE-UP CALL

GOOD MORNING DEVLIN. SHIP STATUS
FOUR HUNDRED AND SIXTY-TWO YEARS
INTO MISSION. SHIP PERSONNEL CUR-
RENTLY AWAKE—ONE. IDENTITY JOHN
DEVLIN. REASONS FOR AWAKENING.
OVERALL HUMAN GUIDANCE REQUIRED
DURING FORTHCOMING FLY-BY . . .

*The starship was approaching another
planet on its long journey through the
galaxy. John Devlin and his fellow passengers had to find a suitable planet
to colonize. And time was running
out . . .*

Also by James White
Published by Ballantine Books:

ALL JUDGMENT FLED

AMBULANCE SHIP

LIFEBOAT

STAR SURGEON

THE ALIENS AMONG US

MAJOR OPERATION

HOSPITAL STATION

DEADLY LITTER

THE
DREAM
MILLENNIUM

James White

A Del Rey Book

BALLANTINE BOOKS • NEW YORK

A Del Rey Book
Published by Ballantine Books

A slightly different version of this novel
was serialized in *Galaxy Magazine,* Copyright © 1973,
UPD Publishing Corporation.

ISBN 0-345-30417-9

Manufactured in the United States of America

First Edition: June 1974
Second Printing: May 1982

Cover art by Rick Sternbach

THE
DREAM
MILLENNIUM

1

His AWAKENING WAS like walking out of a warm room and into a snowstorm. The dream, what little he could remember of it, had not been entirely pleasant but it had been warm. He tried desperately to hold onto it, to pull it back and around him again like a warm blanket that was slipping off his bed, to do anything that would hold back this awful heartstopping cold.

But his mind was working, which meant that his blood was carrying sugar and oxygen to his thawing brain, and his circulatory system had been successfully re-started or he would not have been able to feel the cold in the first place. So he waited patiently while the dream warmth faded to be replaced by the real thing; then he opened his eyes.

In the unlighted cubicle the bright letters on the ceiling display seemed to float in the darkness above his head.

GOOD MORNING DEVLIN. THIS IS A FIRST AWAKENING SYSTEMS CHECK WHICH WILL NOT BE REPEATED DURING SUBSEQUENT AWAKENINGS.
PLEASE INDICATE YOUR COMPLETE RETURN TO CONSCIOUSNESS, VISUAL ACUITY AND MUSCLE CONTROL BY DEPRESSING THE CENTER BUTTON OF THE THREE WHICH ARE CONVENIENT TO YOUR RIGHT HAND.

Devlin pressed hard on the indicated button—which did not move. His heart, which was the loudest thing in the utterly silent ship, became even noisier.

Had the moisture in his breath penetrated the mechanism, he wondered, freezing and jamming it with ice? Were the delicate actuators frozen solid by the years of hyperthermia that had held his body? In short, had the complex life-support system of the starship, which represented the pinnacle of Earth's scientific achievements in virtually every field of knowledge, already developed a malfunction?

He pressed again, much harder.

```
REPEAT, THIS IS A FIRST AWAKENING SYSTEMS CHECK.
WHEN READY TO ASSIMILATE INFORMATION, DEPRESS
THE BUTTON ON THE RIGHT.
```

Devlin reminded himself that he had not used his hand for a very long time and the digits, like the rest of his newly warmed body, would be weak and stiff. As well, the buttons would have been designed to operate with a firm pressure to avoid accidental activation. The moment of calm and logical thinking had an immediate effect on his elevated pulse rate, and this time the indicated button went at the first attempt.

```
SHIP STATUS. SEVENTY-FIVE YEARS INTO MISSION.
ALL SYSTEMS FUNCTIONING.
```

The words hung in the darkness for the length of time necessary for him to read them very slowly, then they were replaced.

```
SHIP PERSONNEL CURRENTLY AWAKE—ONE. IDENTITY
JOHN DEVLIN. REASONS FOR AWAKENING. TO
CHECK FUNCTIONING OF SHIP LIFE-SUPPORT,
REVIVICATION AND COMMUNICATIONS INTERNAL
SYSTEMS. TO CHECK FUNCTIONING OF DEVLIN
VOLUNTARY/INVOLUNTARY MUSCLES, CIRCULATION,
SENSORIUM SPEECH ORGAN AND MEMORY. PERIOD OF
AWAKENING—ONE HOUR.
FOR INSTRUCTIONS DEPRESS BUTTON ON THE LEFT.
```

Devlin pressed the button on the left.

```
BASIC INSTRUCTIONS. SPEAK, EXERCISE,
REMEMBER.
```

There was no sane reason why he should not say something out loud or make some sort of modulated noise like a hum or whistle, perhaps. But he could not do any of those things. The thought of the vast, utterly silent ship stretching away on all sides of his cubicle, guarded and guided by silent computers, was paralyzing his own ability to make sounds, as if by an overwhelming spell based on the laws of sympathetic magic.

```
ADDITIONAL INFORMATION TO INSTRUCTION SPEAK.
THIS PROCESS INVOLVES NOT ONLY CONTROL AND
COORDINATION OF MUSCLES CONTROLLING THE LUNGS,
THROAT AND TONGUE, IT IS A BASIC EXERCISE IN
THE REACTIVATION, ORGANIZATION AND RECALL OF
MEMORY DATA.
SOUNDS PRODUCED FOR THIS EXERCISE ARE FOR
TEST PURPOSES ONLY AND WILL NOT BE ADDED
FOR EVALUATION TO THE PSYCH PROFILE.
```

"I don't believe you," said Devlin.

Satisfied, the display replied EXERCISE.

"Yes, master," said Devlin, beginning to sit up. His head rose perhaps six inches from its padded rest before he collapsed back. By the time his grayed-out vision had returned to normal a new message was hanging above him.

```
ADDITIONAL INFORMATION TO INSTRUCTION EXERCISE.
INITIAL MOVEMENTS SHOULD BE SLOW AND GENTLE.
SUGGEST BRIEF EXERCISE OF LEGS, ARMS AND
NECK MUSCLES WHILE IN RECUMBENT POSITION
FOLLOWED BY ROLL ONTO LEFT SIDE. FIRM PRESSURE
FROM HANDS AND/OR KNEES WILL CAUSE CASKET
WALL TO FOLD DOWN ALLOWING CHANGE TO
SITTING POSITION.
MOVEMENT IS ALLOWED WITHIN THE COMPARTMENT AND
UNOBSTRUCTED SECTION OF CORRIDOR OUTSIDE.
FOR THIS TEST NO SOLID OR LIQUID FOOD WILL
BE CONSUMED SINCE THE ONE HOUR WAKING PERIOD
DOES NOT ALLOW SUFFICIENT TIME FOR WASTES
TO BE ELIMINATED BEFORE COOLING.
```

The display blanked out for a few minutes, then lit with another message.

```
ADDITIONAL BASIC INFORMATION. THIS COMPUTER
POSSESSES NO HUMAN ATTRIBUTES. IT WAS
PROGRAMED BY HUMAN BEINGS WHO ATTEMPTED TO
PROVIDE FOR ALL FORESEEABLE CONTINGENCIES,
BUT IT IS NOT HUMAN. IT WILL NOT BE IMPRESSED
BY ANY ATTEMPT TO DISPLAY UNUSUALLY HIGH
DEGREE OF PHYSICAL FITNESS BY HURRYING THE
EXERCISES, NOR WILL IT FEEL SYMPATHY IF DEVLIN
BREAKS A LEG WHILE DOING SO.
```

"Now," said Devlin, laughing, "I believe you."

```
REMEMBER.
```

"All right!"

```
ADDITIONAL TO INSTRUCTION REMEMBER. THIS
EXERCISE TO PROCEED IN CONJUNCTION WITH
INSTRUCTIONS SPEAK AND EXERCISE. DURING THIS
TEST A DETAILED SEARCH OF THE DEVLIN MEMORY
STORE IS UNNECESSARY. SIMPLY CHECK THAT THERE
ARE NO OBVIOUS GAPS IN THE MEMORY CHAIN AND
CONCENTRATE ON MEMORIES ASSOCIATED WITH THE
PRESENT ENVIRONMENT. RESERVE TIME FOR RECALL OF
AS MUCH AS POSSIBLE OF THE COLD-SLEEP DREAM
SEQUENCES.
RETURN TO CASKET FOR REPROCESSING IN 53
MINUTES.
```

The display rolled away from him as he carefully opened the side wall of his casket and swung his feet to the deck and into the exercise stirrups, but another display was facing him as he sat up.

```
SPEAK. EXERCISE. REMEMBER.
```

The words dimmed slightly as the cubicle lighting came on.

"I'm not really hungry," Devlin lied as his eyes went to the food dispenser. He had been required to fast for twelve hours before the pre-flight cooldown and, in a manner of speaking, he had had nothing to eat for seventy-five years. At the same time his body, although stiff and weak, still looked healthy and well nourished, and the really severe pangs of hunger had begun only when the display had informed him that he was not to eat.

"Psychosomatic malnutrition," he said dryly, "is a terrible way to die."

But he was not even considering using the dispenser. Sound medical reasons existed for not undergoing hibernation anesthesia on a full stomach, and hunger had been a common enough condition on Earth. His present hunger, like the rest of his body, had been frozen and preserved for more than seventy years and the process could be repeated indefinitely. The truth was, he felt fine.

All at once his hunger receded, driven back by a feeling comprised equally of wonder and sheer relief. Seventy-five years of ship-elapsed time had passed and he was alive and well, while back on Earth everyone he had known was long since dead. He shied away from remembering some of them and tried to think instead about the starship, about its inconceivable velocity that was the end result of decades of gentle acceleration and about the polluted and overpopulated planet he had left behind.

EXERCISE. REMEMBER.

There was a narrow area of clear deck on the open side of the casket. The rest of the space in the cubicle that was not occupied by the food dispenser, the ceiling or wall displays was stuffed with equipment associated with the cold-sleep systems and sensors. One of the few tests for joining the mission had been a check for any tendency toward claustrophobia, Devlin remembered, and another had been a test for the degree of dissatisfaction with present—or rather seventy years' past—surroundings.

While he exercised in the narrow space, Devlin wondered how he was supposed to know if there was an obvious gap in his memory. If he could not remember something important, how was he supposed to know that he had forgotten it?

REMEMBER said both displays in unison.

Obviously the computer knew when he had obeyed the instructions to speak and exercise, but it could not tell whether or not he was remembering properly. Telepathic computers were beyond even the resources of Earth science, so the chances were this computer would simply continue reminding him—hoping for the best.

Gradually his stiffness left him and he walked into the corridor. The lighting was switched on but not the heating. Devlin's breath hung like an intermittent fog around his face and he had to pull himself rapidly around the wall-nets to keep warm. But nothing seemed strange to him—no obvious gaps in his memory—about this short corridor in the crew segment of the ship. It was exactly like the corridor in the simulator back on Earth, except there the feeling of weightlessness had been produced by a system of spring wires and localized sensory-deprivation drugs.

If he had been chosen to occupy one of the four colonist segments that were built around the central crew and computer module, he would have had much less room in which to exercise. The others were confined to their cubicles for the duration of the trip.

Feeling warmer but short of breath, he stopped for a moment with his fingers around a strand of netting. As he was about to move off again he saw the other figure, ghostlike, its head surrounded by the same self-generated fog and wearing an open-mesh cold-suit identical to the one he was wearing himself. The figure was standing only a few feet away. He reached forward instinctively, discovering that the figure was his reflection an instant before his hand touched the transparent plastic door and two messages—one of them upside down with respect to the other—appeared on it.

```
ACCESS TO CENTRAL CONTROL. NOT TO BE
OPENED WITHOUT COMPUTER PERMISSION EXCEPT
IN CASES OF EXTREME EMERGENCY.
```

Devlin shivered suddenly and decided that he had had enough exercise. He moved back to his cubicle, trying unsuccessfully not to read the name tag on the door opposite his own.

For a few seconds he stared at the manual override handle which grew from the gray metal like a bright red banana. In an emergency he could bypass the computer controls and initiate the awakening of any person in the ship. He was not, however, supposed to warm up one of the females just because he felt cold and lonely. He shivered again and sought the warmth of his own cubicle.

But the heaters had been turned off in preparation for his imminent cooldown, and his jaws began to ache with the effort of not allowing his teeth to chatter.

```
REPROCESSING IN SEVEN MINUTES.
```

Devlin lay down and the hinged flaps swung up and clicked into position. It was the first noise he had heard since awakening which he had not made himself.

```
REMEMBER. IMPERATIVE YOU CONCENTRATE ON
MEMORIES OF COLD-SLEEP DREAM SEQUENCES FOR
REMAINDER OF CONSCIOUS PERIOD.
```

Devlin had been told often enough how important it was that he remember as much as possible of the dreams experienced during cold-sleep, the dreams which meant the difference between a dead and frigid mind and one that had suspended life, identity and continuity. But he was not supposed to remember the reasons now. There was no time. If he were to be sure of another coherent awakening, he had to concentrate on his last dream.

The display was hazy with breath fog when he closed his eyes. He tried to ignore the goose pimples which crawled like frozen insects all over his body and the picture of Brother Howard which kept getting between him and his dream. It had been warm. He had floated in a thick, warm soup where existence was incredibly violent. Pain, pleasure, hunger, repletion, sex—all were experienced in such raw, savage concentrations that he could not now tell which had been painful and which pleasant. All his senses had been affected as by an abrasive rubbed along a bared nerve. And he had been blind.

As more and more of the dream came back to him he began to realize that the only thing nice about it had been its warmth.

A small change in the quality of the light on the other side of his closed eyelids made him open his eyes. The display had a final message.

GOODNIGHT DEVLIN.

Around and within his body there was a sharp, silent explosion of cold.

2

HUNGER WAS MAKING him take risks. He had lived long and grown large by not taking unnecessary risks, but with increasing size had come a proportionate growth in his hunger and in the number of risks taken to assuage it. On this occasion his hunger was intense and the risks acceptable.

He moved from beneath the cover of the clump of gently waving algae, skirting the overhanging curve of a massive tabulata, and crawled onto the bright area of sea bottom which stretched ahead for as far as his rudimentary eyes could see.

The area was clear of rocks and major growths, but it was not empty. In the middle distance lay the enormous, garishly patterned shell of a carnivorous cephalopod, the pointed rear of its narrow conical body clearly visible. Its forward section was hidden by a self-generated fog of disturbed mud that concealed its head, tentacles and wildly struggling victim. Nearby lay a small group of brachiopods looking disdainful behind the protection of their smooth white shells. The remainder of the area was, as usual, covered by the tiny scurrying shapes of small trilobites scavenging for the plant and animal debris which littered the sand.

He joined them.

But the tiny morsels of organic material did nothing to quell the hunger that raged along every nerve in his body. If anything, feeding which produced something less than satiation served only to make his hunger worse. It was like a conflagration within him which was interrupted only by the brief, hot explosions of fury that occurred when he encountered long-dead husks or fresh remains already picked clean of edible material, or when a smaller trilobite was able to squirm free of the four pairs of appendages serving his wide, underslung mouth.

Such escapes were frequent because he was not by nature a carnivore, and in that continuing fire of hunger and anger, emotions like caution and fear were obliterated before they could properly form.

Then he encountered a trilobite which did not try to escape because it was trapped between the long narrow shell of the cephalopod and himself. The muddy water around the carnivore's head had grown clearer, indicating that it was finishing off its victim. The image registered clearly on his visual equipment and was transmitted accurately to his crude equivalent of a brain, but the warning which accompanied it was like a glass of water on a forest fire.

This trilobite was larger than the others of its kind that were currently infesting the sandy bottom, almost half as big as he was himself, and it had rolled itself tightly into a ball to protect its vulnerable underbelly. He probed angrily with his antenna and head appendages, but succeeded only in removing a few of the small and weaker legs from the tail section. It rolled itself into an even tighter ball and he swarmed over it again and again, his hunger and frustration making it impossible for him to think.

But he did not need to think. A purely defensive and involuntary reflex, triggered off when his victim's tightly rolled body opened briefly to trap and damage one of his antennae, gave him the advantage. It caused him to roll his body tightly around that of his victim. He maintained the hold, squeezing harder and harder while the other's body segments telescoped and their connecting sutures snapped and pulpy flesh began oozing from the organic wreckage.

But the struggle had stirred up the mud and sand around him to such an extent that when he uncurled from the crushed body he could barely see it, although the poor visibility did not stop him from feeding. It did, however, prevent him from seeing that the cephalopod had finished with its victim and, attracted by the disturbance, was seeking another.

It found two.

He was feeding when the forest of tentacles wrapped itself around both his victim and himself and began pulling them into the cephalopod's enormous maw. He went on feeding while the hot, constant flame of his hunger was punctuated by explosions of pain as his appendages were twisted and crushed and torn away, and as more and more of his body segments collapsed under the pressure of the cephalopod's teeth. He was still eating and being eaten when the triple fires of his pain, anger and hunger faded and died ...

GOOD MORNING DEVLIN, said the display. SHIP STATUS TWO HUNDRED EIGHTY-TWO YEARS INTO MISSION. ALL SYSTEMS FUNCTIONING. SHIP PERSONNEL CURRENTLY AWAKE—ONE. IDENTITY JOHN DEVLIN.

"Are you sure I'm awake?"

His dream of being a recently defunct trilobite on the muddy bottom of a Silurian sea was still very much with him, and would require no effort of memory to recall. For a time he had been a tiny organism whose blind fury had been the direct cause of its violent end. But he was now fairly sure the creature had not been intelligent, that its continued survival had been a matter of pure luck and that the impressions he had had of its ability to learn from experience were false. The intelligent dreamer, himself, had given an aura of intelligence to his dream creature which had, in fact, been driven by nothing more than blind instinct.

Hunger and blind instinct were still driving people to acts of violence. At least, they had done so two hundred and eighty-two years ago. He tried hard not to think about the time that had passed and thought instead about the present and about himself.

He was still hungry.

IT IS ASSUMED THAT YOU REMEMBER YOUR FIRST TEST AWAKENING AND THE ACCOMPANYING INSTRUCTIONS. DURING THIS AND SUBSEQUENT AWAKENINGS THESE INSTRUCTIONS WILL NOT BE RESTATED UNLESS THE ORIGINAL MEMORY IS OCCLUDED OR NO LONGER AVAILABLE OR THERE IS EVIDENCE OF SEVERE MENTAL DISORIENTATION.
SHOULD ONE OF THESE SITUATIONS ARISE PRESS FIRMLY ON THE PEDAL BELOW YOUR LEFT FOOT FOR BASIC MISSION RE-EDUCATION MATERIAL.

"No, thanks," said Devlin. He remembered having

to sit for three hours watching that re-education film, which had begun by assuming that the viewer had the mind of a retarded child.

> REASONS FOR AWAKENING. TO GUIDE COMPUTER IN MAKING NON-URGENT DECISION. TO CHECK FUNCTIONING OF DEVLIN MUSCLE SYSTEMS, CIRCULATION, DIGESTIVE TRACT . . .

"Bless you!"

> . . . SPEECH ORGAN AND MEMORY. PERIOD OF AWAKENING FORTY-EIGHT HOURS. CARRY OUT INSTRUCTIONS SPEAK, EXERCISE, EAT AND REMEMBER.

Devlin exercised gently, then released the casket's hinged side. The cubicle's heaters were coating his skin with a film of warmth, making him think of one of his mother's Baked Alaskas—a hot crust surrounding a filling of still-frozen ice cream. But this icy center thawed quickly and he returned his attention to the displays.

> ADDITIONAL TO INSTRUCTION EAT. FOUR MAJOR MEALS OF APPROXIMATELY 1000 CALORIES EACH WILL BE TAKEN DURING THE NEXT 36 HOURS. LIQUID INTAKE WILL CEASE EIGHT HOURS BEFORE COOLDOWN. ADDITIONAL TO INSTRUCTION REMEMBER. RECALL EVERYTHING POSSIBLE OF RECENT COLD-DREAM SEQUENCE. RECALL AVAILABLE MEMORIES OF SHIP ENVIRONMENT BEFORE LEAVING CUBICLE. PROCEED TO CONTROL CENTER WHEN READY.

"No," said Devlin firmly.

He had been told how important it was that he remember his cold-dreams and store them in his waking memory in as much detail as possible. The reasons he had been given for doing so were in part psychological, biological and perhaps even philosophical—after all, he had been dead in every medical sense of the word for more than three average lifetimes.

By its very nature, long-term hibernation anesthesia

could be tried, but it could never be adequately tested. During the years following its perfection as a method of suspending animation for indefinite periods, there had been no shortage of volunteers wishing to undergo the process—people with diseases incurable by the medical science of the day, or those simply wanting to awaken into a better world. But data was still lacking on the biological and psychological side effects, if any, on really long-term subjects.

It had been thought at first that there were no harmful side effects, but the medics responsible for hyperthermia processing on the starship project said they had to be absolutely sure. They were worried, it seemed, by a slight tendency toward disorientation and forgetfulness that was so minor as to be virtually undetectable.

But on a voyage that might last for a thousand years even a tendency toward mental confusion and forgetfulness could be deadly.

Forced as they were by the necessity of finding an answer to a problem that quite possibly did not exist, they could only theorize and try to guard against all theoretical eventualities.

The most generally accepted and worrisome theory was that ultra long-term suspension would greatly increase disorientation and memory impairment and that the harmful effects would not increase proportionately but would mulitply with the passage of time. Extended periods in low temperatures could well bring about a leakage in the electro-biological system which coded and stored the memory impulses, and the end result would be a starship crew-member or colonist being revived in perfect health but without a single thought in his head.

To guard against this purely theoretical disaster, they had decided to revive the travelers at lengthy intervals—one hundred and fifty to two hundred years—during the voyage. More frequent awakenings would have placed a severe strain on the ship's power reserves and consumables. It was also thought necessary to provide a link between the awakened mind and the frigid but not quite arrested mind of the cold-sleeper.

The minds on the ship had to be continuously occupied, insisted the project psychologist. They had to engage themselves with dreaming during the centuries of frigid suspension and, while awake, perform exercises in recall so that the original memory store and linkages would be periodically reinforced instead of being lost.

Dreams were, after all, simply an involuntary form of memory recall.

"But there must be more to it than that," said Devlin suddenly. "Or else that book they made me read on prehistory left a bigger impression than I realized."

He was remembering the shocking clarity of sensory detail in his last dream memory, and he decided firmly that it required no further reinforcing. Saying "No" to the computer might or might not produce dramatic results. But if the thing had been telling the truth in the first place it had probably noted the word only as a sound, proof that he was obeying the instruction to speak, not that he was disobeying the order to recall his dream. That last dream was still too uncomfortably fresh.

Instead he turned his mind to the layout, organization and control of the starship and deliberately ignored the food dispenser as he moved into the corridor to continue his physical exercises. He was a human being in full control of his mind and instincts, not an insanely hungry trilobite.

The display had a new message for him on his return.

REMEMBER. EAT. PROCEED TO CONTROL CENTER.

3

THE SHIP MOVED inperceptibly among the stars and the dreams trickled even more slowly through the minds of its occupants, with one exception. That was the man who occupied one of the two control positions and was not moving at all.

It was not that Devlin did not know what to do. The memory of his training—minimal as would be expected for a fully automated and computerized ship—was sharp, complete and recent despite the fact that in real time it was two hundred and eighty-odd years in the past. Possibly it was the silence which kept him motionless—he was the only thing in the ship that was making a noise—or simply the fact that he was all alone, or the fact that he was not really alone and was afraid of the ghosts of people who were not really dead . . .

Devlin shivered, even though the heaters had long since raised the temperature to a comfortable level, and forced a laugh. Of one thing he could be very sure; the people in this ship would never walk in their sleep.

CENTRAL COMPUTER READY, said the display, as it had been saying since he had taken the control position.

This was a different breed of computer than the one which supervised his awakenings and nagged at him to do the proper physical and mental exercises. As far as this one was concerned Devlin was expected to know his stuff. This was, in short, a highly professional computer which would stand for no nonsense.

Apart from these purely subjective impressions, Devlin thought wryly, it was exactly the same as the

15

other computer—it possessed no human attributes whatsoever, He leaned forward and tapped the button labeled Report.

```
SITUATION REPORT. SHIP IS CLOSING TARGET
SYSTEM THREE TO MAKE APPROACH WITHIN TWO
HUNDRED MILLION MILES OF PRIMARY. FIRST TWO
SOLAR SYSTEMS VISITED OBVIOUSLY NOT SUITABLE
FOR SEEDING AND BYPASSED WITHOUT CREW
CONSULTATION. TARGET THREE REQUIRES HUMAN
EVALUATION OF DATA FOR DECISION. ASTRONOMICAL
GEOPHYSICAL DATA ON MOST SUITABLE PLANET
FOLLOWS . . .
```

Devlin tapped the Hold button to give himself time to think and to control his anger and disappointment.

The starship's course had been plotted to take it through ten solar systems that lay in a fairly straight line which began with Earth, and most of these were thought to contain planets with a high probability of being suitable for colonization. That being the case, their first call should almost certainly have been their final destination, it being natural to assume that the observational data on the nearest target system would be the most accurate, and the probability of finding a suitable world on their second try should also have been high. But the farther they traveled the more they would have to rely on chance, the greater the danger of their developing a malfunction in the ship's hyperthermia caskets, guidance and propulsion systems or even in the periodically frozen organic computers belonging to the ship's occupants.

He remembered the words of old Carewe—the man responsible for the design of the long-range geophysical sensors—who had been angry and disappointed because he was chained to Earth by age and a disease which in a lesser individual would have been terminal.

"This ship is the most intricate, sophisticated, and foolproof fabrication ever to be conceived and built by man," he had told them at the conclusion of his first lecture, "but it is only a bloody machine."

Devlin, too, felt disappointment. But his anger was chiefly due to the fact that the machine had bypassed two likely solar systems without consulting a member of the crew. Perhaps his anger was also due to his fear that the machine could not be trusted, and he wondered what he would do if a playback on the two earlier fly-bys showed that they had bypassed a suitable colony world.

He tried to control this fear and make himself think. The first two target systems had been bypassed without crew consultation, the computer was saying, and it meant just that. But members of the crew could be awakened for other reasons, and he should also have remembered that.

Still without releasing the Hold he called up crew status data. Like the occupants of the colonist sections—who were not supposed to leave their cubicles until after the landing—both crew-members had been awakened once for physical and mental exercise. The display showed a pale blue Exercise Only light burning against each name. His own name was also tagged with his present orange Decision Awakening light, and his crew-mate's name carried the yellow light, indicating an awakening for observation purposes only.

A quick check showed that the observation awakening coincided with the fly-by time on one of the bypassed systems. He knew the crew-member concerned very well. She was not the type to sit idly by if the world they had been passing had been suitable for colonization.

Devlin swung back to the main display. He said, "For all the unkind things I have been thinking about you, I am truly sorry," and released the Hold.

The information came in bright, sharp, silent words. It was a system comprising seven planets held by a sun which was approaching middle age, stable and emitting radiation of an acceptable type and intensity. Six of the worlds were unsuitable, either too close to or distant from the primary, and the display gave brief details of the planetary diameters, gravity, temperature, atmospheric pressure or the lack of it. The remaining one, which was third from the sun, was within the temperature and light zone in which planetary life could evolve, and it had.

He jabbed the button marked Visual and divided his attention between the data display and the pictures on the side screen.

Planet Three was enormous, a rapidly spinning globe composed of semimolten material, superheated liquid and a wide-flung, roiling gas envelope that warmed the planet's two satellites like a second sun. Satellite A was a ten-mile-wide chip of rock which orbited its primary every twelve hours, while Satellite B was much larger, more distant and sedate in its rotational movement and the second most beautiful world that Devlin had ever seen.

He blinked away a temporary impairment of the Devlin visual equipment and concentrated on the data display. In the stillness of the ship his breath sounded like an interrupted gale and his heart was hanging against his rib cage as if it wanted out.

EQUATIONAL DIAMETER 7,540 MILES. ROTATIONAL PERIOD NINETEEN POINT ONE SEVEN HOURS. GRAVITY POINT NINE FOUR EARTH NORMAL. ATMOSPHERIC PRESSURE THIRTEEN POINT SEVEN POUNDS/SQUARE INCH. COMPOSITION SUITABLE FOR HUMAN LIFE. WIDESPREAD FLORA. DETAILS OF FAUNA AWAITING LANDING OF PROBE. NO INDICATION OF RADIATION OR POLLUTANTS PRODUCED BY TECHNICALLY ADVANCED CULTURE.

Devlin jabbed the Hold button so hard that he cracked his fingernail.

Third time lucky . . .

He wanted suddenly to shout so loudly that the silent ship would never get over the shock, so loudly that he would disturb even the slow, frigid dreaming of the colonists. And that wasn't such a bad idea, because this was the sort of good news that should be shared as soon as possible.

It was completely against the rules, of course. The manual overrides were not supposed to be used to awaken people except in cases of extreme emergency, and this was anything but an emergency. But the control center although designed for two people, probably could squeeze six in at a pinch, and they would be able to see their future home for a few minutes before they returned to their cold-dreams, because planet-fall still would be a long way off in time and distance.

The ship would have to go away and come back again.

There was nothing wrong with his memory, Devlin thought happily, because he could remember every word, every line drawn by the electronic pointer and every nuance of Carewe's voice as he had outlined the approach, re-approach and landing sequences. Perhaps the reason he remembered it so well was that the knowledge would be used only when their goal had been achieved—the last few yards in a race before they broke the tape. Despite the sarcastic hectoring manner of old Carewe, who had invariably spoken to them like an Einstein trying to make his special theory comprehensible to a bunch of ten-year-olds, it had been the most popular lecture in the whole training course.

In case the first or second or sixth target star proved unsuitable, Carewe had said, the ship would not, as was customary in interplanetary flights, accelerate for half the distance to its proposed destination and decelerate during the remainder of the trip. To do that would save time but would be very wasteful of power. With their life-suspension techniques they could afford to waste time, but the ship's power reserves had to be conserved for a second or a third or an umpteenth try.

That was why acceleration would be gradual and applied over many decades, until the ship had achieved a velocity just over one-quarter that of light. This velocity would be maintained until the ship reached a system in which a suitable planet was found.

Only then would the ship decelerate, just as gradually checking its tremendous velocity and converting its fly-by into a cometary return orbit, and many decades would pass before general awakening and landing.

Caution diluted his happiness as he thought of the colonists crowding into the control center six at a time. Awakening the first six would be relatively easy. They in turn could awaken the others before returning to the cubicles. But some of them might not want to be reprocessed after only a few minutes of looking at their new world. Some of them would probably want to study the probe data, and others might want to hang around or start celebrating. It was not impossible that all the people on the ship might be awake at the same time, crowding the control center, corridors and cubicles and placing a severe strain on the heating reserves and food dispensers. Intrapersonal difficulties might arise, even arguments.

His instructions, Devlin reminded himself once again, were that no more than two crew-members were to be awake at one time unless an emergency arose that dictated otherwise. Good news like this, and the natural urge to spread it around, was the very antithesis of an emergency. But he might bend the rules just a little and spread the good news to one other person.

His last meeting with her, in biological time, had been only ten hours ago.

They had been sitting on the edges of their suspension caskets in the dormitory which held the colonists who had just completed their training courses—some of them had been cooled for more than a year to preserve their precious biological time while the later arrivals were being trained. Classes had been small; the training could not have been described as intensive, and on its completion cooldown was immediate. The latest batch, like the first, would awaken on the ship somewhere between the stars. She had been sitting facing him, a slim, dark-haired beauty, shivering in her open-mesh cold-suit while she waited for the signal to get into the casket and lie down. She had smiled at him when he smiled at her.

Patricia Morley had been undemonstrative but not unfriendly. When the two-minute warning had sounded he had reached forward to take her hand, meaning to say something which probably would have sounded very trite. But she had spoken first.

"Just suppose," she said quietly and very seriously, "that these caskets malfunction. Do you think we will know when we become permanently instead of temporarily dead?"

Devlin had shivered with more than the cold, and said, "Pleasant dreams."

For a few seconds she had gripped his hand so tightly that he still felt it tingling when the cold explosion came. At that moment he had been remembering the advice of one of the project psychologists who had insisted that pairing-off should wait until planet-fall when the pool would include everyone on the ship, and that pairings among training groups had a much lower probability of success. But right now he wanted to awaken her with his good news and go on from there.

He laughed out loud and released the Hold.

```
ENVIRONMENT OF PLANET THREE B COMPLETELY
SUITABLE FOR HUMAN COLONIZATION ON A
SHORT-TERM BASIS.
```

"What . . . ?" began Devlin. The computer ignored him, but answered anyway.

```
PLANET THREE B IS CURRENTLY ENTERING ROCHE'S
LIMIT AND WILL SHORTLY BREAK UP TO BECOME
A RING SYSTEM OF ITS PRIMARY.
```

Devlin thought about the kind of life they could lead on the Earthlike satellite of Planet Three, the clean air and unpolluted oceans and fresh green vegetation that covered the land surfaces like chlorophyl paint. He thought of the night sky with that tremendous primary shining above them, the fantastic play of light and shade and color when the sun shared the sky with it, and the beautiful spectacle of an eclipse.

"No," he whispered.

```
BREAK-UP TIMING IS DIFFICULT TO PREDICT WITH
ACCURACY. PLANET THREE B ALREADY SHOWS VOLCANIC
ACTIVITY ABOVE THE NORM FOR BODIES OF THIS
AGE AND MASS. SUCH ACTIVITY WILL BECOME
WIDESPREAD WITHIN THE NEXT TWO CENTURIES. HUMAN
OCCUPATION IMPOSSIBLE WITHIN THREE CENTURIES
DUE TO RELEASE OF TOXIC GASES FROM VOLCANOES AND
FISSURES. ELEVATED TEMPERATURES CAUSED BY
POOLS OF MAGMA OCCUPYING LARGE AREAS OF THE
SURFACE IS ALSO A FACTOR. PHYSICAL BREAK-UP IS
ESTIMATED AT LESS THAN FOUR HUNDRED YEARS.
DECISION REQUIRED LANDING/NO LANDING.
```

Devlin swung away from the console and out of the control center, wanting desperately to find something or someone who would make the awful pain of disappointment go away. He stopped outside his cubicle. The big red manual override handle on Patricia's door was within easy reach, but if he had refused to awaken her to tell the good news there could be no excuse for doing so to tell her about this. He swore horribly and went into his cubicle and began pushing buttons on the food dispenser.

The wall and ceiling displays were saying:

```
DECISION REQUIRED IN CONTROL CENTER.
```

He went on swearing at them, but in the end his emotional heat and the warmth imparted by the hot food faded before the cold radiating from his casket, and he returned to the control center. The right decision was obvious.

But he did not take it at once. For a long time he lay watching Three B on the screen. It hung like a great, cloud-wrapped vision of Heaven—a planet-sized egg waiting to be fertilized and to grow and be stillborn. There could be only one decision and he made it, but not until after he had re-run all the data on Three B, called up more detailed information from his sensors, and spent many hours exercising his brain with thoughts that were psychologically very undesirable.

Finally he tapped. NO LANDING, CONTINUE ON PROGRAMED COURSE TO TARGET FOUR.

RETURN TO SUSPENSION CASKET, replied the display. COOLDOWN IN FORTY-TWO MINUTES.

"The sooner," said Devlin bitterly, "the better."

4

THE DAYS WERE long and happy and full of incident, usually the same kind of incident. Day after day he sunned himself on the edge of the swamp, or pastured among the aquatic plants or fed on the palm fronds that were within reach. The changes came too slowly to be perceptible at first, taking many thousands of long, warm, contented days to become manifest.

He was vaguely aware that the deep area of the swamp had become shallower and that when he pushed against the trees in an attempt to reach the higher fronds they tore up their roots or splintered and fell so that he was able to reach down for the food he wanted. Gradually everything seemed to be growing smaller and he became aware, very slowly, that it was himself who was growing larger and more mature.

The internal upheaval of puberty and his first incredibly awkward attempts at mating made him fully aware of his growth and took the calm, contented sameness out of the nearly infinite succession of days. But then even those gargantuan heavings and squirmings became just another aspect of his life, and the days passed in their thousands until the day he nearly died.

He had been sunning himself on a raised shelf of land close to the swamp, sleepily digesting his last gargantuan meal, when the young saurian appeared between his prone body and the safety of the swamp. It was a very small reptile—perhaps only a fifth of his own mass—and stupid enough for the difference in size not to worry it. But its small size and consequent lack of inertia made the attack incredibly fast.

This was his first experience with a carnivorous reptile, and until the razor-sharp teeth raked his flank, the appearance of the saurian had made him feel uneasy rather than frightened. But the savage pain put an abrupt end to his slow, contented thinking and, awkward and uncoordinated, he struggled to his feet while his head swept around in a wide arc so that he could see what his attacker was doing.

The saurian, who until then had been able only to tear at the surface of the enormous wall that was his flank, now transferred its attention to his rear left leg. The teeth sank in like multiple rows of daggers; the jaw locked in position and it began to pull and twist at the upper section of the leg.

An avalanche of pain impulses from the damaged member engulfed the rudimentary brain in the sacral area long before they registered in the fifty-foot distant brain in his head, and that collection of nerve ganglia reacted at once, automatically withdrawing the leg in an attempt to remove it from danger. Already in an unbalanced condition because of the weight and position of his massive neck, withdrawal of the leg from the ground caused him to topple ponderously on to his side and on top of his attacker.

He could feel bones snapping and the other's shrill

hiss of pain as he collapsed, and the sensations continued during the few minutes he needed to regain his feet. By then he could see that the creature's skeleton was seriously distorted and compressed, the bones showing like misplaced teeth in the long, ruptured wounds, and there had been a considerable loss of internal body material and fluids.

The saurian was still alive but unable to move very far, and the scavenging insects and small predators already were converging on it. He did not eat meat and had no reason to stay, so he moved painfully toward the deeper areas of the swamp where he could pasture and cool the fire in his leg and think slow, contented thoughts again.

Once again the days crawled past while he wallowed and pastured and sunned himself in the Jurassic swampland, but there was no mating and very little travel because of his reduced mobility and the raging fire in his leg. Then one day he was unable to get up, and the days succeeded each other once again—but slowly, now perceptibly different and filled with pain.

Fortunately or unfortunately the large carnivorous reptiles did not find him, so he lay undisturbed for a long time. Unable to reach the tremendous quantities of food needed to maintain his gigantic body, he grew steadily weaker. But a long time is needed for a mountain to die, even one of flesh and bone, and the days dragged on while, no longer able to move, he lay with his head turned around so that he could see the thick, angular lump of corruption that his leg had become.

By then a new fire had started along the parts of his body which were in contact with the ground—the slow, persistent erosion of insects and tiny carnivores that could not wait for him to die.

The days passed, far too many of them, and very gradually the fire and the hunger and all the other sensations faded and were gone.

Devlin remained still for the first few minutes after

his awakening, hoping that if he did not move or open his eyes the computer would be fooled into thinking he was still unconscious.

He needed time to think.

His long happy dream life as a brontosaurus and its long and unhappy death which, so far as he was concerned, had ended only a few minutes earlier was worrying him. The images and sensations had been so sharp, and the remarkable lack of compression or vagueness in the dream-elapsed time were frightening. He had been given books to read on a wide range of unrelated subjects that had included pre-history—to give his cold-sleeping brain something to work on, the chief psychologist had told him—but the material had been simple popularizations of the relevant branch of science or period in history. They had not given him any information or insight on how it felt to be a trilobite or a brontosaurus, nor had they described in such exact detail the structure and coloring for the Jurassic Age palm fronds or the various types of aquatic vegetation on which he had lived.

They had certainly not shown him a picture of the improbably marked pink and gray nightmare which had been the young allosaurus that had attacked and ultimately killed him.

To dream the lifetime of a brontosaurus—which could stretch for anything up to a couple of centuries—in such detail indicated a very fertile imagination. Considering the paucity of material available to him and the many, many years of cold-dreaming that stretched ahead, the thought of what might happen in his dream future scared him stiff.

The dreams were supposed to keep his mind alive in an otherwise dead and deep-frozen body, but if the dreams were to become centuries-long nightmares, the mind they kept alive might not remain sane.

He wondered if it would be possible for the dreamer to exercise more control over his dream, to make it more pleasant and to shut out the nightmarish aspects.

In the last dream he, personally, had been aware of what had been going on. He had viewed the events and experienced the sensations as an intelligent being even though the giant saurian, with two rudimentary brains to control its far-flung limbs and masculature, had not enough intelligence to learn by observation rather than experience to avoid danger.

But if Devlin had taken a more active part in the dream he should have been able to make his enormous, brainless and insubstantial monster avoid the allosaurus. Or at least, he should have made it stay where it was on the dry ground for a couple of days while the sunlight and fresh air healed the wounded leg, instead of dragging it through that stinking swamp ...

A dull shock, unpleasant but not painful, jolted through his body and instinctively he opened his eyes.

DUE TO SLOW RESPONSE YOUR AWAKENING HAS BEEN STIMULATED ELECTRICALLY. IF THERE IS ANY DISORIENTATION OR OCCLUSION OF MEMORY REGARDING EARLY BASIC INSTRUCTIONS PRESS FIRMLY ON PEDAL BELOW LEFT FOOT FOR BASIC REORIENTATION MATERIAL.
IF PEDAL IS NOT DEPRESSED IN TEN SECONDS IT IS ASSUMED THAT NO DISORIENTATION OR MEMORY IMPAIRMENT IS PRESENT AND CURRENT MISSION INFORMATION/INSTRUCTIONS WILL FOLLOW.

"You think," said Devlin drily, "of nearly everything."

GOOD MORNING DEVLIN. SHIP STATUS THREE HUNDRED AND TWENTY THREE YEARS INTO MISSION, SHIP PERSONNEL CURRENTLY AWAKE—ONE POSSIBLY TWO. IDENTITIES JOHN DEVLIN AND YVONNE CALDWELL.

Only forty-one years since his last cooldown. It could hardly be another fly-by, and the Caldwell girl was one of the colonists.

REASONS FOR AWAKENING. TO CHECK ON POSSIBLE ORGANIC MALFUNCTION IN CUBICLE THIRTY-ONE BLUE

```
MODULE. TO CHECK FUNCTIONING OF DEVLIN MUSCLE
SYSTEMS, CIRCULATION, SPEECH ORGAN AND MEMORY.
PERIOD OF AWAKENING DEPENDENT ON TIME NECESSARY
TO CHECK MALFUNCTION. NO FOOD INTAKE UNLESS
PERIOD EXCEEDS TWENTY-FOUR HOURS.
```

Devlin had already begun the initial exercises when the display flashed another message.

```
CARRY OUT INSTRUCTIONS SPEAK, EXERCISE,
REMEMBER AND CHECK MALFUNCTION.
```

And another.

```
ADDITIONAL TO INSTRUCTION EXERCISE. COMPLY
WITH THIS INSTRUCTION ON WAY TO CONTROL
CENTER AND TO SITE OF MALFUNCTION. INSTRUCTIONS
SPEAK AND REMEMBER TO PROCEED IN CONJUNCTION
WITH INSTRUCTIONS EXERCISE AND CHECK
MALFUNCTION. INFORMATION REGARDING MALFUNCTION
IS AVAILABLE IN THE CONTROL CENTER.
ADDITIONAL TO INSTRUCTION REMEMBER. AS MUCH
TIME AS POSSIBLE TO BE SPENT IN RECALLING
DAY IN DEVLIN RECENT PAST. RECALL SHOULD BE
COMPLETE AND ACCURATE. IF TIME BEFORE COOLDOWN
PERMITS, RECALL ASSOCIATED MEMORIES AND
CHECK FOR GAPS.
```

"If the malfunction is serious," said Devlin angrily, "I might not be able to think of anything else."

When he reached the control center the colonist status display for the Blue module told him that the colonists had been awakened three times. All the lights were pale blue because the people in there, and in the other three modules, were not required to make observations or decisions or to deal with emergencies. All they could do was exercise their minds and bodies on each awakening and very occasionally eat.

Three pale blue Exercise Awakening lights burned steadily against cubicle 31, indicating three successful awakenings and subsequent cooldowns. But there was a fourth light which winked off and on as if it could not make up its mind.

INFORMATION ON POSSIBLE ORGANIC MALFUNCTION IN
BLUE THIRTY-ONE, said the display. ELAPSED
TIME SINCE LAST WARMUP ONE HOUR TWELVE MINUTES.
CUBICLE SENSORS INDICATED INCREASING PHYSICAL
ACTIVITY AND SPEECH UNTIL FIVE SECONDS BEFORE
COOLDOWN. SENSORS REGISTERED VIBRATIONS
AND INTERMITTENT STRESS ON CUBICLE DOOR. NO
STRUCTURAL DAMAGE. NO CIRCUIT DAMAGE. NO
ACTIVATION OF EMERGENCY HOLD CONTROL. COOLDOWN
INITIATED. DATA RECEIVED FROM ORGANIC SENSORS
UNSATISFACTORY. ORGANIC DAMAGE SUSPECTED.
EMERGENCY WARMUP OF CREW-MEMBER DEVLIN
INITIATED.
WARNING. HUMAN INVESTIGATION OF MALFUNCTION
REQUIRES USE OF THERMAL SUIT.

Five minutes to don the thermal suit, Devlin estimated, and another five to strap on the air-tank and
heater and perhaps another minute to put the tools of
his trade into an insulated container. The organic malfunction could be serious or trivial, but he did not want
the organism concerned to complain later about being
jabbed with a needle which had a temperature close to
absolute zero. Then he needed another ten minutes to
get from the control center to the Blue module and to
crack the cubicle seal ...

DOUBLE CHECK THERMAL SUIT SEALING, AIR SUPPLY
AND HEATING SYSTEM.

He lost another minute doing as he had been told,
but made it up on the way to Blue 31.

As in the other colonist modules, heating was used
only during the periodic awakenings and was confined
to the cubicles. Devlin was not really aware of the absolute, killing cold outside his suit until he bent his arm
to activate the seal release and the revivification Hold
switch. The lining of his thermal suit creased in the
fold of his arm, compressing the insulating foam, and
for a moment he thought that his elbow joint would
seize up and the blood in the area congeal.

At first glance it looked as though the girl was kneeling in prayer beside her casket. Her head and arms were inside, held there by the edge of the hinged flap which for some reason was in the closed vertical position. Obviously she had been trying to climb into the closed casket when cooldown began and the radiation had hit her. That radiation was potent stuff and was designed to achieve molecular arrest and plunge the subject to a temperature close to absolute zero so quickly that cell damage could not occur, and it was focused only on the contents of the casket. As a result her head, arms and body down to a level slightly below the waist had been reprocessed in the normal way while the rest of her body had cooled not so rapidly.

Devlin swore and moved closer to carry out a quick visual examination.

She was small and slim and looked to be about eighteen. Her eyes were open and there were two thin patches of ice on her cheeks where tears had frozen. There were indications of bruisings on the outside edges of her hands and on her knuckles, as if she had been beating at something with her fists, but he saw no other outward signs of physical injury.

Very carefully he lifted her into the casket—in the cooled-down condition human tissue was brittle and highly susceptible to damage. She lay with her knees projecting above the edge while her arms reached grotesquely upwards, like one of the undressed female window-display models he used to stare at as a growing boy when he thought his mother wasn't looking. They, too, had been cold and stiff and unbelievably lifelike, but none of the window-display staff had thought of giving the mannequins plastic tears. When he was sure that all of her body was in radiation focus he went outside and cancelled the revivification Hold.

Like the cooldown treatment, the radiation designed to reverse the process was also potent stuff, and deadly to anyone who was already revived.

When he went in again she was not yet conscious. He moved her into a more comfortable position and replaced the arm which was hanging over the edge of the casket. The heaters had raised the temperature sufficiently for him to do without his suit, and by the time he had opened the helmet she was coming awake. He pulled off his gauntlets and put his hand to her forehead.

"Relax," he said gently. "Do not make any sudden movements."

Her eyes opened and she said, "I'm cold. My legs are asleep, and my hands . . ."

"That," lied Devlin quietly, "is because you woke up before they did."

Her respiration was normal and the partial and premature cooldown had not affected mentation, but, considering her position at the time, that was not surprising. He thought that her arms must have slipped over the opposite side of the casket during the cooldown instant and dropped back inside when she had slipped backwards.

Suddenly she smiled and said apologetically, "I was stupid. It wasn't claustrophobia or anything—I just wanted to see Brian for a minute. The display said we were three hundred years older and I thought something might have happened to him in all that time. I wanted . . . I even beat on the door with my fists before I realized how stupid that was. By then only a few seconds remained to cooldown, and I rushed to the casket so quickly that my knee hit the flap and knocked it closed and the computer thought I was in it and—"

"So that's how it happened," said Devlin.

She nodded and said, "I'm still very cold."

"I'll get you some warm food," said Devlin, going to the dispenser. "Don't move. I'll feed you. But talk as much as you want to."

"The computer didn't say that I could eat," she began doubtfully.

"Doctor's orders," said Devlin.

She obviously enjoyed the hot meal even though she seemed to be increasingly ill at ease and her color was high. Apparently she had become aware that there was a man in her cubicle who was not her Brian and that the suspension garment was little more than a collection of holes held together by fine wire. But the flush stopped short below waist level and a few inches above her wrists, and the area of bluish white skin bordering these lines of demarcation was increasing perceptibly as he watched.

Circulation had already ceased at the extremities and she had only a few minutes to live.

"Brian is doing fine," said Devlin, keeping his eyes on her face. "If anything had gone wrong in his cubicle I would have been awakened to deal with it, just as in your case. But I'm afraid all you'll be able to do is dream about him for a while."

She smiled again. "All I seem to dream about is being a lady dinosaur."

"They made you read that book, too?"

She shook her head slowly. "They told me to, but I didn't and read a historical romance instead. Learning about dinosaurs isn't useful to a colonist so I didn't bother, but I still dreamed about being one so clearly that ..." She broke off. Her breathing became labored and uneven and she looked suddenly frightened. She said, "I'm terribly cold. What ... what's happening to me?"

"You'll be all right," said Devlin reassuringly, and he put his hand on her forehead again. "You're doing fine."

A few minutes later he closed her eyes and left the cubicle.

He tried not to let her face and figure and her manner register with him as he shut down the computer outlet and suspension equipment, and for a while he thought he had succeeded. In the old days he used to have no trouble forgetting that kind of thing—perhaps because there had been so much of it. But recently his memory had become unusually retentive, even when he was only remembering dreams, and he could no longer trust himself to forget.

By the time he had returned to central control and stowed the thermal suit, less than two hours had passed since his awakening. The status display for the Blue module now read Organic Failure against cubicle 31. Devlin tapped instructions for his own cooldown in one hour and returned to his cubicle.

His instructions were waiting.

```
REMAINING TIME BEFORE COOLDOWN TO BE SPENT
REMEMBERING ONE DAY IN DEVLIN RECENT PAST.
RECALL SHOULD BE COMPLETE AND ACCURATE AND
SHOULD INCLUDE ASSOCIATED MEMORIES. IF TIME
AVAILABLE IS INSUFFICIENT COOLDOWN HOLD SHOULD
BE ACTIVATED UNTIL RECALL IS COMPLETE.
```

5

EVERY DAY HE awoke in a room which was not very much larger than the starship suspension cubicle which, at that time, was still in his future. His room expanded considerably when the bed folded into its wall recess to become a set of well-filled bookshelves—glassed in, of course, to keep the books from falling out when it was being used as a bed—and contracted again when the dining table and stool came out. But he did not notice the cramped conditions, or the pitifully few touches he had been able to give the place to express his individuality, or the taste of the food which he pushed in the general direction of his face, because normally he did not come fully awake until he had been up and about for at least an hour.

By that time he had tidied up, converted the room to its daytime mode and unlocked the waiting room in readiness for morning office hours. The waiting room was the largest of the three, holding up to nine people uncomfortably, and his office was the smallest. Into this shoebox was fitted an examination couch, a combination desk and drug cabinet, and a folding chair for patients who were well enough not to have to lie down.

Behind his desk the imitation window was transmitting a picture of the surrounding buildings that rose like bottomless pillars from the early morning smog. The clock on his office wall was showing six-thirty when the patients began to arrive—hobbling, sniffing, coughing and occasionally bleeding.

In a medium-sized block of apartments containing two thousand rooms and an average of three potential patients per room, infections of the upper respiratory tract were circulated like money. To these cases he dispensed face masks that the majority of them would not wear, with small doses of the indicated medication and sympathy. The sympathy was an optional extra—his option, not his patients'—and the dosage varied in direct proportion to the amount of sleep he had had the previous night, the quantity of residual alcohol still in his system, and various psychological factors.

When the patient was old and/or disturbed he tried to dispense constructive sympathy no matter how rotten he felt, because that was the only form of treatment available to him and he was always trying to bring down the suicide rate in the buildings.

The first of the walking wounded arrived on the arm of a girl who helped him on to the examination couch and returned to the waiting room without speaking. Devlin judged the patient to be in his early twenties, still partially in shock and, judging by the outraged expression on his face, a bystander. The right leg of his evening coveralls was bloodstained below the knee and had been ripped open to show an even more bloodstained towel which had been knotted tightly around the wound. The pale green material of the coveralls toned with the greenish shade of the patient's face, but clashed horribly with the primary color soaking his leg and right slipper.

"D-don't cut the towel, please," said the patient as Devlin folded back the sodden material. "My mother ... It's organic wool, she says, and very expensive."

Devlin nodded and began undoing the knot.

"I suppose," said the patient, "that you're wondering how I got it?"

To the contrary, said Delvin under his breath, I am agog with disinterest. But as the medic for the building it would do no harm to be polite and pretend that this particular wound, out of the hundreds he had already treated this week, was unique in all its aspects. To the patient—especially if it had been his first—it was unique.

He nodded again and said, "Please lie face downwards."

While Devlin sprayed the area with painkiller and began probing the wound for traces of coverall material that might have been carried inside by the bullet, the patient outlined the circumstances that had led to his accident.

"It wasn't my affair, you understand," he began angrily, "and they were too old for it, anyway. Besides the old fools were practically in the Lunar insertion on Mix 82—the rec hall bars had run out of everything else—and were incapable of telling the difference between an insult and fair comment. You know that stuff—it's supposed to be a harmless euphoric, but hydraulic fluid flavored with fruit juice has the same effect. I don't think they were even talking clearly enough to be insulting, but they insisted on having an affair there and then just to show us young folks that ... that ... I couldn't quite follow their reasoning."

"If they were high on 82 I'm not surprised," said Devlin with feeling. "Move your foot up and down and flex your toes, please."

"This was three hours ago," resumed the patient. "It was still dark but there was enough moonlight to see a

man the regulation thirty yards away. My girl and I
went with them to act as official witnesses and to see
that the Maxers didn't interfere. We didn't expect them
to be able to hit each other and we were right, but one
of them got me and—"

"You demanded satisfaction," said Devlin wearily.

"Well, no," replied the other. "They expected me to,
of course, and I never saw two old boys sober up so
fast, but the situation was complicated. One of them
was my old man and the other was my girl's old man.
My mother wouldn't approve of me having an affair
with Dad, and this girl I'd like to keep permanently. If
she called me out I wouldn't like it at all.

"I don't approve of affairs of honor between men
and women," he added seriously.

Devlin squirted wide spectrum antibiotics into the
entry and exit wounds and began to tape a dressing in
places before he spoke. "You are a believer in men
upholding the honor of women, but not in women
upholding their own?"

"No. Not exactly."

"Maybe it is just that you can't abide male property—the female of the species, in this case—being
able to shoot back. Maybe you think that it is unfair to
young, or even old, males?"

The patient tried to turn his head to look at Devlin,
despite the fact that it was physiologically impossible
for the human neck to travel through one hundred and
eighty degrees. He sounded very angry as he said, "Are
you suggesting that I'm some kind of Maxer? Listen,
Doctor. You belong to one of the few professions that
don't wear the belt and don't suffer loss of status by not
wearing it. But that does not give you the right to insult—"

Devlin, who was putting the finishing touches to the
dressing, paused to put his hand on the other's shoulder. He said seriously, "I did not mean to insult you
and I unreservedly apologize. But I had an old man,
too, and for a while there I was talking just like him.

And I agree with you about mixed affairs—women are neither physically nor temperamentally suited to fighting death duels with men—and I think you behaved as a responsible citizen should. I also agree that men should wear the trousers, but I disagree with the idea that the proper way to hold them up is by wearing a gun belt."

The patient was silent for a few minutes, and the color of his neck and ears became a less angry shade of pink. He said, "Your apology is accepted without loss of honor by either side." Less formally, he went on, "Some of us have to wear belts, Doctor. As a salesman I must wear one to talk to armed executive-level people that I have to do business with. If I went dressed like a sheep they wouldn't let me in to talk at all. At the same time, if I went in with too many studs on my belt they would think that I was the touchy kind who would as soon fight as sell, or the type who sells by intimidation, and I wouldn't get many more appointments.

"I don't want a belt loaded with studs, anyway," he ended. "People are too touchy about their honor these days."

"You can sit up, now," said Devlin, then added, "Just to satisfy my curiosity, how did you extricate yourself from last night's business without staining your escutcheon?"

For a few seconds the other would not meet his eyes, then he said apologetically, "I didn't actually tell a lie, you understand. It was just that these two old boys were blasting at each other so enthusiastically that it sounded like a re-take on operation Overlord, and an armed vidge from the next block could have thought that a Maxer attack was developing and decided to loose one off. After all, there is no proof that the bullet came from—"

"No need to apologize," said Devlin, holding up his hand. "If you stop to think for a minute you'll realize that I prefer people to talk their way out of trouble—it makes less work for me. As for the wound itself, come back in three days unless it begins to feel hot. And rest—don't do anything more energetic than watching television for at least a week. After you are back on your feet, wear a wound disk on your belt at least a month."

He pressed the stud controlling the office door and, as the girl was helping the patient out he called, "Next."

While he was dealing with the succession of sniffs and coughs that followed, Devlin kept remembering that young and unusually sensible patient and the two glimpses he had had of the girl. He decided he liked them well enough to arrange an evening meeting with them in the rec hall for a longer and more wide-ranging discussion. But there was the danger of his other patients thinking that he was playing favorites.

Even greater was the danger that, by talking too much to any of his patients, he might give someone the idea that he was not simply a medic but a medic with psychiatric experience and, just possibly, a cabinet full of the hallucinatory or personality-change drugs that were the institutional psychiatrist's stock in trade.

If the rumor got about that he was a psychiatrist neither his time, his property nor his person would ever be his own again.

His last patient was last because, judging by the condition of the pad she was holding to the side of her face, she had deliberately waited until the others had been attended before coming in. Any number of the coughers and sniffers would, Devlin was sure, have given up their place in line for her. She was in her early twenties. The half of her face which was not hidden by the bloodstained pad was beautiful, and it was obvious from her expression that the facial injury was merely a sympton of much deeper trouble.

Even the symptom was serious enough—three deep, incised wounds running from the cheek bone to the line of the jaw and apparently inflicted with a not very sharp knife. There was a question he had to ask even though he knew what the answer must be.

"Is this a police matter?"

She shook her head.

Devlin tried to conceal his disbelief. He said, "Very well. These are deep cuts which require sutures. I can do the job myself, but frankly, my needlework isn't very neat. A good-looking girl like you needs specialist attention for this sort of thing, and I still have friends at Sanator Five who will help you jump the line and—"

She was shaking her head again.

Leave this one alone. Devlin told himself firmly. *You are not a psychiatrist.*

Go away, himself replied, *and mind your own business.*

None of the waiting room seats were occupied so he could give her extra time without being accused of playing favorites. He said, "Most of the rumors you hear about institutionalized medicine are wildly exaggerated if not completely untrue. I did my training in Five and served there for six years and have kept in touch with some of the residents—one of whom is an expert in invisible mending. He'll see that you are not treated as just another statistic ... Don't shake your head like that or you'll start bleeding again."

The trouble was, Devlin thought angrily, that the rumors about the big hospital complexes were *not* exaggerated. But he wanted to play favorites in this case and use his influence to get her special attention, because the thought of her going through the rest of her life with three ugly puckered scars on the side of one of the most beautiful faces he had ever seen was not to be borne. It would be like watching an old leprosy case burn itself out when the medication was available to cure the condition without wastage.

"I don't understand you," he said quietly. "If it isn't a police matter was it a family fight? A jealous lover? Why not have plastic surgery?"

She stared silently at him for a moment, and Devlin

thought that it was her polite way of telling him to mind his own business, then she said firmly, "Because I did it myself."

Devlin cringed inwardly. It had taken determination to inflict that first cut, but three of them . . . !

He did not have to ask any more questions because she badly wanted to talk about her problem to someone, even though it had only one highly unsatisfactory solution. Her trouble was that she could not keep a boy friend.

". . . the first two I hardly got to know at all," she said quietly. Having decided to talk at last, the words were pouring out. "Somebody decided that I was too good for them and wanted me for himself. One of them died and the other was badly wounded. I wouldn't even speak to the somebody who had challenged them, and for a while I wanted to apply for a belt myself. But I hadn't known them long or well enough to want revenge. I was just angry. Then I met a sheep boy, from this building, who was nice and considerate and sometimes boring about his eye condition which kept him from wearing a belt. They couldn't call him out, but they made life miserable for him in other ways—usually by insulting me in front of our friends—so that he applied for a belt anyway. I broke it off before he could get killed, too.

"The next one was a very good shot," she rushed on, "but tried to avoid trouble. Two young men who thought I was too good for him but an ideal piece of organic property so far as they were concerned, died. I didn't want that; it didn't prove anything except that our society has gone mad. So I thought that if I became a less desirable piece of property I would not be the cause of so many people dying or—"

"Surely there was an easier way . . ." began Devlin, then stopped. His hand was covering the mutilated side of her face and he could see that she had been not only a lovely piece of organic property, but that her expression reflected a character that was determined, self-assured, well balanced and compassionate, with the compassion predominating. Obviously a girl like this would have given a lot of thought to her problem before coming up with her terrible answer.

Devlin swore long and luridly behind a calmly clinical expression and went to work. It was almost an hour later, after the neatest and most painstaking piece of surgery he had ever performed, that he said, "Let me have a look at it tomorrow. And don't try to smile or you might open the . . ."

He broke off again, feeling his face begin to redden with embarrassment. What could she possibly find to smile at?

"I'm sorry," he said awkwardly. "The trick of putting my foot in my mouth I usually reserve for the rec hall, after a couple of quarts of Mix 82."

Her eyes showed sympathy for Devlin's embarrassment, making him feel worse than ever, as she said, "No need to apologize, Doctor. But if you are in the rec hall tonight and feel like doing acrobatic tricks with your foot, I'll be somewhere in Yellow area with my parents. They will probably need some cheering up."

Devlin stared at her for a long time, thinking that he could understand why people wanted to fight over her. Her parents needed cheering up . . .

He nodded finally and said, "I may see you then, provided that I am capable of seeing anything by that time. But if there is a younger male at the table I shall stagger past."

He had a sharp, mental picture of her as she had opened the surgery door, then reality faded in with a message from the ceiling display.

COOLDOWN IN FIFTEEN MINUTES. IS MEMORY RECALL COMPLETE?

"My day, said Devlin, "is hardly yet begun."

The computer would take no meaning from the words, of course, and would accept the instruction as being performed if he did nothing. But he had been asked to remember a day in the Devlin lifetime in complete and accurate detail and, whether he was driven by a sense of duty, a vestigial conscience or a tendency towards masochism, he would try to do just that. So he rose, tapped for a one-hour Hold and returned to his casket.

As the cubicle heaters came on again he sighed and resumed his not very pleasant daydream.

6

HE HAD ONLY one private visit to make that day. It was on the edge of the city more than seven miles away and, although he did not like the thought of a round trip of fifteen miles, he had to take some risks if he were to build up a private practice. The high-density central areas provided resident medics for each block of apartments, but it was listed as an essential service covered by the rental and the salary of the doctor concerned was not high.

Private patients occupied family dwellings rather than living in two-thousand-room apartment buildings, and they had to be very rich or very brave or very well liked to be able to survive at all in such small defensive units. The Bennetts were an unusual combination, Devlin had discovered during his two earlier visits, they were both rich and well liked.

Before leaving his office he called city security to check on route safety and found there was only one major trouble spot between his block and the Bennett home. Two large rival bands of Maxer mercenaries had started a shoot-out in the early hours at a shopping complex about four miles away. Casualties were reported to be heavy and ambulances were standing by, but they could not go in because of the danger of their being hijacked and used by the combatants as armored personnel carriers—APC's. City security forces could not go in because the situation was complicated by pockets of property-owners and members of their night staffs who were trying to defend various buildings against both Maxer factions, and the forces were being used merely to contain the trouble until it burned itself out. People with business in the area were advised to stay clear for at least three hours unless equipped with vehicles possessing overall armor and gas-filtration apparatus.

Devlin mentally plotted a course which would skirt the trouble spot, grabbed his bag and headed for the elevator.

His armored car had been visited during the night or the late morning. On its near-side flank someone had written with a very small finger "Please wash me" in the grime that coated the white paintwork, and all the doors were open. No fittings were missing or damaged, however, and the medical stores were disturbed but otherwise intact. Possibly someone had investigated the unlocked car on the off-chance of finding hard drugs. But much more likely one of the children from the block, sent by his parents to play in the relatively fresh air and safety of the early morning, had been indulging his curiosity as well as practicing his script.

He drove as rapidly as possible along streets that were peaceful and thronged with shoppers, and only once did he pass a suddenly deserted area indicative of an affair about to reach its deadly climax. He did not stop to offer assistance because the city hospital service had that responsibility, and professional poaching was frowned on. It was an unusually quiet morning. He heard less than a dozen shots above the traffic noises, and none of them had been close. He was tempted to open the heavy metal hatches covering the vehicle's tiny windows and drive by direct vision instead of letting his face bounce against the periscope, but his sense of caution prevailed.

It was the generally held belief that the people responsible for the greatest amount of disorder and destruction in the city did their work at night and so tended to sleep late, leaving the streets safe for law-abiding folk during the early part of the day. Like all good rules, Devlin knew from experience, this one had its exceptions.

When he arrived at the Bennett home he was checked and passed by the oldest boy, whose angry brown eyes seemed to be the only spots of color in his face. There was a man in a high white collar already there. He seemed to be one of the new, relaxed breed of clergymen who occasionally swore or cracked jokes or talked a bit dirty if the situation seemed to warrant it. Even though they did very good work in many places, Devlin did not completely approve of the type. An agnostic himself, he still preferred the ministers of the religions he did not believe in to be the proper, old-fashioned kind. He nodded politely.

"My name is Howard," said the minister quietly, "Brother Howard. You cannot help him."

"Can you?" asked Devlin, maintaining his politeness with an effort. It was beginning to look as if the elder Bennett had roped in a faith healer for his son.

But the Brother was looking sympathetically toward the boy's father as he said "Probably not, Doctor. But I shall try."

Until then Devlin had not given much attention to the boy's father. Far too much of his mind was being taken over with thoughts of the two patients he had treated in this morning's surgery. Now he turned a more clinical eye on the father of the patient.

He saw at once that Bennett had more on his mind than a young son with a septic hand which was responding nicely to treatment. He was moving about normally and saying the right things while his expression changed properly to match his words. But all the time his eyes had been and were strangely empty. The mind, which should have been looking out of them, was somewhere else while the body was switched to auto-pilot.

Without speaking, Devlin hurried into the boy's room.

He had confined Tommy Bennett to his room in an attempt to make him rest the hand and to keep the dressings as clean as possible, but now the bandages were smeared with dried watercolor—sometime during the two days since Devlin's last visit the boy had been playing with his paintbox. That was of no importance now, of course, because much more primary color was on the floor by the window and on the white woolen bedspread on which the boy was lying.

The boy looked pale and serious and apparently uninjured, but that was because his red dressing gown was buttoned up to the neck so that a second look was necessary to see the wide, sticky area covering his chest and abdomen. Devlin looked away, noticing the starred window and the small red-flecked crater in the opposite wall, and cursed. He had made the mistake of liking young Tommy.

Devlin could imagine the boy standing by the direct-vision window, watching the smoke rising from the distant trouble spot and listening to the shooting. One of the shots had been wide, and with a high-velocity weapon a bullet traveled forever. He could imagine Tommy's father picking him up and laying him on the bed, or perhaps it had been his mother who had had to do that.

Whichever one, they both needed help—a couple of large-caliber tranquillizers to begin with, and possibly a course of personality-change drugs—PCs—which would give them a calmer, more fatalistic personality for the next few weeks to allow the shock to be absorbed in easy stages. But he could not, of course, give them that kind of help. No medic who did not work and live in one of the big Government hospitals was allowed to prescribe such drugs and, if he did, no pharmacy outside such an institution could have filled the prescription.

Any drug used for the cure or alleviation of psychiatric conditions could be misused and, in the absence of the more common hard drugs, were continually in demand. The price, until the drugs had been withdrawn many years earlier from all but the maximum security hospitals, had very often been the life of the doctor who had carried or stocked them in his surgery. The only course left open to Devlin was to refer the Bennetts to a psychiatric hospital for treatment, where the waiting list might not stretch for longer than a few months and where, if they elected to risk the out-patient department, they would be lucky not to be robbed of their medication on the way out. In short, he could not help them at all even though he had to go through the motions.

But when Devlin left Tommy's bedroom, Bennett was still not really there even though he was being polite to the Brother and Devlin while they expressed their sympathy and asked if there were anything they could do to help him; it was evident that he wanted them to go away.

Devlin caught the Brother's eye and said, "Can I give you a lift anywhere?"

"That is very kind of you, Doctor," said the other, and they began a brief conversational disengagement.

When they were on the street the Brother said quietly, "Mr. Bennett probably wants to curse or cry or break things or, more probably, try to console his wife. He could not do any of those things with us there. So I really don't need a lift, Doctor. I live only a few miles away and at this time of day unaccompanied pedestrians are in very little danger."

"I have to divert anyway," said Devlin, "and I don't have any other urgent calls."

He help open the door on the passenger side, then walked around the car checking for tire damage or the attachment of foreign and possibly explosive objects, then he climbed in himself. But for a long time he made no move toward starting the car, nor did he speak.

"Perhaps," said Brother Howard, when the silence had begun to drag, "you would like to break a few things yourself, Doctor?"

He did not sound impatient at the delay, just sympathetic and angry.

Devlin did not reply.

When the other man spoke again his anger was under control so that only the sympathy showed in his voice. He said, "Perhaps you would like to ask questions, then? A great, sweeping question like 'Why?' Or a more detailed one like 'Why did a young boy like Tommy Bennett have to be killed?' Or perhaps you are the kind who ask questions like 'Why is the human race—which has reached an undreamed-of peak of scientific achievement, personal affluence and more than enough leisure to allow cultural and philosophical advancement to catch up with those material achievements—why is it trying to tear itself apart?' Or maybe you would like to ask the God that you don't believe in what He thinks He's playing at?"

Angrily Devlin started the car and moved slowly through the Bennett security gate before he said, "Perhaps you would like to answer the questions I haven't asked. Or maybe you are looking for the answers to some of them yourself?"

He could feel the other's eyes on him while he stared into the driving periscope, then the Brother said drily, "Well diagnosed, Doctor."

They drove for several minutes in silence, with Devlin beginning to feel more and more ashamed of himself. The other man had been trying to help him, applying a little practical psychology by inviting him to blow off steam. Lacking the proper medication, it was a very good procedure and the other was expert in practicing it. But Devlin, of all people, should have realized that even an expert can be vulnerable.

"I'm sorry," said Devlin suddenly. "I don't know why the human race seems bent on individual and collective suicide when, as everyone agrees, we never had it so good. And I'm sorry that I don't share your belief that this is all a transition stage, an unpleasant wait or training period for something better. But if you wouldn't mind my asking a personal question, what made you become a soul-saver? Why not a socio-technician, a psychologist or even a medic? Those are jobs which usually attract the, well . . ."

"The do-gooders," said Brother Howard, "the sheep who want to do something useful but are too yellow to wear a belt while doing it. There is no need to spare my feelings, Doctor, because you are in the same category. But why, when you were in a position to do the most good for the greatest number of people, did you leave a respectable, secure job in a big hospital to take a block practice?"

Bennett must have been talking about me, Devlin thought. He said, "I suppose because I was processing up to two hundred patients a day—mostly major reconstructions due to car accidents—and I couldn't remember a single one of them by bedtime. I was even losing the inclination to check with Recuperation to see if any of them had survived. As well, when I came across a patient who was wandering around lost in a maze of hospital red tape I got angry at him for his stupidity, regardless of how serious his injuries were. I was beginning to think like a clerk.

"And if you want to know why I became a medic in the first place," Devlin went on, "it was because my father told me at a very early age that death and injury would always be with us, and that the people who helped alleviate the pain would always have work to do and a measure of respect no matter what kind of insane society evolved in the future."

"That was very good advice," said the Brother, and

then went on, "I trained for a job that I wanted to do very much—I was sure that I would be happy in it. But the job became more complicated, difficult and morally disturbing. I won't go into all the details now, if you don't mind."

Devlin nodded. "We have something in common, then—we were both looking for job satisfaction. Or maybe we are merely being selfish in looking for the gratitude and respect of individuals—seeking personal gratification—instead of the impersonal thanks of the many."

"Do you want an argument?" asked the Brother.

"Yes, please," said Devlin.

"Sorry," said Brother Howard. "I'm inclined to agree with you, Doctor. We may well be selfish while practicing altruism. But we are helping things, not making them worse."

"Nothing can make them worse," said Devlin.

Somethings whanged off the side of the car at that moment—a stone or a spent bullet from somewhere. When the noise was not repeated Devlin began to relax again.

"Why can't it get worse, Doctor?" said the Brother. "I'd like to know why you think that."

Devlin took a deep breath, then said, "I hope this isn't a lead-in to a conversion pitch, Reverend. Nothing personal, you understand, but I hate to see wasted effort. But to answer your question, I don't think that things can get worse, or much worse, because we have never had it so good and, at the same time, we have never been so universally unhappy. People are bored. Instead of building they are tearing down—even though they themselves know that it is stupid to do so. Pressures of all kinds are building up in them, both individually and as social groups. You can't tell people to do things anymore; they react, push away from you and each other. They want a change, or they want out, or they don't know what they want except that it isn't ... this. One of these years the pressure will be too much and there will be a great, sick, explosion that will take out even the sensible, responsible kind who are trying their best to run things at present.

"The way I see it," said Devlin seriously, "we have reached the peak of our cultural and scientific potential. It is as if we were a great overripe fruit. We started as a pretty sour and green culture which was prone to war and disease and social injustices. Gradually we grew in intelligence and self-awareness and empathy and personal freedom. The growth continued with society becoming richer, more colorful, sweeter and softer in every way. Now we are ripe."

"And?" asked the Brother.

"After ripening," said Devlin, "fruit rots."

"And you hope for nothing after that?"

"Oh, I'm stupid enough to go on hoping."

"For what?" pressed the Brother.

Devlin was silent for a moment, trying to find words which would not make him sound ridiculous, then he replied, "We are a big, overripe fruit which is under increasing pressure. Maybe, before we fall completely apart, there will be enough pressure on us to squeeze out a pip."

The Brother gave a strained laugh and said, "A good analogy, Doctor."

The laugh and the tone sounded so odd that Devlin glanced aside from his periscope, and when he looked back there was a car nosing out of a side street. He braked hard, skidded, but stopped broadside-on to the other car without hitting it. A large, fat man wearing a belt got out of the car. Devlin muttered under his breath and prepared to do some serious apologizing.

"This was my fault, Doctor," said Brother Howard, climbing out on the other side. "I distracted you."

They stood together for several minutes while the other driver told them what he thought of their stupidity at not looking where they were going. If they had been wearing gun belts, the other driver would have been in the wrong but, as things were, sheep were never in the right.

Devlin was used to this kind of thing and so, no doubt, was the Brother. No actual damage had been done, and the tongue-lashing probably would not last for long because a line of vehicles was beginning to form. He amused himself by counting the number of times the fat man repeated himself and wondering if the over-tight belt was upsetting the other's digestion.

But a small crowd had gathered, including a boy of fourteen or fifteen who was also wearing a gun belt. It was plain that the things which the fat man was saying to the two sheep, or at least to the Brother, were beginning to embarrass the young citizen—so much so that he was about to join in.

Brother Howard had noticed the boy as well, Devlin saw, and seemed to be just as anxious as the Doctor was not to be the cause of an affair. The Brother stepped forward and held up his hand.

"Don't you dare interrupt me, you stupid sheep," said the fat man furiously. "Your profession will save your life but not your honor, if you ever had any. A sheep like you should be—"

"I prefer," said the Brother quietly, "to be called a shepherd. In any case, the condition of sheep is a temporary one which can be ended at any time, for any desired period of time." He swung around and walked to the boy. Very politely and correctly he said, "Pardon, Citizen. I would be obliged if you would lend me your belt."

"But Reverend . . ." began the boy.

"I would be obliged if you would retain your weapon, Citizen, and lend me your belt."

The fat man had paled when the Brother had turned wolf suddenly, and Devlin realized that he had probably been greatly relieved when two sheep had climbed out of the car a few minutes earlier. If a full, belt-wearing citizen had been driving, there would have been an affair on the spot with the possibility of the fat man being killed. There was, after all, an awful lot of him to aim at. Probably he was not very fast, either, and knew that he would have died unless he publicly accepted all blame for the near-accident. But relief had made him vicious rather than gracious, and now that he had the double relief of shooting at a suicidal maniac it was unlikely that he would be satisfied with inflicting a token wound.

"Excuse me, Citizen," said Devlin desperately to the fat man. "My friend has had a very severe mental shock—a young boy who ..."

"It is my considered opinion," said Brother Howard, joining them again with his hands hanging very still below his empty, borrowed belt, "that you are self-indulgent in food and alcohol, vastly overweight, completely lacking in manners and the worst driver that I have ever seen. If you wish to dispute this opinion, be prepared to defend yourself."

For an instant Devlin felt a wild hope that the fat man would pass out from a cerebral haemorrhage before he was able to draw. His face had gone an improbable plum color. But no, Devlin saw him begin to draw, very clearly. Less distinctly he saw the man's gun wrist and nose broken, not necessarily in that order, by the blunt edges of two flesh-colored blades that had been the Brother's hands. Clearly, because it was the last and slowest blow, he saw a set of stiffened fingers sink into the other's diaphragm—a blow that would have been fatal but for the thick layer of adipose in the area.

Devlin brought a litter from his car and made the fat man as comfortable as possible while the Brother returned the boy's belt. Judging from the conversation, he had gained a convert as well as a hero-worshipper. But when they were moving again Brother Howard looked very depressed.

"There is no permanent damage, Brother," said Devlin reassuringly, "but he will need hospital treatment."

"I know, Doctor," said the other apologetically. "But

it will put you to considerable inconvenience, and ...
and I am ashamed to say, I took sinful pleasure from
that incident."

"No comment," said Devlin.

"You're very kind, Doctor," said the Brother. "Oh,
you can drop me here, please. And maybe we can meet
again soon and continue our discussion. I mean that.
I'm not just being polite."

"You're an interesting man to know, Reverend," said
Devlin. "But you still won't make a convert."

"Maybe I'm only looking for recruits," said the other
airily.

"There's a difference?"

"There's a big difference," said the Brother as he
slammed the hatch.

The man he had known in the casualty department
of Sanator Five had recently transferred to another hospital so that it was long after dark before he could un-
tangle himself from the red tape. Devlin could recall
every minute of the ride home, during which every
vidge on the way seemed to take a shot or throw a
piece of homemade nastiness at him. By the time he
had freshened up and gone down to the Yellow area of
the rec hall, the pre-midnight activity level had reached
the noisy and nasty stage, with non-affair brawls breaking out all over. The girl and her parents were occupying
a four-piece table but were about to leave.

Although he could not apologize directly for his late
arrival—that would have implied that two citizens and
their daughter had been awaiting the pleasure of a
sheep—the atmosphere thawed considerably when he
mentioned the incident that had delayed him, and they
stayed talking about nothing in particular for about
half an hour. They called him Devlin, of course, because he was off-duty and not a full citizen, but otherwise they were friendly and very easy to talk to. The
girl's father had vidge duty from midnight, however,
and wanted to see the others secure before he left for
the roof.

Devlin wanted to say that he would look after his daughter for an hour or so and see her safely to her apartment, but that would have embarrassed them. A man without a belt was not considered capable of looking after anyone in this situation, and they would have been forced to tell him so.

He remembered the look of concern in her eyes as they rose to go, and every wrinkle in every strip of tape which held that incongruous dressing on to the damaged side of the otherwise lovely face. Especially he remembered her voice as she said, "We may see you tomorrow night, if you happen to be here then."

Devlin had nodded, making a mighty resolution to be nowhere else.

She had said. "Goodnight, Devlin."

The display was saying COOLDOWN IMMINENT. GOODNIGHT DEVLIN.

7

FROM THE TIME he became aware of himself in relation to the others around him he knew that he was different. He had been scrawny and malformed from birth, and his condition had not been helped by minimal food intake during the early months of his life. Then, every feeding time had been a battle with siblings stronger than he for a place at their mother, who did not seem to care whether he had enough or not. His had been a long and unhappy childhood completely without warmth or affection or security, and his even longer approach to maturity was a period of unallayed misery.

The other tribes and large family groups occupying the forest drove him away because he was a stranger. His own people tolerated his presence because he had the right tribe smell, but otherwise would have nothing to do with him.

Unlike them, he was not good in the trees. He did not have the stamina for a rapid, sustained climb to safety when the predators of the forest floor tore at the lower branches. He grew cautious and was always alert for the approach of the carnivores so as to have more time to climb to safety. As the days passed he was able to watch the quick, happy, over-confident ones being smashed against the tree-trunks by enormous paws, or the ones with the long, sleek fur shaken from ill-chosen branches to be ripped apart before they could hit the ground.

For some reason the predators had become more than usually active in that area of forest, and the number of males in his tribe was diminishing. Like himself, the females were more cautious and tended to survive these attacks.

But the days passed and he grew as strong as he would ever be, and the tribe was strutting and squabbling and grappling its way through the mating season. Over the long, unhappy years he had learned that for him to take part was to risk serious injury or death. Even in a group seriously depleted of males, he was tolerated but not wanted. He thought about it very seriously and decided he did not want to be injured or to die. Then a female recently made mate-less passed within a few feet of him . . .

She screeched and fought and tried to get away from him at first. He felt the painful nipping of her teeth and the long scratches she left on his face and almost hairless body. But the pain stimuli was swamped by the roaring flood of raw, mindless instinct which drove him at the female. He knew that they were making too much noise, and they were attracting the attention of their tribe and probably that of nearby carnivores. But his fear was as insubstantial as the pain of the scratches and bites, because now the urge to join and mate which drove him had triggered off a response in the female and she was no longer fighting.

Caught in the biological trap and shaken by diminishing explosions of sensation, he became aware that he was still being attacked. Fear and pain returned as the female left him and he realized that virtually the whole tribe was surrounding him, struggling for a chance to scratch and bite his body. He struggled frantically to escape, but the angry circle was always there, nipping and scratching and pulling him down when he tried to climb. They were herbivores lacking the physical equipment to inflict killing wounds, but they had hate and persistence and numbers enough to kill one of their fellows if it became necessary.

Apparently it was necessary to kill him for the present and future good of the tribe—an instinctive attempt to avoid the possibility of other scrawny weaklings being born to them—and they would do it no matter how long it took them.

But suddenly the attack stopped. He lay quivering with pain from the tight lacework of bites and tears that covered his body, unable to see the damage because his eyes had been lost early in the attack. Then the explanation came as something large and heavy flattened the undergrowth beside him. The predator, unlike the members of his tribe, did have the natural weapons to kill effortlessly and efficiently.

A darkness that was not of his blinded eyes descended with merciful speed, and the cold was invading every molecule of his being, until the cubicle heaters drove it back.

GOOD MORNING DEVLIN. SHIP STATUS FOUR HUNDRED AND SIXTY-TWO YEARS INTO MISSION, SHIP PERSONNEL CURRENTLY AWAKE—ONE. IDENTITY JOHN DEVLIN.

"Wait. Wait a minute," said Devlin through chattering teeth. "There's something wrong. Let me think, damn you!"

REASONS FOR AWAKENING. OVERALL HUMAN GUIDANCE REQUIRED DURING FORTHCOMING FLY-BY. TO CHECK FUNCTIONING OF DEVLIN MUSCLE SYSTEMS, CIRCULATION, SPEECH ORGAN AND MEMORY.

The idea which had been trying to reach the surface of his mind sank again without a trace. Overall human guidance required—that sounded serious.

PERIOD OF AWAKENING INDEFINITE. FOOD INTAKE PERMITTED SUBJECT TO WASTE ELIMINATION PROCEDURE BEFORE COOLDOWN.

"Get on with it," said Devlin irritably. The display kept telling him the same thing after each awakening—in case of memory impairment, no doubt. But if anything the cold-sleep seemed to be sharpening his memory rather than dulling it.

PRESENCE IN CONTROL CENTER REQUIRED IN ONE HOUR. THIS PERIOD TO BE SPENT CHECKING PHYSICAL AND MENTAL FUNCTIONS. CARRY OUT INSTRUCTION EXERCISE AND REMEMBER.

He surprised himself by being able to ignore his anxiety over the nature of the ship emergency and by recalling several incidents from his seventh birthday. They were sharp and clear because it had been his last happy birthday, and for that reason he usually tried not to remember it. But as he moved through the preliminary physical exercises his mind kept jumping all over the place, from his latest dream to his recent past in the training center, back to the brontosaurus sequence, to Tommy Bennett and Brother Howard and the girl in Blue 31. Each time his mind jumped the person or incident flashed up bright and clear—like lights in a pinball machine. He could see and feel every sensory impression associated with it, and he knew that if need be he could concentrate his mind and expand on any of the incidents until he had a complete sequence, equally sharp and clear in every respect.

"There's something wrong," he said again.

Memories, or memories of dreams, should not be as sharp and clear as that. Loss of mental ability was thought to be the greatest single danger, they had been told, threatening the success of the voyage. But Devlin's memory, and presumably his ability to think, was not impaired after four centuries in cold-sleep—the exact opposite was happening, in fact. His memories were gaining a clarity usually associated with hallucinatory and sensation-heightening drugs, and his dreams . . .

He did not think that he could take any more such dreams. The last one had been so vivid that he sweated just thinking about it. The creatures inhabiting the dream had been completely unfamiliar to him. He doubted if they were pre-men, or even pre-monkeys, and the predators had been shaggy and shapeless to his terrified eyes and could have been descended from anything. He had certainly not read about anything like them.

And neither had the dead girl in Blue 31 read anything about dinosaurs.

Since he had been forced to watch her die, Devlin had tried to forget the incident. But now, for some reason, it was becoming impossible to forget anything. Suddenly he was back in Blue 31, hearing her talking and seeing her die from a combination of galloping gangrene and massive thrombosis, and feeling all the emotions that at the time he had tried to suppress.

Her last dream had been of being a female dinosaur and her last thought was of her Brian. She must have known Brian very well and she had known nothing at all about dinosaurs. She had deliberately avoided reading about them. Why, then, had she dreamed about them and not about her Brian?

Why had Devlin, not even once, dreamed of his Patricia?

Was everyone on the ship having the same dreams?

He stopped exercising, his breath making an intermittent fog around his head while he sought a way through the even thicker haze of speculation that filled his brain. If everyone was having the same dreams, and that could be checked by awakening a statistically meaningful number of the others and questioning them, then the dream material had been artificially produced despite everything they had been told during training.

They had been told that the ship could not carry enough direct mental stimulators and recordings to keep their minds occupied during the centuries-long voyage. But would that still apply if only one set of recordings was being used for everyone? And what about the memory-sharpening effect which he had noticed recently? That suggested the use of hallucinatory drugs. And was he really undergoing cold-sleep for hundreds of years at a time just because a computer display told him so?

Was he, perhaps, still under training? Was this frigid, silent structure all around him in Earth orbit and his reactions, along with everyone else's, being continually observed and monitored?

"If you must question," Brother Howard had told him on one occasion, "question everything."

Devlin was still asking questions of himself when he took one of the control positions an hour later.

```
SITUATION REPORT. SHIP IS CLOSING TARGET
SYSTEM FIVE. OTHER SYSTEMS NOT SUITABLE FOR
SEEDING AND BYPASSED WITH THE EXCEPTION OF PASS
THREE AUTHORIZED BY JOHN DEVLIN.
LONG-RANGE SCAN INDICATES TARGET FIVE MARGINALLY
SUITABLE FOR HUMAN COLONIZATION DUE TO HIGH BUT
NON-LETHAL LEVELS OF TOXIC ELEMENTS IN THE
PLANETARY ATMOSPHERE. SURFACE GRAVITY ONE
POINT ZERO FIVE EARTH NORMAL. ANALYSIS OF
RADIATION PATTERNS INDICATES PRESENCE OF
INTELLIGENT LIFE-FORM POSSESSING NUCLEAR
TECHNOLOGY. COMPUTER DECISION TAKEN TO LAUNCH
HIGH VELOCITY PROBE FOR CLOSER INVESTIGATION,
```

COMPUTER DECISION TAKEN TO AWAKEN CREW-MEMBER
DEVLIN FOR OBSERVATION AND EVALUATION OF DATA.

"I should damn well hope so," said Devlin. "But
thanks, anyway."

CLOSE-RANGE PROBE SCAN OF SYSTEM AND PLANETARY
SATELLITES CONFIRMS PRESENCE OF INTELLIGENT
LIFE-FORM POSSESSING ADVANCED SPACE TRAVEL
CAPABILITY. PROBE SOFT-LANDED SUCCESSFULLY.
PROBE DETECTED, IMMOBILIZED AND RETAINED
FOR INVESTIGATION BY NATIVE LIFE-FORM.
PROBE NO LONGER TRANSMITTING.
PROBE DATA AND EVALUATION OF MOST RECENT
OBSERVATIONS OF SPACE ACTIVITY AROUND OUTER
PLANETARY SATELLITES INDICATE THAT LIFE-FORM
IS EXTREMELY HOSTILE.

"By-pass, stupid," said Devlin. "What's the problem?"

THREE SPACE VEHICLES CLOSING ON COLLISION
COURSE. HIGH ACCELERATION, RELATIVELY SMALL
SIZE AND PRESENCE OF UNSHIELDED RADIATION
IN NOSE CONE AREAS INDICATE OBJECTS CONTAIN
NUCLEAR WARHEADS.
OVERALL HUMAN GUIDANCE REQUIRED.

Devlin stared at the words on the display screen, felt
the sweat pop on his hands, forehead and at the base of
his spine. It was probably a test. Almost certainly it
was a test. But was it a test?

There might be no danger at all. Their ship, possibly
the last hope of a race which was stewing in its own
physical and psychological effluent, might not be about
to be torn into its component atoms by an alien nuclear
device. Probably the threat was nothing more than a
near-perfect simulation.

But he kept remembering Yvonne Caldwell, the girl
in Blue 31. Her death had been a too-perfect simulation. If he really were being tested and he made a mistake, like the stupid accident in the girl's cubicle, this
could well be a test for destruction.

8

ALTHOUGH ITS HOME world had been plentifully equipped with highly sophisticated and dirigible forms of nastiness, the ship had been deliberately designed and built without any form of offensive or defensive armament.

The idea had been that in the highly unlikely event of a meeting in space with an extra-terrestrial race possessing a technology equal to or greater than that of Earth, friction was unlikely to occur. Any race that had achieved interstellar flight, and that possessed the background of social and scientific cooperation that such a high level of technology implied, should be civilized in every sense of the word. Such a race would not, the ship's designers and psychologists had been sure, be expected to react with hostility toward strangers simply because they were strange. The computer had other ideas.

```
FIRST VEHICLE ORBIT INTERSECTION THREE HOURS
FIFTY-THREE MINUTES. SECOND VEHICLE THREE
HOURS FIFTY-SIX MINUTES. THIRD VEHICLE THREE
HOURS FIFTY-NINE MINUTES.
```

Devlin rubbed his palms against his coveralls and wondered if the ship and project designers had made any other fundamental errors, even though this error could make the others irrelevant.

Do I need help?

Awakenings, except for reasons of the direst emergency, were forbidden. Ship consumables were strictly limited so that periods of awakening were kept as short as possible. Loneliness, however, or a need for human conversation or contact, was not considered to be an emergency. In a voyage which had lasted over four centuries, Devlin had spent less than four days of biological time in the ship. As a result his memory of the final briefing was only four days old despite all the dream lifetimes that had occurred since then.

Especially sharp was the memory of their instructions regarding emergency procedures.

"... we can conceive of no emergency that would require more than one person to be awake at any time. Your ship is self-guiding and its systems are either self-repairing or they possess multiple backups, so that awakenings should be for exercise, observation and, of course, decision on the suitability of the target planet before deceleration is applied.

"If awakened for any other reason," the instructor had gone on, "it will be up to the individual concerned to decide whether or not he needs additional human assistance. But to avoid situations where, say, a crewmember awakens others for moral support, or to try to pass responsibility for solving a tricky problem to one of the colonists, who will be less qualified than he is to handle it, we have made it the rule that the first crewmember to be awakened is deemed to be the senior during the emergency.

"If absolutely necessary he can call on additional human assistance or advice," the instructor had added, "but he cannot transfer responsibility to another. Ideally he should make the decision himself and save on the consumables."

The display was reminding Devlin that dire emergencies would occur in three hours forty-seven, fifty and fifty-three minutes' time. He decided to sweat it out alone for a while, rather than awaken Patricia or some of the others to watch him do it. He requested the data obtained by the probe before it stopped communicating and a fast re-run of transmitted visual material up until that time.

Like the Earth which his memory insisted he had left only four days ago, this planet was habitable, densely inhabited, but not really suitable for human or any other kind of intelligent habitation.

Even the world's two airless moons, which had never been capable of sustaining any form of life, were covered with city-sized blisters filled to bursting with beings who had exchanged their larger and more crowded planetary prison for ones that were smaller, but that offered fractionally more living space.

He had thought that the Earth had been polluted, but it had been like an eighteenth-century garden compared to the visual data sent back by the probe. Nothing lived on the planetary surface. Nothing moved on the land or sea except robots which tended vast, inland lakes of wastes or tracts of bright, artificial greenery protected by domes whose natural sunlight, because of the stinking and near-opaque atmosphere, had to be augmented by massed batteries of artificial lighting. Hundreds of other dome cities floated on or under the turgid oceans, which were also covered by vast carpets of greenery. In several areas there was evidence of robot activity around an area of sickly yellow or brown that was, presumably, a diseased section undergoing cure or destruction.

Not unexpectedly, the natives of this world looked like something which had crawled from underneath a very damp rock.

Steady, thought Devlin, *your xenophobia is showing.*

There were lots of chances to see the natives in action as, covered by opaque protection suits, they retrieved the probe from the planetary surface, subjected it to elevated temperatures and a variety of what were presumably anti-bacteria sprays and, finally, transported it to a sub-surface laboratory staffed by people whose physical charms were no longer concealed by protective clothing.

If they had had tentacles or pincers or antennae he would not have felt so bad about them, but they were so nearly human in shape, that they made him want to be sick.

They had narrow cylindrical heads joined to the chest by a very flexible neck of the same diameter as the head, which was hairless and seemed to have much more skin than it really needed. Among the loose folds and creasings of skin there were the fleshy gashes of eating or breathing orifices, a couple of flowerlike proturberances which were probably ears and, set on top of the head, two large yellowish blisters which could only be eyes. The shoulders and chest were uniformly rounded, and from the waist the creatures spread out like giant, wrinkled pears balanced on two short legs fringed with misshapen toes or atrophied tentacles. The arms were long and thin, sprouting from just above waist level, and were jointed at elbows and wrists. Beyond the wrist the limbs were multi-brachiate, with three distinct groups of fingers evolved for rough, medium or very delicate work.

Their skin was pallid and greasy and partly covered by small patches of color which might have been clothing or badges of rank. The placement of their eyes made them incline their heads toward each other when they spoke, giving the impression of aggressiveness, and the sounds they made were like the gobblings of a turkey.

The probe's vision pick-up showed one of the aliens gobbling and waving its arms at three others who looked and sounded much less agitated. Perhaps they were the first creature's subordinates being attentive.

Suddenly one of them held up an arm level with its face and gave it a peculiar, whiplike jerk. All the groups of fingers made small, crackling sounds like a body falling into dry underbrush. There was absolute silence for a few minutes, then the voluble one reached toward the vision pick-up and the picture died.

Devlin stared at the blank display, aware that he had been jumping to conclusions. The agitated one had not been the boss then, but a subordinate who could have been arguing with its superiors for a course of action that had been overruled. Perhaps it had wanted to maintain the vision channel with a view to establishing communications, and its chief had been worried about security. Devlin tapped for a slow-motion re-run of the final ten minutes, studying not only the four beings but the items of equipment which were within visual range.

He could make nothing of the equipment and all four aliens looked exactly the same to him—but he discovered another conclusion to jump away from. The soft, fleshy heads were not heads at all but simply a flexible platform for the beings' main sensory organs. The head was the solid rounded structure which he had mistaken for a chest, and the arms grew from the shoulder area and not the waist. The creatures were really unhuman and the realization made him, for some odd reason, feel much better disposed toward them.

Even though they had launched three nuclear missiles against the ship?

Cursing, Devlin cleared the display of slow-moving aliens and their distorted, low-key gobblings. In all probability the probe had been dismantled by now and was no longer capable of responding to signals from the ship. Nevertheless, he would have liked to communicate with these aliens, even though their world was too over-crowded to be of any use as a colony site. However briefly, Devlin would have liked to talk to them instead of fighting with them.

Especially, he thought cynically, *since I have nothing to fight them with.*

For a few minutes his fear receded, replaced by the wonder and curiosity of seeing and listening to members of an extra-terrestrial intelligent race, but then it came flooding back. His palms were sweating again as he tapped,

WHAT CAN WE USE AS A WEAPON?
PLEASE CLARIFY.

"You stupid computer," raged Devlin. "You know what I want . . . !"

But did it? The ship was unarmed and, while its

computer was capable of recognizing a threat in the shape of oncoming missiles, it had no programed instructions for turning its ploughshare power sources and equipment into swords.

Should he awaken someone?

Devlin shook his head angrily. He had to *think*. He must make sure that, before he called for assistance, he had done everything possible to help himself.

He tapped,

LIST ALL POWER SOURCES AVAILABLE
WITHIN THE SHIP. LIST SYSTEMS NOT DIRECTLY
CONNECTED TO LIFE-SUPPORT WITH POWER AVAILABLE.

But before the display could react he hit the Cancel button. He would be stupid to waste time watching the computer talking about the ship in great and probably useless detail.

LIST POWER SOURCES AND SYSTEMS WITH LONG-RANGE
EFFECTS, he tapped, then added, OMIT
COMMUNICATION SYSTEMS.

PLEASE CLARIFY.

Devlin took a deep breath and exhaled it slowly. The computer was *not* stupid, he reminded himself. It could give only the answers which it had been programed to give, and then only when the questions were properly phrased. It was the computer's programers who had been remiss, four centuries ago.

He tapped, LIST SYSTEMS FOR PREVENTION OF
ACCIDENTAL DAMAGE OR INJURY TO VESSELS OR
PERSONNEL MAKING A CLOSE APPROACH TO THE SHIP
SHORTLY BEFORE ACTIVATION OF DRIVE.

PLEASE CLARIFY SHORTLY.

MINUS THREE MINUTES.

BROADCAST WARNINGS ON SHUTTLE FREQUENCIES
ORDERING VEHICLES AND PERSONNEL CLEAR OF FLIGHT
PATH AND BEYOND FIVE MILE RADIUS OF SHIP.

WARNING LIGHTS MOUNTED FORE, AFT AND AT FIFTY-
YARD INTERVALS AROUND THE HULL. FLASHING
LIGHTS ON SECONDARY DRIVE REACTOR ORIFICE.
FLUORESCENT PAINT IN AREAS WHERE STRUCTURAL
PROJECTIONS ENDANGER SPACESUITS. . . .

Devlin turned his face away from the display, fighting despair. He had had a vague idea of finding out
ways in which the ship could be dangerous to objects
or people approaching it by discovering the safety
devices and systems and then switching them off. But
as the list of safety measures lengthened it became
more and more obvious that the greatest danger to an
object in the vicinity would be if the ship rammed it.
He turned back to the display and reached for the
Cancel button, then stopped.

. . . IN THE EVENT OF A MAXIMUM THRUST TEST
OF THE SECONDARY DRIVE TO SIMULATE AN ABORTED
LANDING, VESSELS AND PERSONNEL ARE WARNED TO
REMAIN BEYOND A MINIMUM DISTANCE OF FIVE MILES
ASTERN. RADIATION HAZARD SIGNALS ARE BROADCAST
ON ALL SHUTTLE FREQUENCIES. FLASHING LIGHTS ON
SECONDARY DRIVE REACTOR ORIFICE ARE . . .

He had almost forgotten about the secondary drive
which was needed only during the final approach and
landing. It was a relatively unsophisticated piece of
equipment using a nuclear reactor and water as fuel,
but anything which got in the way of the jet would become severely overheated and, in the case of a dirigible
missile, its control and guidance systems would be dis-
rupted by a concentrated beam of ions and its warhead
might very well go prematurely critical.

Directing the drive at three missiles in turn while
they were within effective range would call for some
very fancy maneuvring on the part of the computer, for
beyond a distance of five miles the secondary drive jet
would be something less than a hazard. Eagerly, Devlin
called up the relevant figures, then slumped back in his
couch.

The fantastically high closing speed of ship and missiles was such that only a few seconds could be allocated to dealing with each of them between the times needed for changes of attitude. That was scarcely enough time to warm their metallic hides, much less detonate them a safe distance from the ship.

He had to face the fact that the ship could not fight. But could it evade? Devlin began tapping again, trying to find out exactly what the ship had in the way of legs to run with.

There was the main drive which had provided the gentle and continuous acceleration that had built up to their present velocity of one-quarter lightspeed. It had been shut down until they found a suitable planet and they had to use it again to decelerate and return. The secondary drive, whose legs were designed for sprinting rather than marathon running, delivered three G's during final approach and landing.

According to the computer, the missiles had been launched from a satellite of the alien home planet nearly three months earlier. Devlin did not know exactly how advanced the aliens' equipment was, but he assumed that the ship had been detected and its course through their system plotted anything up to a year previously. The missiles had been launched on an intersecting course but, like the ship, were no longer under acceleration. Perhaps they were nothing more than large, sophisticated bullets, incapable of further trajectory modification. In that case he could duck with a very good chance of avoiding trouble, and the sooner he ducked the better his chances would be.

He strapped himself more securely to the couch and, without giving himself a chance to have second thoughts, requested three minutes three-G thrust on the secondary drive at right angles to the present course. Theoretically the evasive action would have been equally effective if he had accelerated towards the missiles, or even decelerated and allowed them to pass ahead of him, but psychologically it was more comforting to turn away from the attack and the people who had launched it—especially when the display was showing graphically the narrow margin by which the ship would avoid disaster.

According to the display, the missiles would pass within fifty to sixty miles distance unless their courses were modified. Should the aliens be capable of this, the display gave the times involved—a little over six minutes for the ship's course change to become apparent to the attackers, an unknown number of seconds or minutes for the aliens to react and recompute trajectories, and just under three minutes for their radio signals to go out to the missiles.

Devlin watched the display anxiously.

```
MISSILE ONE MISS DISTANCE FIFTY-SIX POINT THREE
MILES. MISSILE TWO MISS DISTANCE FIFTY-ONE
POINT SEVEN MILES. MISSILE THREE COURSE
CORRECTION INITIATED. MISSILE THREE ON
COLLISION COURSE. ESTIMATING CONTACT TWO HOURS
FIFTY-SEVEN POINT EIGHT MINUTES.
```

Devlin swore. The missiles did carry enough fuel to make course corrections. But only one of them had done so—the one which had been due to strike last and which therefore had more time to maneuver. This move might be an indication that the aliens' computing facilities were being overstretched or simply that they were so confident of hitting the ship that they were refusing to waste time diverting all three missiles.

To give himself time to think he tapped for a replay of the sound and visual material from the probe, and stared at what he thought might be a good alien and the three bad aliens.

His first impulse had been to order random attitude changes and periods of thrust which would give the aliens' control-and-guidance people a lot of work to do and, just possibly, would reduce missile three's capacity to maneuver. But a random attitude and course change would take them toward the missile at times. He could not afford a near miss because the radiation, although it might not be fatal as far as everyone aboard was concerned, would probably injure the people in cold-sleep who were positioned below the outer hull. Then too, the computer would have to carry out all the random movements in reverse order if the ship were to regain its original course and reach the next target system.

The ship was moving deeper into the alien system and closing rapidly with the missiles, which meant that the reaction time of the missiles' guidance people to ship course changes was also reducing. But if he could make a drastic course change within that reaction time, using the secondary drive at its full emergency thrust of five G's, the aliens might assume that the ship was incapable of any greater evasive effort than the three G's already used and their counter computations, necessarily hurried, might be correspondingly off. Devlin did a few quick calculations and decided that a two-minute five-G burn within the reaction time would pull the ship out of danger.

The computer did not agree.

Devlin found himself fighting back anger and a bout of hysterical laughter as the ship's computer did its best to mutiny. It did not want him to apply five-G's thrust to the ship, it flashed, because this should only be done in the event of an extreme emergency shortly before landing on unsuitable terrain. The ship's systems would be severely overstressed by five G's. This would not matter if the ship were landing shortly afterwards, but it could be dangerous for the occupants if it had to resume the voyage after such a period of maximum stress. The display went on to list the dangers of such an action, detailing the effects on power reserves, life-support systems and long-range sensory equipment. Every time Devlin tried to tap out an instruction he got nothing but warning lights, and the minutes were rushing past.

"Damn you," he said to the side display, which was still showing the four aliens talking and gesticulating in slow motion. "We aren't invading you. We wouldn't touch your stinking overcrowded system with a barge pole!"

But a calmer, more controlled corner of his mind knew that the aliens had a point of view, too. They were simply reacting to the apparent threat by a strange ship which was storming into their system with intentions that they could only guess at. If the positions had been reversed, Earth people would probably have done the same.

He tapped again for emergency acceleration of five G's, and the warnings and precautionary telltales began flashing again. He tapped for four G's and received no objections at all.

With his finger poised above the Execute button he stopped, canceled, and tapped for four point five G's. Still no objections. He tried edging it up a few decimal points while extending the period of thrust, and the arguments started again. Apparently the computer would cooperate at four point five G's for three minutes and no higher.

He needed nearly two hours to power-up the secondary-drive reactor and to check its focusing coils, and by that time it was obvious the first two missiles were being allowed to go wide. The third was still on a collision course and closing rapidly. When the ship took evasive action, the time-lag needed for the light carrying this information to reach the aliens and for the radio signals bearing the course correction to reach the missile was just over four minutes. Any dodging that he could do would have to be done within that time.

He called up a picture of the area of sky from which the missile would come.

The aliens, if they were using their oddly equipped heads, would pre-time the missile to explode at the nearest approach. The detonation signal would go out to the missile at the last possible moment and be based on the latest available course data—which would be less than four minutes out of date.

Precisely four minutes before estimated impact the thrust from the secondary drive rammed him deeply into his couch. There was nothing on the display screen but stars and, in one corner, a distance figure that was blurring rapidly through the eight hundreds. One minute, two minutes, three minutes passed and it seemed that the missile's rate of approach was slowing—but not, Devlin was sure, quickly enough. Not until the distance closed to under one hundred miles was he able to recognize individual numbers, not until the forties that the missile showed any signs of slowing, and there were only a few seconds remaining before estimated impact when the figures crept out of the low twenties and into the 'teens. They hesitated at sixteen miles distance, then withdrew to seventeen, eighteen ...

An intolerably bright point of light appeared near the center of the display screen, and by the time Devlin had blinked away the after-image it had become an expanding patch of mist which was almost too diffuse to see. He waited for a shock wave to hit the ship, but it did not even shudder.

"The inverse square law," he said, laughing with relief, "is wonderful."

He felt happy as the ship went through the secondary drive maneuvers that would return it to the original programed course heading towards the next target system; he was delighted that the near-miss had not—so far as the status displays were concerned—had any ill effects on the ship, its systems or the cold-sleeping colonists whom he had been instrumental in saving. But he also felt a vague uncertainty and a feeling of surprise that he had been able to accomplish so much. True, his memory had recently become much more retentive and the lecture material on computers during training could, perhaps unconsciously, have been available in his mind. Whatever the reason, he had, for a few crucial minutes back there, felt he knew exactly what he was doing.

At best he was a hero, Devlin thought dryly, and at

worst a crew-member under observation who had passed a difficult test. Trouble was, he found it difficult to believe that the aliens who had tried to kill him were the product of a simulator. And if he was a hero, he deserved a pat on the back from someone.

He did not get it from the computer.

```
COURSE CORRECTION COMPLETE. SECONDARY DRIVE
REACTOR POWERED DOWN. WARNING. REACTION MASS
REMAINING FOR PLANETARY LANDING BELOW MARGIN FOR
SAFETY.
```

If it had been a test, he might not have passed.

9

IT SEEMED TO Devlin that all his life had been spent trying to pass tests, failing most of them, and then trying to escape the results of the failures. He was trying to escape the latest failure by escaping into cold-sleep, but the computer was being awkward.

```
NEGATIVE TO REQUEST FOR IMMEDIATE COOLDOWN.
CARRY OUT INSTRUCTION REMEMBER. COOLDOWN IN ONE
HOUR THIRTY-FIVE MINUTES.
```

Devlin did not want to remember anything, neither his own past life nor the bright, pleasant and often agonizing dream lives. Although the process of memory was one of the Devlin organic systems that was capable of being checked by a temporary Hold, it could not be switched off.

Not only was it becoming impossible to forget anything of importance, even the most trivial incidents were coming back to him with a clarity and intensity that made him wonder if someone—or some medically programed thing—were feeding him psycho-augmenter drugs. He did not know and he could be sure of nothing. His only means of defense against a recall of too-painful memories was to concentrate on one of the less unpleasant days in his life.

The day which he had decided to recall had begun pleasantly. He had seen only three patients in the office that morning and had no private visits scheduled. During the preceding two weeks there had been a sudden upsurge in block security casualties and affairs of honor within the building, but now they were entering a period of relative sanity that, experience had taught him, might last for a few days. His last patient had been Patricia Morley, the girl with the lacerated cheek.

"It is healing nicely," Devlin said as he renewed the dressing, "but there will be scars. Are you sure you won't have plastic surgery?"

"No," she said firmly.

This was her fourth visit to the office and he had twice spoken to her in the recreation hall, so that their time together totaled no more than three hours. Her face was no longer giving her pain and, although she still considered her reason for inflicting the wound a good one, she was normal enough to want to hide the scars behind a no-longer-necessary dressing. Very soon she would no longer need him as a doctor. Devlin was glad about that, but a little worried in case she might have to swap him for a psychiatrist.

Sufferers in silence, even those who could do so without complaint or outward show of distress, were still sufferers.

Clearly she wanted to talk about her problem which was, fundamentally, a non-surgical one. She was not a wailer, a martyr to misfortune or a potential suicide. Devlin would not in the least have minded listening to her, but in their present surroundings the conversation stayed on a much too clinical level.

"It's a fine, sunny day," said Devlin. "I advise you to get some fresh air and exercise in the district park."

She laughed at that because the fresh air of the city was anything but and compared unfavorably with the cooled and filtered hurricane that whistled continually from the building's main air ducts.

"It is three miles away," Devlin went on, "which should be exercise enough if you go on foot. But to make sure that you are following doctor's orders, I shall call at the park on my way back from morning rounds. If you look to be on the verge of exhaustion I shall offer you refreshment and a ride back."

"As a form of exercise," she replied, "it beats the nightly epilepsy to music in the rec hall. All right, Doctor, I'll follow the prescribed treatment. But isn't this a very complicated way of asking for a date?"

"It *is*?" asked Devlin, then more honestly he added, "It is."

But there were very good reasons for his circumspection, Devlin thought as Patricia left his office, and she understood them just as well as he did. In the rec hall there was too much noise and not enough light for their few chaperoned meetings to be generally noticed. But driving her away from the block in his car after passing through the security checkpoint which, at this early and safe time of the day was manned by over-talkative oldsters, would cause comment. Giving her a lift back in his medic's vehicle, considering that her dressing would make her look like a walking casualty, would not give rise to any talk.

There was also the fact that as a member of a non-belted profession he was nominally a citizen, but actually, so far as the younger belt-wearers in the block were concerned, he was a sheep pretending to be a citizen. The girl had already suffered too much as a result of young citizens offering her unwanted protection and, in at least two cases, killing her men friends. They could not, of course, challenge Devlin to an affair; but there were many ways in which they could make life unpleasant for him if he made them envious or even annoyed at the thought that a jumped-up sheep might win a girl a citizen had lost.

Devlin wanted to help the girl and he liked her company, but he was cautious by nature.

The city park for that area was a tiny island of greenery surrounded by an enormous car-park provided for its users. The car-park was three-quarters full, Devlin noticed as he found a slot close to the main entrance, which meant the park itself was relatively uncrowded. He also saw, without really noticing them, the signs warning against the carrying of weapons inside the park and the city security men in full riot gear who lost interest in him as soon as they saw his walking-out whites. Beetlelike inside his air-conditioned armor and with his features hidden by the reflections in his visor, the security sergeant waved him past the search point just as he had waved on the black-garbed figure who had preceded Devlin by a few seconds and who had halted inside the entrance.

Hearing Devlin's footsteps behind him the man turned suddenly, then smiled. It was Brother Howard.

"Good morning, Doctor," he said pleasantly. "I was hoping to meet you again. Do you mind if we walk together?"

"I'm meeting someone . . ." began Devlin.

"I understand," said the Brother, holding Devlin's gaze until there could be no doubt that the doctor was telling the truth. Then he looked at his watch and went on, "But you strike me as being a methodical individual, Doctor, who would be inclined to make appointments, professional or social, exactly on the hour. It wants eighteen minutes to the hour, and if you could spare me those few minutes for a talk . . . ?"

He kept pace with Devlin, waiting.

The truth was, Devlin realized suddenly, that he did not know how long the girl would take to reach the park. She might even have changed her mind about coming. He was tempted to be very impolite to the

Brother. But the man had not been impolite to him, merely a little bit too insistent, and Devlin had survived this long by being as polite as possible to everyone.

"My pleasure," he said.

But the Brother said little during the first few minutes, and Devlin began to relax and enjoy the slow, silent pacing among the flower beds and under the trees.

Unlike the other parks in the city, the trees in this one were real. Transparent plastic protected the first few yards of their trunks against vandals and name-carvers. The flower beds, which had less obtrusive, electronic protection, were real as well, judging by the delicate and natural scent leaking into the air and the number of bees in the area. The turf underfoot was fresh, green and springy; it had to be a hardwearing synthetic to remain in that condition after the daily pounding it had to withstand from the district's collective feet.

A sudden burst of firing—irregular spacing, less than a mile distant, suggesting an affair between a couple neither of whom could shoot straight—reminded him that beyond the real trees and flower beds there was an unpleasantly real world.

Beside him the Brother sighed and said, "I realize that I am rushing things, Doctor—coming much too quickly to the point. But there isn't much time. I hope you will forgive me and, well, make allowances."

Devlin made a non-verbal noise, a guarded grunt which, he hoped, would bind him to nothing.

Seriously, the Brother went on, "I won't insult your intelligence by asking if you are happy with things as they are, Doctor. But just how unhappy are you?"

"With things as they are?"

Brother Howard nodded. "As detailed a list as you can manage."

Devlin began to laugh, then stopped, his amusement changing suddenly to irritation. He said, "There is a long list of things I'm unhappy about. Arming so-called responsible citizens before they have reached maturity, much less achieved a sense of responsibility. I don't like the way the majority of these citizens treat the sheep, or the way the Maxers overreact if someone so much as sneezes without using a tissue, or the way city security can't seem to be able to keep the peace without waging total war on all and sundry. No, that isn't quite fair to the security people, but it is pretty obvious they can't trust anyone who is not another security man, and they don't bother to hide that fact.

"Oh, I know that the citizens and Maxers started out with the highest possible motives," Devlin went on angrily. "We were on the verge of anarchy and it was thought that sober and responsible citizens bearing arms would be able to curb the worst excesses—the wholesale muggings and murders and bombings. And the idea of maximum rather than minimum response to violent crime worked for a while, too. But then the citizens and the Maxers began looking for wrongs to right, and when they could no longer find even a minor wrong they . . ."

Devlin broke off, took a deep breath, and continued, "I don't like the mass processing of patients and the complete depersonalization in present-day hospitals, or the lack of sympathy and the increasing loneliness that overcrowding brings. You have only to walk through a crowded rec hall at night to know what I mean.

"Curative treatment for these social ills should have started many generations ago," Devlin went on bitterly. "I realize nothing can be done at this late date, but I don't have to like the situation. In my profession one is conditioned to dislike illness, I suppose, and I especially do not like the illness, the rot, which is afflicting society these days. The sickness goes through to the center and from the top to the bottom. There is no secure place, nothing to hold on to, nobody in authority who is fully trustworthy, nowhere to go that is any better. I'm generalizing, of course. There are bound to be some individuals or groups trying to do something, but they are the exceptions that prove the rule, and they will eventually go soft and rotten like the rest of us. Their psychiatrists or friends will explain the folly of remaining firm while everyone else is going loose. They will be given, or elect to take, one of the personality-change series that will chemically tailor their minds to fit happily into present-day society. Sheep into citizens or vice-versa with a couple of color-coded pills!"

Brother Howard nodded and opened his mouth to speak, but Devlin went on savagely. "And now you will say something ponderous about confession being good for the soul, then lead into a lecture designed to show me the error of my ways—"

"Like Hell I will!" began the Brother, then stopped to look past him at the girl who was hurrying toward them.

Devlin had not realized they had walked around to the main entrance again. He introduced her to the Brother, then added, "We were talking about—"

"No need to explain," she said, frowning. "I could hear you from the gate. It sounded like the beginning of a hand-to-hand affair."

"Nothing like that," said the Brother reassuringly. "We were simply continuing a discussion begun some time ago and, much as I would like to finish it, I realize that I am intruding ..."

He was intruding, but a full minute passed and he was still standing there, looking from Devlin to the girl and pleading silently for them to deny it. Something was bothering the Brother, and Devlin's curiosity was beginning to outweigh his irritation. He looked enquiringly at the girl.

"There is no need to cut short your discussion on my account," she said.

The Brother's sigh was clearly audible. He said, "Thank you, ma'am, and Doctor. What I was really asking a few minutes ago was whether you were unhappy enough with the situation here and now to want to escape from it. I can offer you, perhaps both of you, a chance at something much better—"

"Another thing I dislike about present-day society," Devlin broke in harshly, "is the way people can have their minds changed against their will, by personality-change drugs or by subtle argument or by people offering new methods of escape through hallucinations or heightened metaphysical experience. I do not think, Brother, that you will ever convince us that we would be better off dead and in Heaven."

Brother Howard was waving his hands in agitation. They were the same hands which had sent an armed citizen to the hospital, but Devlin was too angry to care. He did not want to embark on an interminable argument about the afterlife, comparative religion or any other metaphysical means of life-support. All he wanted was to be alone with the girl and talk and hope that something would develop, despite the pressures of the sick society in which they lived. He would dearly love to escape, but not by using the Brother's method. Taking the girl's arm he began to turn away.

"Wait, Doctor, please," the Brother said very seriously. "When we spoke last you accused me of trying to convert you, and I denied it. I still do. But I have been thinking about our meeting and . . . Well, I've had a chance to sleep on it, and I've come to a decision. The reason I wanted so badly to speak to you again was because of your ripe plum analogy. You said that the human race was at the peak of its scientific and cultural abilities, but that we were too rich, too ripe and were about ready to burst. What happens if someone takes a firm grip on that plum, and squeezes hard?"

"You would be left with a nasty mess," said Devlin.

"And the stone would shoot out," added the girl.

"Exactly," said the Brother.

They stood for several minutes in silence broken only by the sound of bees and some distant shooting. When the Brother finally spoke he sounded awkward, diffident, but very sincere.

He said, "I've already told you that I am not seeking converts, but recruits. I am recruiting the colonists and crew for a starship."

10

HE HAD EXPECTED to see a ten-thousand-person block wrapped in a security blanket three guards deep and packed with computers, simulators, medics, instructors and all kinds of technical and non-technical support staff as well as hundreds of other candidates under training. Instead he saw a small, three-story building with boarded-up windows and pitted walls symptomatic of a structure that has suffered a near miss. Many city security men were nearby, but they were grouped around a dozen or more armored vehicles which were parked in the space where the adjoining building had been.

The security guard at the entrance paid them very little attention, but that was because his eyes were on one of the most sophisticated weapon sniffers that Devlin had ever seen. And when the Brother ushered them into a ground-floor office—the building did not have an elevator, and the room's occupant was obviously incapable of climbing stairs—the old man sitting behind the impressive desk computer showed no interest in them at all.

There was too much skin and not enough underlying tissue on his shrunken skull for any facial expression to show, Devlin thought. A face like that belonged in a terminal geriatrics ward, but the depth and power of the voice was surprising.

"My name is Martin," he said. "Sit down, please, and relax while Brother Howard wires you up. Don't talk until he is finished, and don't ask questions until I have finished asking mine—that way you will probably find that you need not have asked them in the first place."

Silently and with the gentle but impersonal touch of an experienced medic, Brother Howard fitted Devlin and the girl with psych collars and positioned the leads and sensors as accurately as if their skulls had been shaven and marked. Devlin knew that he should object because the collars were diagnostic tools that could be dangerous in the hands of someone who was not a high-level psychiatrist, and he had no idea of the incredibly old man's professional qualifications, if any. But he was too intrigued, or perhaps too much of a moral coward, to argue.

He cleared his throat and said, "You're full of surprises, Brother."

The Brother smiled, gave both collars a final check and sat close enough to Martin so that they could look at both of them without twisting their necks and perhaps pulling out the collar connections.

Devlin swallowed nervously and said, "I'm not sure that I believe everything I've been told. But if I did believe it . . . well, I'm no superman."

The old man nodded and said, "For this particular exercise I am completely disinterested in supermen, or superwomen. Instead I am seeking standards that may be too high or too low for you to reach, because whether you attain them or fail them, you fail. And now that my words have made you sufficiently worried and confused for your mental reactions to be as revealing as possible to this over-sophisticated bundle of scrap . . ."

"Excuse me," said Devlin, "but isn't it wrong to reveal so much about the purpose and mechanics of a test to the subject?"

"Maybe," said the old man, "I'm a very stupid psychiatrist."

"But I wouldn't bet on it," said the Brother dryly.

"Very well," Martin went on. "We know that you

are not a superman. What else are you not? Have you ever been a citizen? And don't shake your head or you'll loosen a sensor. Use your tongue."

"Sorry. No."

"Was the reason cowardice, irresponsibility, or a sense of vocation for your present profession?"

Devlin took a deep breath and tried to control his irritation, even though he knew that the sensors were picking it up and telling the old man all about it. He said, "In order, probably yes, definitely no, and I was ordered to take up this profession."

"Go on."

"I was afraid of wearing the belt of a responsible citizen," Devlin replied. "I think that too many citizens are strutting braggarts and completely irresponsible. I became a doctor because, in my father's opinion, I was unsuited to any other job."

The old man nodded, but there were too many lines on his face for his expression to be readable. He said, "Your father isn't being assessed, Doctor, but his opinion of you might have some relevance."

"It has a lot of relevance," said Devlin, "because I did as I was told. According to my father, however, I was too impressionable, too soft, too prone to falling over my own feet to have any real coordination between eye and muscle. He did say that I showed intelligence at times. He thought that I might be stampeded into wearing a belt by some real or fancied insult, but if I did my opponent would almost certainly win because, even if I refused to shoot because I might hurt or kill him, I might not be able to draw my weapon without dropping it on the ground or shooting myself in the thigh. He was also fond of saying that society was going to Hell and that there was nothing permanent but death and taxes. There was nothing I could do about the taxes, he told me, but the more widespread the armed protests and honor killings became, the greater the need for doctors would be."

"Was he a citizen?"

"No."

"I see," said Martin. "But we'll leave your father for now. Have you ever been a Maxer? Ever been in a sheep fight with illegal weapons or hands? No? Well, how about a heated argument? You're beginning to sound like a supersheep, Doctor, and that also is an abnormal condition that could ..."

"Try not to feel so angry and insulted, Doctor," Brother Howard broke in, his eyes moving over the desk displays. "My colleague is very short of time, which often means that he is also short of tact and good manners. Forgive him and remember that the qualities and characteristics that we are testing for are not those which you yourself might consider important, or even admirable.

"The meek are going to inherit the earth, Doctor," he said seriously. "Not *this* Earth, of course. But they *will* inherit."

"I shall try to remember that," said Devlin skeptically; then, to the old man, "Yes, I have had arguments with other sheep, too many for me to remember with accuracy, but no fights. I take my turn on block security duties, but have never had to shoot anyone. I believe that the best form of defense is defense. I was never a Maxer for the same reason."

"I see," said the resonant voice coming from Martin's pendulous, bloodhound's face. "Have you ever been friendly with, or related to, anyone who subscribed to the philosophy of maximum response?"

"We're back to my father again," said Devlin.

"How long was he a practicing Maxer?"

"Seven, maybe eight minutes. Just after they had cut my mother for saying they were a bunch of—"

"So he was provoked. Casualties?"

"Three dead, two requiring hospitalization and one with psychic damage that caused him to resign his citizen status."

"So he killed three, injured two and scared the other one into becoming a sheep," said the psychiatrist.

"What age were you when he told you about it, and how often did he describe the incident?"

"I was ten," said Devlin. "I found out about it much later. He didn't speak of it at all—except once, maybe, when he told me that the most dangerous thing in the world was a coward driven to desperation."

"You felt proud of him?"

"Yes. No. I'm not sure."

Turning to the girl, Martin said, "My apologies for taking the Doctor before you, Miss. It is just that I was expecting to interrogate your friend, and you were not expected—"

"What about my mother?" asked Devlin. "Isn't her influence important?"

"It is," said Brother Howard, "but since she died sixteen years ago as a result of the Maxer incident just described, when you were only ten, her influence isn't recent. Besides, her death meant that full psychomedical records became available to us so that her effect on you could be estimated with a fair degree of accuracy. Your father, on the other hand, did not break any laws, never caught any serious diseases, managed to avoid major injuries and is still alive somewhere."

"But this means that you expected me here!" Devlin burst out. "If you had already studied my—"

"Thoroughly," said the Brother, nodding toward the psychiatrist. "Miss Morley being with you was a bonus. We have called up her records and she, too, is colonist material. But please be quiet, Doctor. My colleague is busy."

Devlin nodded carefully so as not to dislodge the sensors, his mind suddenly at least as busy as that of the psychiatrist's—so much so that he missed Patricia's initial answers. If the material in Central Records were available to these people, then they had the support of Population Provisioning and Control, which in turn had a great deal of influence with Security and Health. In all probability, then, the squadron of security armor outside was not simply on standby in case a disturbance might break out in the area; they were there to protect this building.

It made the Brother's starship story much easier to believe.

He wondered about the Brother's reference to Martin, the ancient psychiatrist, as his colleague. Was the Brother really a Brother? By the time Devlin had decided that he was—his conversation and reaction after the Bennett boy's death were too good to be false—Martin had finished with the girl.

"Bearing in mind that we are not looking for superhuman physical or mental abilities," he said, his eyes moving slowly from Patricia to Devlin and back, "I consider both of you suitable for further indoctrination—as crew-members rather than colonists. The major factors in reaching this decision are that both of you are intensely dissatisfied with your present life-styles and would like escape from them, and neither of your personalities is basically violent. More simply, you would like to change things but are unwilling to hurt people to do it.

"The decision regarding your crew status was a close one," he went on, his voice seeming to vibrate inside their very bones, "because you, Miss, gave indications of future instability should you be unable to find a permanent male dependent. You, Doctor, although the Brother had already decided on your suitability as a colonist, are a drifter who is dissatisfied with everything including yourself. You know that some kind of decision to change is necessary, but you are too lacking in self-confidence to make any decision that involves only yourself. If you two had not been complementary personalities and potential mates the crew-rating decision could well have gone against you. My congratulations."

Devlin could feel Patricia's eyes on him. He opened his mouth to speak, but the psychiatrist went on, "We cannot fit you into a training schedule for another two weeks, however, so the Brother will spend as much of the intervening time as possible with you answering your questions and outlining project philosophy. To begin with, this will be done in your own living block. You can arrange a cover among yourselves. Miss Morley requires spiritual as well as medical comfort, perhaps, and needs frequent visits of a Reverend during rec periods. You have quiet talkers, I presume?"

"Yes, but . . ." began Devlin.

"I'll try not to intrude," said the Brother.

". . . we scarcely know each other," Devlin ended.

There was a moment's silence, then Martin said firmly, "You are introducing an unnecessary complication, Doctor. I can solve it—in fact, I already have—but it might be better for both of you if I let Brother Howard explain. Unlike me, the Brother still has a little romance left in his soul . . ."

But the answer was delayed. When they left Martin's office the Brother signaled for silence and motioned them against the corridor wall. Eight white, coffinlike containers, on wheels for easy movement, were being pushed toward the rear of the building where Devlin could see one of the large riot ambulances backed against a loading ramp. The men pushing the containers, which were beaded with moisture and radiating intense cold, were silent.

"So that's what you do with the unsuccessful candidates," said the girl, shivering.

"They are the successful ones, Miss," said the Brother, "in suspended animation for holding in orbit. In that condition they are not a drain on the ship's consumables. Thus we can train them in small numbers over a considerable period and store them until we have a full complement, and there is less risk of a security leak . . ."

He talked about the training program and nothing else while they left the building and began the drive back to their own block. Perhaps, Devlin thought, the psychiatrist had handed the Brother a chore which was highly embarrassing for a man of God who believed in free will instead of endocrinology. Or maybe the

Brother's enthusiasm for the project was as honest as it sounded and he had simply forgotten about Devlin's earlier question. But he had to break off talking as a small explosion nearby rocked the car, and the armored shutters dropped into place.

The period of temporary sanity had come to an end.

Devlin reduced speed and drove on his periscope for a few hundred yards until a larger and softer explosion showered the car with debris and the blast jerked it to a halt. Through the dust which had settled on his outer lenses he could see that the front of a building had fallen into the street and that traffic was blocked in both directions. From somewhere farther ahead there was the sudden whump-crash of a rocket opening up a vehicle, accompanied by sounds of shouting and screaming; but his own armor muffled the noise so that he could not tell whether the people were protesting or in pain. He cut the engine, sat back and loosened his safety harness.

"We could be here for some time," he said; "you'll find sandwiches on the shelf beside the instrument cabinet."

"A lot of them," said the Brother appreciatively. "But of course, Doctor, you were planning a picnic in the park, off an imitation log table under a real tree. Very romantic."

"And practical," said Devlin, "considering the mob around the park food dispensers. Which reminds me— you were supposed to give us a romantic answer to a practical question back there."

The Brother smiled and said, "I was hoping that you would not insist on an answer, that you would let things happen naturally. Two people whose psych profiles are as complementary as yours would only have to spend a short time in each other's company to become inseparable. But informing people of this fact tends to make them think that their free will is being taken away, that they have no choice in the matter. They then tend to react in an abnormal fashion to each other out of sheer contrariness. To prove that they still have a choice, they sometimes insist on making the wrong choice."

A smooth talker, this Brother, Devlin thought. But the truth was he had already made his choice. Had the girl made hers?

"Pairing is forbidden until after the landing, in any case," Brother Howard went on, "so you will have plenty of time to consider. We could adjust your personalities so that you would become a latter-day Romeo and Juliet. But personality engineering is one of the things you will be escaping from . . ."

He broke off as a long burst of gunfire made speech impossible. During a short lull which followed he tried again, then gave up. Devlin looked from the Brother to the girl while she looked steadily at him. Then the firing rose to a crescendo, interspersed with the small, soft explosions of gas grenades, the sounds of screaming, jeering and the tinkle and hiss of thrown fire-bombs. The girl reached forward and gripped his hand.

It was not a panic reaction. Her hand was cool and steady, her grip just tight enough to let him know that she did not want to let go. The car's filters, which were never one hundred percent effective, were leaking a sharp and not unpleasant smell composed of smoke and a barbecue odor. Quite suddenly all was quiet except for the screaming.

In the distance they could hear the sirens and intermittent whining of the heavy Sanator ambulances as they used their jet-lift to jump intervening traffic. Brother Howard reached toward the hatch handle.

"No," said Devlin harshly. "We can't give medical assistance to compare with the heavies, and they'll be too busy to let you give any other kind. Oh, they'll give you a white coat if you insist, but not the body armor to go under it, and they'll be very annoyed if a surviving protester makes another casualty out of you. Believe me, I know."

More quietly he went on, "But they are very well

equipped and expert at their job, Brother. And good at separating the potential survivors from the others on whom hospitalization would be wasted. So just be patient until the ambulances and the law have gone, then there will be plenty of work for you to do. After all, it is the unsalvagable ones who really need your help."

The Brother nodded and loosened his grip on the handle while the girl suddenly tightened hers on Devlin's hand.

"This," she said, "is a terrible way to live."

The hours that followed were not pleasant to remember because they were spent helping the Brother to comfort the dying. But later, when they were together in the block rec hall and talking about the starship with miniature hush-mikes and earplugs, they had forgotten the incident.

It had been very easy to forget just then because the process that was supposed to happen naturally was well advanced, and Devlin for one had no control over it. Incidents like that had been nothing new to them, after all, and it had been a happy and interesting day apart from the riot ...

COOLDOWN IN FIVE MINUTES.

Devlin shivered and thought about the enormous, complex ship and its interminable voyage, about the colonists, whose hours of life were sandwiched between decades of frigid sleep and about his suspicions that something had been done, or was being done, to their cold-sleeping minds. His memories and dreams were much too vivid and complete, suggesting that they were being artificially stimulated. Were they where they thought they were, or was this simply an advanced simulation and final weeding out process for the candidates?

Of one thing he was sure. This, too, was a terrible way to live.

11

THE MOST PERSISTENT memories of his early life were of confinement and restriction, both in the clothing he had to wear and the limitations placed upon his movements inside and around the castle. As he grew older he came to realize that the stairs had been too large and steep for his child's legs and undeveloped sense of balance, and as he grew older still he learned about the faceless people who might kill him if he strayed alone beyond the protection of the outer walls.

He never did fully understand why he had to be continually smothered in satin and frills. Even in bed he had to wear more clothes than most of his people wore in midwinter, and he wore a cap with earmuffs which was like a jewelled cloth crown.

A laughing, leather-kilted and strong-smelling giant called Hawn told him it was because he was more important than everyone else and had to be protected—against sickness, damp and the attacks of enemies. Later, when the giant Hawn had shrunk to normal size he said much the same thing, but he usually tried to change the subject by hitting or prodding him with a wooden sword—though never painfully. When he was full-grown and Hawn had become a wiry little man with graying hair who laughed but seldom, such questions were left for his advisers to answer, and the swords used to change the subject were no longer of wood.

But age, or perhaps an unwilling pupil, had made Hawn shrewish of late.

"Slashing and cutting is a waste of effort, armed as you are, Sire. To slash with a light sword you must move your shield clear of your body, leaving it unprotected. Move it aside only enough to aim and stab, and never block a blow directly. A strong thrust from your enemy will go through your shield unless it is very thick and heavy, and in that case the weight will tire and slow you down. A light shield used to deflect, not block, an attack and with a sharp edge that enables it to serve as an additional weapon is best, Sire—provided you do not become angry and begin waving your sword around your head as most of the others will be doing."

"Yes," he said, whirling the sword around his head and cutting another notch in the wood of the practice stump.

"Carving pieces off your enemy may give you pleasure, Sire," said Hawn with irritating patience, "but an aimed thrust in the vitals is instantly disabling and fatal. You have no need to skewer your enemy—a finger's length in any vital area, followed by a twist before withdrawal, will do it. You should practice at every opportunity, Sire, until it becomes habit."

"Very well, Hawn," he said coldly. "I shall keep a cool head and kill an enemy with every blow, but I think you are a calculating and cruel man."

"No, Sire," said his master-at-arms. "A wounded enemy is a dangerous enemy. If he is also a thoughtful enemy he will know that his wound, even though it may not be disabling, will go bad and kill him slowly with fever and vomiting and endless thirst. You have not yet seen a battle, Sire, or its long aftermath when the wounded are brought home to their friends who try to bind and poultice them and try to make them live, to no avail."

"Enough!" he said angrily. "I shall try, then, to be cool-headed and kind in battle. Now guard yourself."

For several minutes he cut and thrust at his master-at-arms while the old man parried or ducked every single blow. Then gradually the cool, calculated methods of attack that Hawn had tried to instill came back to him and he saw his aged opponent becoming more and more worried. But by then his anger had faded and he was no longer trying to kill the irritating old man.

When he told his mother about the incident that evening, how Hawn had complimented him on the excellence of his attack, she was far from pleased. For the first time she told him how his father had died—not as it was recorded in the library, of wounds received in a glorious and heroic battle, but from a deep scratch in his arm made by the dirty stave of a dying foot soldier. The scratch had gone bad and, after many weeks, so had the arm. It was smelling and corrupt and dead before his father was.

Unlike his mother and Hawn, his advisers were old and wise and never irritating. They gave quiet and thoughtful approval to his idea—or had it, perhaps, been their idea?—that a man should not run like a child to his mother for advice and that he should think of fathering an heir to his kingdom. He overheard a highly insulting remark, which he was probably meant to overhear, about his peace-loving grandfather being a great and glorious queen, and everyone had laughed just an instant after he did.

But later they became serious and talked about the noble ladies he might choose to marry, and the political and territorial advantages which each possible candidate would bring him. The discussion was cold and calculating and very like one of Hawn's lessons. But he did not mind because they also discussed, for the first time, the desirability of installing royal concubines while a suitable queen was found for him.

Except for the irritating bullying of Hawn and the equally irritating acquiescence of his advisers, he was very happy during the eight years that followed. His domain was free of disaffection, plague and war.

The war started because of a chance remark by a traveler to one of his advisers, a remark he was not supposed to overhear. The advisers had boasted that from the highest tower in the palace their king could not see to the borders of his lands, and the visitor had replied that this was so only when rain was falling to the eastward.

Even on the clearest days the hill, which was just inside the border of the adjoining kingdom, was only a tiny swelling on the eastern horizon, misty with distance and visible only from the highest tower. The hill was densely wooded and uninhabited and unlikely to be considered of value by the monarch to whom it belonged, but this visitor had not been the first to joke about it. Of itself the thing was unimportant, a tiny pimple on the face of his fair land—but even a small pimple could itch.

When he mentioned it in council, Hawn laughed uproariously, then said, "The simple solution, Sire, would be to plant a grove of trees between the palace and the offending object ..."

Hawn broke off, silenced by the look on his lord's face. Realizing that their king was not jesting and that he knew exactly what he wanted, the council began deliberating on the best way of getting it for him.

Very tactfully they suggested to him that he could not simply take the small and worthless piece of his neighbor's territory without very good reasons for doing so, reasons that would add to rather than diminish the respect in which he was held. Granted that the constant reminders of the presence of the hill were embarrassing, but perhaps at the back of his mind he might also have realized that it overlooked a large area of his kingdom and, should his neighbor intend taking up arms against him—and there was no evidence to the contrary—the hill would confer a military advantage. In fact, it was considered imperative that a small, well armed but secret force should be deployed on the border as close to the hill as possible, to guard against the possibility of an observation post being set up there. They would probably need half a year, which would allow time to recruit and train men and would give the people time to feel sufficiently threatened to support the war.

They saw his baffled expression, and once again it

was Hawn who spoke. He said, "The men will be equipped with plain shields and armor and will carry no identifying standards. We will see that they are undersupplied and that they will find it necessary to live off the land. This means that much livestock in the area will disappear, usually at night, and it will be easier to rob our own people than the others across the border—although they, too, will find sheep and chickens missing from time to time. Soon the other king will send some of his soldiers to investigate these occurrences, but before that there will be complaints and much anger from our own people who have suffered. Cause and effect will become confused in their minds, which are not very bright, Sire, and they will appeal to you for protection. The appeal will have general support, and when the other king's men clash with ours—"

"These nocturnal raids," he said sharply. "Will any of my people be hurt?"

"No, Sire," said Hawn. "Unless they think more of their chickens than they do of their miserable lives ..."

During the months that followed he had second thoughts about the war which he had engineered and which was rapidly becoming inevitable. When the first news of the growing trouble on his border reached the capital, he tried to give orders that would recall his soldiers and allow the situation to get better—but it was a small, inner voice which never had the cooperation of his lips and tongue. When word reached him that his anonymous men were taking more than chickens and sheep, that they were taking wives and daughters as well and killing anyone who objected, he grew angry with himself. He also grew publicly angry and rode among his people, who more and more often hailed him as their protector. Sometimes their cheering was able to drown the quiet, nagging voice of his conscience, of both his consciences.

He was dimly aware of a strange mental ghost called Devlin, that gibbered unheeded when his real thoughts and decisions were leading him into danger. It kept reminding him that the brachiopod, too, had represented a deadly danger and his trilobite had crawled within reach of its tentacles. Then there had been the incident with the young allosaurus, and the insane jealousy of the tree-dwelling pre-simians, and the time he was wounded by a big cat and had plastered the bloody tear with filthy, matted grass instead of washing it in the sea and allowing the Sun UV to heal the wound. But warning him of danger was like trying to influence the actors on a television screen, whatever that was.

The specter was inside him, thinking strange out-of-context thoughts and giving unheard advice, but it was not really a part of the spoiled, forty-year-old boy who rode at the head of his small army against a self-manufactured threat.

Eastward, his domain extended to the river that passed within a mile of the lower slopes of the offending hill. The river was only a few feet deep, but the banks were lined with prickly bushes. One of them must have scratched the belly of Hawn's horse as it was climbing the bank, because the animal reared suddenly, throwing its rider and then dragging him by one stirrup as it floundered and splashed downstream. Two of Hawn's men gave chase and managed to head the horse up and on to the bank, but by that time the master-at-arms had drowned.

Looking at the slack, wet face and the heavy armor which Hawn had taken to wearing as his ageing joints stiffened, he felt anger at the man's ridiculous and ignoble death. The laughing giant of his childhood should not have ended his life like this.

"Leave him until after the battle," he said sternly, then more softly for the benefit of his soldiers, "If you remember his teaching when you meet the enemy, he still lives."

They re-formed and moved toward the base of the hill where the other army was already gathering.

Every soldier in his service had been trained—taking into account the differences in personal armor and weapons—in the same way as his monarch. Even the pike-men, who did not matter very much to either side in a battle, had been instructed in Hawn's methods of cool-headed and calculated attack and personal defense. The long and terribly unhandy pikes, which until then had been little more than sharpened branches, had been shortened and thickend and a cross-piece added near the base so that they had the handling characteristics of both a long-sword and a short spear. In use, a pike-man was supposed to knock aside his opponent's lighter and longer pike with his short, heavy one, or catch the thrust in his cross-piece and steer it past his body, then close and dispatch his enemy before the other could shorten his grip for a second blow.

There were hundreds of bruised ribs among his men to prove that, in training at least, the method was effective.

There was no sign of cooking fires from the other side, so obviously their prince wanted to settle the affair before the midday meal. The prince, who was leading an army slightly more numerous than his own, had taken the field because his father was too old and heavy to mount a horse safely. The fact that losing this battle would mean him yielding to little more than a boy—and a very boastful boy, at that—had weighted heavily in his decision to adopt Hawn's new and in some ways not quite honorable ideas.

In leisurely and dignified fashion he aligned his forces —pike-men to the fore, mounted soldiers who were the personal troops of two of his most trusted lords protecting his flanks, and the rest of the nobles, their men and his own guard surrounding himself. When his formation was complete the two armies would remain facing each other within hailing distance until trumpeters on both sides announced their readiness to fight.

After that they would advance toward each other and fight until one side or the other decided that an unacceptable number of casualties had been sustained, then they would yield the field to the victor, parley to achieve a settlement of land or gold and go home. Most of the fighting would be between pike-men and foot soldiers, but a few of his nobles would be able to exercise within the safety of their resplendent armor while he and his guard stood decoratively in the middle of his army until the issue had been decided.

But his formation was still incomplete when trumpets blared on the other side. Their nobles, personal troops and the prince's guard with the prince himself at the center began trotting quickly along the rear of their pike lines, pennants fluttering on their lances and plumes undulating like flying caterpillars. Not until they had rounded the flank of their pike-men and lowered their lances to charge did he realize that Hawn had not been the only radical military thinker.

The young prince was hotheaded and anxious to prove himself fit to lead and rule, but he was doing a very strange and a very dishonorable thing.

Instead of merely trying to win a battle, the prince intended to kill the opposing king.

The king's pike-men had not been expected to withstand a charge led by heavily armored horsemen and they did not do so. But they did remember Hawn's training and some of them managed to fend off the lances and stab at the horses, or jump at the last moment to the safe side and stick their pikes between the animal's forelegs, bringing the horse and its rider to the ground, where a dazed and heavily encumbered man was easy to kill.

He saw the center of his pike line collapse, saw the opposing lines of pike-men begin to walk forward, saw his flankers galloping from each side along the narrowing gap between the opposing lines with the obvious intention of following the enemy horsemen through the gap they had made and taking them in the rear. Then he, whose royal person was supposed to be inviolate, was fighting for his life like the lowliest pike-man.

One of the opposing nobles leading the attack was charging down on him, lance leveled and visor open for better accuracy. He tried desperately to move aside, but was hampered by the press of his guards. Then suddenly there was a horseman between his attacker and himself—his guard captain, judging by the helmet crest—who screamed shrilly as a bloody lance-head sprouted from the small of his back and he rolled off his horse, taking the enemy's lance with him. But the other was already drawing his heavy sword to aim a two-handed swing.

He slashed in panic at the man's helmet, saw the plume begin to drift groundward, then managed to get his shield up in time to block the swing. The shock nearly paralyzed his arm and he was left with a splintered shield dangling loosely from its arm-straps, and his enemy was raising his sword high above his head for the final killing blow. He remembered Hawn saying that a shield should be used to deflect, not block, a heavy weapon, and that an angry or excited enemy exposes himself during an attack.

He spurred forward, took aim at one of the dimly seen eyes below the opponent's open visor and thrust to full extension. His sword met with very little resistance and he thought that he had not been able to reach far enough, but he twisted it before withdrawing as Hawn had advised. His enemy's weapon tumbled into the long grass and the man followed it, beating frantically at the sides of his helmet with his mailed fists. Then there was another lance reaching toward him across the riderless horse, so that he could not get to close quarters with the new threat. He dug his spurs into his mount and pulled back hard on the reins—another Hawn-taught trick—so that the horse reared and took the thrust meant for him. He had already disengaged his feet from the stirrups by the time the animal fell squealing and threshing to the ground, taking the broken lance with it. He jumped clear and ran around the riderless horse in time to see his opponent reaching for the sword in his back scabbard.

With both hands reaching behind the back of his

neck, the unarmored gap at his armpits was at least three inches wide. He had an instant's pause to take aim—a thrust, twist and withdrawal. As the man fell he snatched the other's shield and for a few minutes had to fight with one of his own Hawn-trained guards who took him for an enemy. The look on the man's face when he discovered who he was fighting was so ludicrous that he laughed out loud—a great, bellowing guffaw which sounded terribly out-of-place in the middle of a battle.

This was the stuff of which legends were made, for it was evident that his enemies were intent on killing him as well as on winning the battle—a most dishonorable intention. He was matching their dishonor with his cold and calculating fighting methods.

As the attacks on his person became fewer he took to helping his guards, stepping forward to make a flanking attack when a man or group was hard-pressed, relieving them with deadly, calculated thrusts, that left a dead or rapidly dying enemy before moving to another part of the field. He did not have to do this very often, but later there was hardly a man who did not boast proudly that the king, personally, had saved his life during the battle. Later the scribes elaborated on these stories and added details of a fight in which the king had slain the opposing prince in single combat.

There were many suits of beautifully decorated and costly armor tumbled about in the long, trampled grass leaking blood. But he had not been responsible for all of them. Anyone, perhaps even an over-zealous pikeman, could have slain the prince on that confused and bloody morning. It was a strange battle with only the enemy making the noise. Only they did the charging, the shouting of battle cries and most of the dying. If it were not stopped, soon not enough of them would be left to bury their own dead.

"Hold! Enough of this slaughter!" he called suddenly and pointed with his sword toward a group of opposing nobles and their remaining personal soldiers who were fighting hopelessly a few yards away. "Enough! I call on you to yield with honor!"

On his return to the palace that evening he was hailed as the greatest warrior of all time, and the festivities in celebration of his victory went on for three days. He had been called their Protector and now they added "the Merciful" to his name because he had not killed each and every one of his enemies. A little later they added "the Peacemaker" because of the alliance he negotiated between his country and its former enemy.

With the prince slain and the old king ailing and ruling with difficulty a country which was poor and ripe for revolt, he helped his erstwhile enemy with gold and grain in return for an agreement that their kingdoms would eventually merge with the marriage to him of his former enemy's only daughter—an exquisitely beautiful child of nine—when she arrived at a suitable age. This would probably mean that he would have to give up his concubines, for a while at least, but in ten years' time he would be much older and that might not be such a great hardship. He had one problem, however; his young queen-to-be did not like him.

Her father explained that she had dearly loved her older brother, the prince, who had taken her about on his horse and told her tales of great and glorious deeds of valor. In a way their companionship had been like the early relationship between Hawn and himself, except that she had been an impressionable girl-child and the prince had not lived long enough to become boastful and irritating to her maturing mind. But her father assured him that childish memories and feelings were short-lived and that when the time came she would be honored to wed such a great king.

And he was a great and well loved king to his people. Apart from that single morning's battle there were no more wars in his reign. Adjoining kingdoms, worried by the fighting prowess of his small but well-trained army, had to be reassured. Threats of combined aggression had to be countered by various devious methods, none of which were honorable and many of which were utterly despicable. He had to be constantly on guard against the devious threats of groups within his own court. But his kingdom prospered and his reputation for honesty and mercy and nobility grew, it seemed, in direct proportion to the depths of dishonor to which he sank.

As the years went by, the costly robes that he used to find so irksome gave girth and stature to his wasting body, and when the time came for his wedding he had begun to feel uncertain in ways which he would never have believed possible.

He was beginning to feel old.

But he was not yet old enough to be unaffected by the glory and pageantry of the wedding, or by the obeisance of the nobles of two powerful kingdoms that were now one. And he would have had to be senile indeed not to be affected by the sight of his young queen. She had been a beautiful child, and he had discounted as diplomatic exaggeration the stories of her increasing beauty as she approached womanhood. But then he saw her on the eve of their wedding and knew that the courtiers had been stupid, insensitive and blind creatures who had not done her justice.

During the three years following the wedding she was the most-loved person in the kingdom—the king was respected and feared as well as loved. She was incredibly lovely and regal and gracious and faithful—and as cold toward him in the privacy of their chambers as the ice that covered the northern wastes. During those three years she gave him two strong and healthy sons, and a great deal of irritation.

He could not express his irritation in public, or even admit to its existence within the palace, because his queen was too well loved for him to make her appear anything but perfect. The trouble was that she was perfect to everyone but him. Her disposition was pleasant toward the servants and guards, she laughed a lot and her gaiety was unforced; and to nobles and serfs alike she showed consideration. But the king she did not love, and she did not want to be his confidante or his companion either.

Several times he tried to explain about the bloody confusion of the battle in which her brother had died, but on each occasion it was obvious that the impression left by the scribes who had recorded the event and who had not even been there, was much deeper and longer lasting than the words of her king.

Sheer loneliness and the need for companionship if not understanding made him consider recalling one of his concubines, but that would have made him look ridiculous—not because the practice was frowned on, but because there was no woman in the kingdom more beautiful and desirable than his own queen. So he returned to the lonely life of being a feared and respected and powerful monarch, and he took pleasure in only three things.

Two of them were his sons, who were growing taller and stronger and more handsome with each passing day. The third pleasure came from playing the devious, dangerous and dishonorable game which would, if he won, ensure the continued existence and future long life of the first two pleasures. For the life of a king, even one who was well loved and generally referred to as "great", was an uncertain thing.

He could not know for certain who had been responsible, but for the few seconds in which he was able to think he thought sadly that this act would cause grave instability in the kingdom and that his queen must have loved her big brother very much. Then the knife which had been driven upwards into his back at waist level was given an expert twist as it was withdrawn and, briefly, he suffered more pain than he would have believed possible.

12

GOOD MORNING DEVLIN.
SHIP STATUS SIX HUNDRED AND THREE YEARS INTO
MISSION. ALL SYSTEMS AND/OR BACKUP SYSTEMS
FUNCTIONING. SHIP PERSONNEL CURRENTLY AWAKE—
ONE. IDENTITY JOHN DEVLIN.

Six hundred years! All systems or back-up systems . . . ! That meant there had been system failures since his last awakening. But how many, and how serious?

REASON FOR AWAKENING. TO CHECK FUNCTIONING OF
DEVLIN MUSCLE SYSTEMS, CIRCULATION, SPEECH
ORGAN AND MEMORY. PERIOD OF AWAKENING FOUR HOURS.
CARRY OUT INSTRUCTIONS SPEAK, EXERCISE AND
REMEMBER.

"Mary," said Devlin furiously, "had a little lamb." He began the careful movements of his back, arms and legs which would allow him to get out of the casket. The process of remembering was involuntary, and the memories were painfully sharp.

Devlin gritted his teeth and moaned at the remembered pain of that knife-thrust, at the burning agony which was like a fire inside his cold and shocked body. He tried to push the memory away, to escape the king's life as well as his death and return to his own life and memories. Instead he found himself watching that same king in action from a distance of a few dozen yards; he was holding the broken pike which had transfixed him. He was moaning and holding it as steady as his fading strength would allow because if it moved the pain became even worse.

Devlin fought off that dream memory, too, and suddenly he was babbling at the streaming roof of his cave while a fever raged through his hairy body, then he was a dying mountain of flesh and bone somewhere in the Jurassic period and a near-mindless crawler on a warm sea-bed which was eating and being eaten ...

"Stop it!" he shouted. "You're driving me insane ... !"

```
ADDITIONAL TO INSTRUCTION REMEMBER. EXTENDED
PERIOD OF VOYAGE RENDERS DETAILED INSTRUCTIONS
UNNECESSARY DUE TO INABILITY TO FORECAST
PRESENT MENTAL STATUS OR PROBLEMS WITH ACCURACY.
SUGGEST DIVIDING AVAILABLE TIME BETWEEN RECALL
OF PAST WAKING AND COLD-SLEEP MEMORIES.
TRY TO RECALL ACTUAL EVENTS AND DREAM INCIDENTS
WITH AS MUCH CLARITY OF DETAIL AS POSSIBLE.
```

"I can do that," said Devlin savagely, "without even trying."

He had been repeatedly told during training that the ability to remember was vital and that it must not be allowed to weaken lest the human seedlings in their star-traveling metal pod drift forever as cold-sleeping and mindless vegetables. But that, apparently, was not to be the danger. Far from losing his memory of past real and dream incidents, they kept returning with a clarity and intensity that terrified him.

While he had been thinking back to that training session, he had been *in* the room, hearing every word the instructor had said, aware of the sounds of attention and inattention of the people around him, feeling the abrasive pressure of bristles against the backs of his fingers as he rested his chin on his closed fist ...

This, he thought fearfully, *is what total recall is like.*

Everywhere that his mind's eye looked, it was dazzled by the bright intensity of the images and the sharpness of sensory recollections. It seemed to be worse when he closed his eyes, so he kept them open and tried desperately, and vainly, not to use his mind at all.

But then his hand rested briefly on the edge of the service panel and it was as if two full-sensor films were being superimposed. There was the sight and feel of the panel's edge, the open casket and the display which was still reminding him to exercise and remember. But also, equally sharp, was the picture of one of the lecture rooms and an instructor saying, "... the duration of the voyage will be measured in centuries, but the biological time which will elapse—that is, the time during which you will be conscious and your metabolism functioning normally—will be measured in days, and not very many of those. That is why the food and air must be strictly rationed; the water is recycled and no problem. You must not eat unless advised to do so by your cubicle display, no matter how long in real time it has been between meals. Food synthesizers, seed stores, domesticated animals in cold-sleep will remain sealed in their special module, which can be opened only on landing.

"So it will be the duration of waking time that dictates your food intake," he went on, "and you should not increase your hunger by staying awake longer than the alloted time, even though there is provision for delaying cooldown in an emergency. For the same reason you must avoid using the resuscitation overrides to warm someone before his or her allotted time ..."

The instructor smiled, showing teeth which were pointed in a style that had been fashionable three years earlier. Devlin remembered the digestive upsets and lacerated tongues that that particularly stupid fad had caused in its time, and then the instructor was talking again.

"It is not our intention that you arrive on your new planet suffering from malnutrition, but you must exercise restraint in the matter of—"

One of the group, a colonist whose name was Clarke, broke in with a question. He asked, "Suppose we are lonely rather than hungry. Suppose we feel the need, after all those centuries of time, of a little female company—or male company, as the case might be. Are we forbidden to—"

"You are advised most strongly against it," said the instructor very seriously. "By now you should be aware that your period of deprivation, counted in biological time, will be a matter of days or at most weeks. Try to pay attention. This matter will be explained in greater detail during the project philosophy lectures, but two reasons can be mentioned now.

"The first," he went on, "is that such premature couplings will involve a heavy expenditure of energy, which in turn will demand an increased intake of food. The second, and much more important reason, is that while we have proved to our complete satisfaction that repeated coolings and resuscitations in no way impair the male and female reproductive systems, we are still unsure of the results on such a delicately balanced organism as a recently conceived fetus. For this reason conception must not take place during the voyage . . ."

Inevitably the recollection opened up a line of thought which filled the cubicle with bright, remembered pictures of gargantuan grapplings and couplings from his dream past, many of which he seemed to be recalling for the first time, which were too incredibly savage to be pleasant. But occasionally there were incidents—snatches of the king's love-life when he was young and his emotional reactions less complicated and controlled, and a memory of a small, dark, incredibly passionate girl from he knew not where—that were very pleasant indeed. But he could not hold on to the pleasant dream incidents because the raw, violent episodes were pulled in again by strong chains of association.

He sat for a moment on the edge of the casket, his eyes squeezed shut and his limbs trembling despite the exercises and the cubicle heaters. But closing his eyes blotted out only the cubicle around him, not the supersharp pictures that his mind kept throwing on to the dark red screen of his closed eyelids.

What had they done to his mind . . .

"... During the voyage you will be thrown on to your own mental resources," Martin, the aged chief psychologist was saying. "You must use your minds because what you don't use you lose. We cannot use them for you in spite of the wide range of psychomedication presently available to us.

"While it is possible to include mechanisms capable of administering medication of this type during the voyage," he continued, "it is imperative that the cubicle systems be kept as simple as possible to reduce the possibility of long-term component failure, and adding dispensing equipment of this kind would place a serious strain on the overall system. In any case, the temperature and radiation changes used during the hibernation and resuscitation processes could, over a long period, cause chemical changes in the medication with unforeseen and perhaps fatal results.

"You must also remember that you have been chosen because you are normal people," he went on, playing the beautifully modulated instrument that was his voice in such a fashion that what should have been an insult came across as a sincere compliment. "We have sought long and diligently for people who are normally motivated, normally nasty, normally accident prone and even normally stupid. It is not, and never has been, our intention to make supermen or superwomen out of you. Geniuses, supernormal people, are like rare chemical elements—they tend toward instability. We cannot afford to be too sophisticated, to have too much finesse. There is too much danger of component failure for us to risk people failure as well. So you are as stable as we could make you.

"You are like lead—or no, that is a trifle too stable. Think of yourselves as mud, but mud in which something will grow . . ."

With the remembered words came the memory of

the all but imperceptible sighings, rustlings and creakings of the other colonists-to-be trying to remain silent, and the sharp, fearful excitement of what they were going to do. But something had gone terribly wrong.

Devlin opened his eyes and looked intently at his immediate surroundings, trying to fix his mind as well as his eyes on the here and now.

If he could believe that wrinkled husk of a psychologist, or any of his instructors, or even Brother Howard, then his mind was his own. During the early stages of instruction he had been questioned under hypnosis, but this fact had been admitted by the medics concerned and the procedure had been simply a means of speeding-up the acquisition of his personality data. A number of physical tests had been carried out under anaesthetic—but those, he had been assured, had been aimed solely at establishing genetic and general health factors. A wide variety of medication and direct electrical stimulation were available which could heighten sensation, improve memory and even insert memories that had not previously been there. But these procedures, he had been told, had not been used on the ship's personnel.

If he believed that, what explanation was there for the diamond-sharp dreams about subjects and events and people of which he knew that he had no previous experience? The trilobite sequence, the brontosaurus, even the incredible details of his dream of being a great king—his mind had contained no such source material before he joined the ship. So it must have been implanted afterward, perhaps was being implanted every time he underwent a cooldown.

Suppose the things they had told him were generally true, but just to be on the safe side they had decided to ignore the simple approach in his case. Perhaps someone had second thoughts and the result had been that, instead of fading and needing constant exercise and renewal, Devlin's mind and memory were growing sharper and more retentive with every cooldown. It had grown so sharp that he was, he realized, utterly terrified of going into cold-sleep again.

Abruptly he wanted out of that cubicle and away from the process that was driving him mad. If there had been post-hypnotic commands against leaving the cubicle when not ordered to do so, they had faded over the centuries because he was able to use the manual override on the seal without any hesitation whatever. Then he was in the corridor, his breath hanging like misty ballons around his head, trying to think.

If he were, as he suspected, a special case, then the circuitry that had been feeding his mind with dreams, and the mechanism for administering the supportive medication, should be capable of being switched off. He did not have the technical training to recognize one of the circuits or mechanisms or switches if he saw it but by careful scrutiny he should be able to see differences in the wiring and telltales coming from his cubicle and those of the others. If he had an extra strand of cable or length of plumbing, then he could always cut it if he could not follow it back to a switch.

Such a course would be very dangerous, stupid even. But the risk was acceptable because he refused to undergo cooldown again if there were the slightest chance that those incredibly realistic dreams would return.

For a few seconds he cringed as the remembered knife tore into his body and he was crushed by the cephalopod and a score of other violent deaths overtook him, then he fought desperately to force those memories away and return to reality. It was the cold that saved him finally, reminding him that he must go to the control center and switch on the heaters and put on coveralls before he did anything else. But he had gone only a few yards when he had to stop.

· A man's body had been concealed by a cabinet which projected from the wall of the corridor. The body was held between the wall-net and the metal plating, its arms and legs outstretched and shining with the intense cold. Devlin could see that as much as possible of the body's surface was in contact with the cold metal and that the man had, of course, died from exposure. The reason for the death, as opposed to the cause, was equally easy to see.

The eyelids were held open by two pieces of adhesive tape.

Devlin, it appeared, had not been the only one to be singled out for special treatment, and this man had chosen to die rather than go on dreaming.

13

FOR MORE THAN an hour Devlin checked and rechecked the control center telltales, searching for some clue to the identity of the man and the place he had come from. He concentrated really hard on the search because he badly needed something safe to think about—even though he knew when the search was ended he would have to face the question of why the man had killed himself with cold; that would mean thinking about the dreams again.

But the colonist-status displays showed the pale blue color that indicated awakenings for exercise only. Except for the negative indication beside the name and number of Yvonne Caldwell, and he had switched off that particular system after the girl had died, there was no evidence of a cubicle malfunction that should have been apparent if a cold-sleep casket were empty.

For a wild moment he wondered if the man belonged to their ship, if he had wandered in from outside and the whole thing was, after all, just a complex simulation in which they were all being tested. Then he remembered the dead girl who had dreamed of being a female dinosaur. Could she have been undergoing the same kind of psychodrug program as the dead man and himself?

Two colonists and one crew-member had been or were being fed advanced and possibly experimental forms of psychodrug. Of a complement of over two hundred, what were the chances of any three people chosen at random being special subjects? Just how many people on the ship were undergoing the treatment? And why didn't the dead man's absence from his casket register on the status board?

Without being able to work the answers out exactly, he knew that a fairly large proportion of the ship's personnel would have to be undergoing the treatment for the first two he had encountered to be special subjects.

But wait. Were the three subjects a truly random sampling? The girl was; she had suffered an accident with her cold-sleep casket and died before the side-effects of the treatment had become manifest. But the dead man was a different matter. Here was a subject whom Devlin had found because the treatment had driven the man to his death in the corridor. One could argue that if a large number of colonists were being treated then the ship should be filled with permanently cold, and dead, bodies.

Perhaps it was.

Devlin shook his head violently, trying to discard that ridiculous idea and to jolt his mind into producing a more reasonable one. The status board and its associated casket monitoring system were designed to show the condition of each and every person on the ship. The dead man either did not belong to the ship, in which case it was all a complex simulation, or he was a colonist who had somehow devised a way of leaving his cubicle and concealing his absence from the casket monitoring system. Devlin's first step would be to find out who the man was if he did belong to the ship, and an examination of his cubicle should then show how he had been able to fool the monitor.

It occurred to him that a simple answer would be to

open all the cubicles in turn until he found, or did not find, one that was empty. But he dismissed that idea as too impractical and time-consuming. Instead he would try to identify the man by searching his new, recently improved memory, and he would be looking at events and people in his own past—a fairly safe and pain-free area in which to explore.

Devlin put on warm coveralls and returned to the section of corridor containing the dead man. He detached him from the wall-net and towed him back to the control center where he placed the body on the spare couch. For a few minutes he focused a heater on the man's head and shoulders, then he carefully removed the tape from the eyelids and pressed them down until they were half-closed.

The heat had made the features look expressionless but natural. He tried harder to remember them.

Most of the lectures had been given in small rooms with rarely more than a dozen people present. Devlin concentrated on recalling a particular sequence, and gradually the still features of the dead man became overlaid with the mobile, incredibly wrinkled face of the project's chief psychologist. The old man was seated at a desk behind which there was a wall-chart containing information and hundreds of small photographs of the ship's personnel.

"... You people represent the final intake for this ship," Martin was saying in his deep, resonant voice. "There will be no chance for all of you to get to know each other before the end of the trip, but we are fairly sure that your predecessors and yourselves will be fully compatible—"

"Excuse me, Citizen, a question."

Devlin turned around to look at the questioner—a small, beautiful, dark-haired girl whose timidity was apparent in her tone and overly respectful manner. No person would normally address another as "Citizen" unless he was wearing a gun-belt, and Martin was as beltless as any sheep. She was, Devlin recalled with a rush of hindsight, the girl who would accidentally kill herself in Blue 31, and who might have been lucky to die when and how she did rather than living until her dreams drove her to it.

He forced his mind back to the girl's question, not looking at the mind-picture of her so much as at the other faces of the group, which should have included that of the dead man.

He did not see it.

The psychologist must have nodded because the girl went on, "So ... surely we will be compatible. I mean, it cannot be your intention to transplant all the conflict and viciousness of our society to ... to ..."

She had lost her timidity, Devlin noted, just before losing her voice. He faced to the front again as the psychologist replied:

"To be perfectly frank, our intentions are not clear even to ourselves. Certainly we do not intend to turn loose all the social and psychological ills of Earth on your future home, but we cannot be absolutely sure we will not. We do not believe we will because we are selecting and educating normal, average people.

"This appears to us to be the safest course," he went on pleasantly, "because supermen and superwomen are unpredictable during long periods in non-stress situations. Their treatment and the training of their offspring are likewise uncertain, because all their children are unlikely to be superchildren and the superparents may be unable to accept that fact. The result would be personalities subjected to abnormal pressures during the formative stage, and pressures of abnormal kindness or abnormal cruelty can be equally damaging. The high probability exists that the genetic background of the parents, the characteristics which made them superior in the first place, are in themselves abnormal and that a strength in one area is usually balanced by a weakness in another.

"Since we are unwilling to export unnecessary abnormalities to the stars," he continued, pulling up the corners of his lipless mouth and modulating his tone to express humor, "we have decided to educate—I prefer the word 'educate' to 'train'—people who are moderately honest, moderately unselfish and even moderately abnormal . . ."

The words, the tone, the smallest changes in expression of that bloodhound's face came back to him the way sensorama plays were supposed to, but did not. Devlin went back a few minutes to look at the memory sequence again, but this time he was concentrating on the chart containing the photographs behind the old man.

Perfect recall, Devlin discovered at once, did not improve the eyesight. He had to go back over the episode three times before he was able to remember a photograph, indistinct with distance, which might have been that of the dead man. The adjacent color coding indicated that he was a colonist due for cooling in Red 23, and the status board gave his name as Thomas Purdy.

What, he wondered once again, *have they done to my mind?*

But the question brought on a rush of too-perfect dream-memories and, in self-defense, he returned to the memory of the lecture. The psychologist, Martin, did not seem to mind interruptions, so Devlin was able to listen again to Patricia, who had been sitting beside him, and to the Caldwell girl. They had started by asking questions but had progressed to a three-way debate on the advisability of sending untrained personnel on such an important mission.

He could not remember anyone asking if it were possible, once having joined, to quit the project. Judging by his own feelings and those of Patricia, everyone was so glad to have been given the chance to run away from everything that the thought had not entered their heads—which said a great deal for the effectiveness of the initial selection procedures. But suppose some of the personnel chosen were expendables, guinea pigs who would be tested to destruction so as to increase the chance of survival for the others.

The most important items to be tested, so far as the project was concerned, were his mind and memory.

The memory of his first decision awakening came rushing back—the intense, almost physical pain of his disappointment at having to pass that beautiful but doomed world. Then came the fly-by of Target Five, the evasive action he had taken and the memory of its physically repulsive and warlike natives.

He had already convinced himself that the ship was real, that it was light-years from home and that the things he remembered when he was awake were real. But now he was reversing, or at least weakening, that conviction. If his dreams were as sharp and detailed and intense as his waking memories what, if anything, was real? Was it any more difficult to produce a full sensory hallucination of a space battle with extra-terrestrials than a Middle Ages near-massacre or the adventures of a giant saurian?

Possibly not. But there was one essential difference between his dream and his waking shipboard experiences. During the former he had no control over the incidents which occurred. No matter how hard he tried there seemed to be no way of altering the results. With the latter, however, he had a choice. He had the power of deciding, for instance, whether he would leave the dead Purdy on the couch or carry him back to his cubicle.

He was on a real ship or on a completely real simulation of the ship. In either case anything that happened to him between the present moment and the time he returned to cold-sleep, or died, was real. He left the control center and headed for Purdy's cubicle to see how the other had managed to fool the computer into thinking that he was still in residence.

The manual override allowed him to open the cubicle without initiating the resuscitation sequence, and the answer was obvious as soon as he bent over the casket.

But the question still remained—how had Purdy let himself out of a colonist cubicle? Where could he have picked up the highly specialized knowledge to do so?

Purdy had been desperate, but logical. Unsure of the extent of the computer's sensors, and incapable of finding a way of killing himself that would be effective before a crew-member could be roused to go to his assistance, he must have examined the personnel status board, and found the answer in Blue 31.

Devlin had switched off Blue 31 when the occupant died. With the sensors out of action there was no way for the computer to know whether the girl's body was or was not still there, so Purdy had moved it to his own casket. The sensors did not operate during cold-sleep, only while resuscitation was in progress to monitor the physical condition of the occupant, so the substitution had gone unnoticed. But when the occupant of Purdy's cubicle became due for revival, the substitution would be noticed—but as a substitution. It would be flagged as an organic malfunction for the attention of a crew-member, probably Devlin himself.

Except by then Devlin might also show as an organic malfunction, because the dead Purdy could be in Devlin's casket while he himself was dead in another part of the ship and long past caring.

Purdy had shown him the way out.

On his way back to the control center he passed the open door of his own cubicle and the closed one with Patricia's name on it. He had been trying not to think and trying especially hard not to remember, but he knew that he had other problems to face than the simple, mechanical one of committing suicide. That was why he was going to return Purdy to the man's own cubicle, for a short time, anyway, so that he would have the control center to himself while he tried to face his problems.

Until recently—a few weeks or six centuries ago—he had done his best thinking when he was alone.

But something was happening in the control center

when he returned from Purdy's cubicle for the second time. One of the repeater screens was glowing with a message, but he was too far away and the angle was too acute for him to read it. By the time he reached his couch the message had gone, to be replaced quickly with another.

```
REASONS FOR AWAKENING. TO CHECK POSSIBLE
MALFUNCTION IN CREW-MEMBER JOHN DEVLIN. DEVLIN
IS ABSENT FROM HIS CUBICLE AND OVERDUE FOR
COLD-SLEEP REPROCESSING. TO CHECK FUNCTIONING
OF MORLEY MUSCLE SYSTEMS, SPEECH ORGAN AND MEMORY.
```

"Patricia ..." began Devlin.

```
ADDITIONAL TO INSTRUCTION CHECK DEVLIN POSSIBLE
MALFUNCTION. IN THE EVENT OF SUSPECTED
PSYCHOLOGICAL MALFUNCTION, DO NOT RISK MORLEY
PHYSICAL DAMAGE BY CLOSE CONTACT. INSTRUCTIONS
EXERCISE, SPEAK AND REMEMBER TO PROCEED IN
CONJUNCTION WITH INSTRUCTION CHECK DEVLIN
MALFUNCTION.
```

Patricia had been awakened to discover why he was absent from his cubicle, and the computer had warned her against the possibility of finding his mind rather than his body malfunctioning. That meant the project's psychologists and programers had also been aware of this possibility. Very carefully Devlin kept his mind on his present surroundings and his eyes on the entrance to the control center.

It would take her half an hour to finish her resuscitation exercises, find his cubicle empty and come to control. He wondered if she would be as terrified of going to sleep as he was or if she would be able to help him find an answer different from Purdy's.

14

HER FACE WAS still and calm and lovely, and as stiff as so much chiseled marble. When she spoke her voice was under the same tight control.

"What are you doing out of your cubicle? Are you all right?"

Devlin nodded and tried to smile. He said, "There's nothing wrong with me. At least, nothing more serious than a case of self-induced insomnia . . ."

Suddenly she launched herself at him, knocking him backward onto his couch. Her arms were wrapped around him so tightly that it was difficult to breathe, and she was trembling. He did not have to be a medic to be able to diagnose desperation rather than desire. With one arm he held her as tightly as she was holding him, feeling the warmth of her body through the metal mesh. With his other hand he stroked her hair which, because it was long and thick, still retained the icy cold of the cubicle.

"What's wrong," he asked softly, "bad dreams?"

Her face was pressed too tightly against his chest for her to speak, but he felt her nod.

"I was hoping," he said, "to meet someone on this ship who was *not* troubled by unpleasant dreams. It might have helped disprove a theory of mine."

When she did not reply for several seconds he said, "We'll talk about it. You'll be all right, you'll see. And there is one answer, at least. It is a bit drastic, and only to be used as a last resort, but it *has* been used at least once . . ."

Devlin trailed off into silence. Although she was still trembling, holding her on the couch was very pleasant. Despite his confusion and anxiety about the ship and his terrible fear of going to sleep again, he began to react physically to the situation. As the fear and confusion ebbed, the other memories rushed in to fill the spaces—memories of incidents in his own past as well as a flood of dream episodes of a similar nature involving females that, in many cases, were not even human. All at once his need for her became so great that he, too, began to shake ...

Suddenly, violently, she pushed herself away from him and the couch, crying silently and shaking her head.

"What's wrong?" he asked angrily. But he knew the answer as soon as he asked the question. In fact, virtually every item of the dream material was supplying its own answer. Very few of those episodes had been pleasant for the female concerned.

"Put on a coverall," he said more quietly, "and sit on the other couch. I know what's bothering you, and I ... won't."

She relaxed enough to smile briefly, then she tightened up again. Devlin turned his head away as she began pulling on the coveralls, wondering why he felt embarrassed watching her dress when he had not felt that way on seeing her undressed. When she returned to the couch a few minutes later, he told her of his confusion regarding the voyage, or the simulation of the voyage, and of his uncertainty as to whether everyone or only an unlucky few were having dream trouble. He told her about the solution which Purdy had found to the problem, then he waited for her reaction.

She said finally, "I'm glad you're all right."

He turned then, furious at her stupidity in putting the whole problem on a personal basis, then silenced his tongue behind clenched teeth. It was obvious that she was concerned for the other people in the ship, and personally afraid of what had been happening to her mind. But unlike Devlin, she was concerned for other people first and for Devlin most of all.

"I'm sorry," he said, "I shouldn't have ... well, let's

both try to relax and talk about the problem without thinking too much about it. That sounds stupid—what I mean is if our thinking brings back something really unpleasant, let's sidetrack it by thinking of something nice. Remembering a difficult piece of music heard at a concert is probably a good way. Nothing terribly unpleasant ever happens at a concert."

"Except," she said, smiling, "if there's a bomb hoax or the music is so boring that I remember going to sleep."

"You just said a dirty word," said Devlin. "But do you have any ideas? We have one answer, but suicide isn't a good answer."

"No future in it," she said.

They were beginning to sound like a couple of comedians, Devlin thought. He wondered who they thought they were fooling.

"I agree with you," she went on, her reaction to their lapse into levity making her sound much too serious and pedantic. "The circumstances surrounding the deaths of colonists Caldwell and Purdy are such that it seems unlikely that the ship is a simulation. However, whether it is or is not a simulation is of secondary importance. What we must do is try to establish whether the dream trouble is happening to everyone or only to a few of us, and if so, how many and why?"

Devlin nodded. In a matching tone he said, "We could probably establish the number of disturbed dreamers by studying the status board, calling up the details of their awakenings and checking if any of them resisted, by even an hour, the return to their cold-sleep. We know that the colonists are supposed to be unable to open their cubicles; but they have ways of delaying cooldown, and a check on the consumables will tell us if they stayed awake inside their boxes rather than breaking out to do a Purdy-style body swap and commit suicide—"

"Does that mean," she broke in, "that you think some of the people in the cubicles are already dead?"

Devlin shook his head. "I don't see how they could have managed it. If they killed themselves prior to or during a cooldown, it would have been flagged as a malfunction, and a crew-member would have been awakened to investigate. You were awakened, remember, to check on a possible malfunction in me."

She was silent for a moment, then she said very seriously, "I'm frightened. Some of those dreams were so bad that if I deliberately recalled them I, too, might think that suicide was the only answer. But I don't want to think that even if Purdy did. Maybe he was in an earlier intake. We don't know what kind of person he was, whether he was nice or nasty or stable or otherwise.

"Perhaps he was flawed in some fashion," she went on quickly. "I realize this is wishful thinking and not logic, but he was a different personality from you and me. I don't want him to influence us too much, or the people who awaken later—the ones who have this dream problem—will discover Purdy and us and be convinced that suicide is the only answer.

"There might even be a chain reaction of suicides," she ended grimly, "until nobody is left alive on the ship."

Devlin reached across and took her hand. Obviously there was a difference between physical contact to give comfort and to seek pleasure, because the memories which had threatened to overwhelm him earlier merely stirred restively and went back to sleep, and she did not pull her hand away.

"Suppose Purdy was the first to encounter this problem," he said, "and we are the second. I didn't know him, either. But there is one difference between his case and ours. He did not have anyone to talk to. It could be an important difference."

She nodded wordlessly, and Devlin squeezed her hand. He said, "First we check the status board . . ."

It took many hours of concentrated, repetitious effort to call up and study each awakening in turn, and to check each one of them for differences that might indicate that a person on that particular awakening was behaving abnormally by not returning to his or her casket at the specified time. But they could find no evidence of it.

Devlin decided that they should make spot checks on the cubicles and look for the evidence at first hand. It would have been much faster if they had split up to make the checks, but somehow it was easier, when they worked together, to keep each other's minds off unpleasant memories.

Opening a statistically meaningful number of cubicles and performing the sequence of operations that would allow entry without initiating warmup of the occupant took an additional three hours. But it was the purely mental strain of controling their minds—of seeing cold-sleepers time after time without allowing themselves to think about the terrible dreams which must have been going on inside those frozen heads— that was much more tiring than the physical effort involved. When they returned to the control center, still without the evidence they had been seeking, their voices were slurred with fatigue and they kept yawning in each other's faces.

But their fatigue was filled with the fear of going to sleep, an abnormal fear which kept them moving about when they should have been resting in the couches. To help them stay awake they ran another detailed check on the status board and found nothing, except for one minor abnormality which had been plainly visible from the beginning.

Devlin pointed it out and said wearily, "I'm stupid. But surely it can't be as simple as all that. And if that is the only difference between us and the others, what the blazes does it mean?"

Her face was pale with weariness so that the scar tissue on her cheek stood out like an embossed pink star when she said, "I see what you mean. The Caldwell girl doesn't come into it because she died accidentally a long time ago, and the only thing Purdy had in common with us was that we three have been awakened more often than the others."

"Right," said Devlin, "Purdy and we have had one extra awakening. He had a test warmup during the first few years of the trip to check on the accuracy of the resuscitation timers. I had an extra awakening to attend to the Caldwell girl, and you were warmed because of me. That means ..." He yawned violently, then went on, "that means the trouble could affect everyone in the ship at their next awakening. We are not special cases, we have simply had an early warning."

"We have to help them," said the girl urgently. "We have to tell them what to expect—"

"They'll know what to expect as soon as they waken, dammit!" Devlin broke in. "What you mean is that we have to think of an answer for them when they do waken. But I'm too damned tired to think of anything."

"I'm tired, too," she said angrily, "and it keeps me from saying exactly what I mean. I meant that we must find a better answer than Purdy's."

"How long," said Devlin sharply, "do we have to find it? How long can we stay awake?"

She did not answer and he could see his own fear mirrored in her expression. Apologetically, he said, "I'm sorry. If we don't stop snapping at each other we'll have to send out for a couple of belts. Let's try, despite our tiredness, to think about Purdy's answer. Let's examine it, and the situation which drove him to it, in detail in case there is something there that we can use ..."

They had to assume that Purdy had been terrified by his dreams to an extent greater, or at least equal, to that which they had and were experiencing and that he had tried hard to find another answer. Probably he had tried so long and so hard that he had reached the same stage of physical and mental exhaustion that they had. But Purdy had been all alone. He had not been so selfish as to awaken someone else to share his troubles, but he had not panicked.

Knowing that he had to sleep sooner or later, he had delayed sleeping for as long as possible by taping open his eyelids. Then, after stripping off his coverall, he had gone to an extremely cold section of the module and arranged himself so that the greatest possible area of his body's surface was in contact with the cold plating. The taped-up eyelids and the freezing cold metal would have kept him awake for some time, but eventually he would have fallen asleep and dreamed briefly before dying from exposure . . .

"This extreme fatigue which we feel, and which Purdy presumably felt, bothers me," Devlin went on thoughtfully. "All of us were fit at the beginning of the voyage, which is only a matter of days ago in biological time, and we have not been working so hard on the ship that we should be ready to drop from exhaustion like this."

He paused, squeezed his eyes shut and shook his head violently, trying to shake his brain cells into increased activity, then he went on, "Suppose the project people made a fundamental error in thinking that the long periods in cold-sleep were enabling us to rest—a justifiable assumption, in the circumstances. But let us suppose instead that the cold-sleep preserved the body's fatigue toxins along with everything else, and that we haven't in fact slept properly since the day before we entered the cold-sleep caskets on Earth. Sleep deprivation causes some odd mental effects—disorientation, reduced self-confidence, that sort of thing."

"Are you suggesting," said Patricia, smiling, "that we should have been awakened periodically and told to go to sleep?"

"Yes," said Devlin, "If they wanted us to stay mentally alert."

He did not smile.

Despite her fatigue she saw what he was driving at and began shaking her head, violently.

"I know how you feel—I feel the same way myself," said Devlin. "But we won't be able to think properly about anything until we've rested, even if it is only for a few hours. And we must not be asleep at the same time. One of us will stay awake to keep watch on the other, to awaken him or her if the sleep appears to be disturbed. We won't be in a cold-sleep casket, unable to stop dreaming. At the first sign of distress—I'll explain about the mechanics of sleep, the eye movements behind the closed lids that indicate natural dreaming, and so on—the other person will rouse the sleeper.

"We have to try it," Devlin ended firmly. "I'll go first."

But as soon as he said the words his fatigue disappeared driven away by the terror of dozens of remembered dyings. He could see that the same terror had the girl in its grip and, when she spoke, his strongest emotion was one of shameful relief.

"If we are going to try it, I'll go first," she whispered. "You have a better idea of the symptoms to watch for if I ... I ..."

But it was not easy to make her relax. She kept fighting sleep for what seemed like hours, even though Devlin spoke softly to her, held her hands and finally reran a close-range probe sequence from his first observation awakening which showed the beautiful, parklike scenery of the satellite of Planet Three. Gradually her eyes began to close more and more frequently and remain closed for longer and longer periods. Her breathing became deep and regular after she passed the restive period on the threshold of sleep, but there were no indications of disturbance or distress.

Devlin rubbed his eyes and thought, *Poor Purdy ...*

Watching her, he wondered what was going on in the mind behind that lovely tranquil face, and if it were possible that the fearfully sharp and intense dreams which they had both experienced could go on without some outward sign. He did not think so, and gradually he began to feel a little envious of her escape. He remembered the young king tired after a strenuous training session with Hawn, or lying exhausted in the arms of his favorite, or of the feel of sunshine and warm mud on his enormous, leathery body as he dozed in the shallows of a prehistoric lake ...

He came awake to find her shaking his shoulder and smiling. She said, "I don't know how long you've been asleep, but I've had nine hours. As a sentry you're a total loss!"

15

"How DO YOU feel? Any unpleasant dreams?"

She shook her head. "I feel fine."

"Me, too," said Devlin. "But we should try to remember as much as possible—the difference, that is, between cold-sleep and the normal kind of dreaming. It might help us to understand what is going on."

Devlin had never been very good at recalling dreams. He had been convinced that he did not dream at all until he discovered during medical training that everyone dreamed, whether they remembered dreaming or not. But now, with very little effort, he found that he could bring back the memory of what his mind had been doing while he had been asleep.

There had been chaotic flashes of dozens of unrelated incidents as his sleeping mind sorted and sifted through the records of his last waking period. His mind had tried to impose some kind of order and sense on them, with the result that people and places and incidents and timing were mixed in a fantasy world that was ridiculous rather than frightening. Then there had been dreams which had been logical within themselves—events, imagined or remembered, which fairly shouted out his fears regarding the voyage and his own reduced probability of surviving it. His cold-sleep memories had obtruded, as well, but not seriously enough to frighten him awake—and there had been one odd sequence involving Brother Howard.

The Brother had been talking very seriously to him, and Devlin had replied occasionally. But in spite of the conversation, the whole sequence had been completely silent.

Finally he said, "Find anything?"

"I don't think so," she said. "But then I'm not sure what I'm looking for. There was nothing in the dreams as frightening or intense as in the cold-sleep kind, although I'm pretty sure that if I tried I could recall them in just as much detail. My memory seems to be enormously improved. Some of the incidents—one involving Brother Howard, for instance—were completely ridiculous. I'm very hungry."

"What did you say?"

"I'm hungry," she repeated. "And I know that we shouldn't really be awake and should not, therefore, draw on the ship's consumables. But being practical . . . well, Purdy and the Caldwell girl will not be using their allowance and we could—"

"A good idea," Devlin broke in, "but I didn't mean that. What I wanted to know was if the dream about Brother Howard was silent? Did he talk during it, but you couldn't hear him or yourself speaking?"

She did not reply, but her expression was answer enough. Once again he wondered what had been done to their minds.

After a long and baffled silence he went on, "Well now, it seems that we can stay warm and eat and sleep for about two weeks without using anyone else's rations. That should give us enough time to come up with an alternative answer."

She nodded and he went on, "I feel happier thinking about this in my own language, but if I forget something or seem to be going wrong, don't be afraid to interrupt, right? Now suppose we treat our problems as a dangerous and possibly lethal symptom of a disease. The first step would be to find out how the infection, or whatever it is, was introduced into our systems before we can begin negating its effects . . ."

The possibilities, Devlin went on to explain, where that it had been deliberately introduced by mechanical means, either before the voyage had started or during it. If the former, then it had delayed-action effects that were only now becoming manifest; if the latter, the effects were cumulative and the method of introduction was probably incorporated in the cooldown processing or else it was taken with the food or water . . .

"In that case," she broke in worriedly, "we shouldn't eat or drink."

"When we get hungry and thirsty enough," said Devlin wryly, "we'll find good reasons why it could not have been introduced with the food and water. But right now we have to search the ship's cold-sleep and life-support systems for indications that some form of medication is being introduced. We must also search our memories for clues to some form of treatment that might have been given us before we left Earth.

"I don't know what we are looking for exactly," he went on. "It could be a hallucinogenic drug, direct modification of memory by psychoradiation techniques—they were getting very good at that sort of thing before I left the hospital—or post-hypnotic verbal or visual triggers for an implanted memory sequence placed during training. It could be a mixture of all three, or combined with others which we can't even guess at.

"One good thing about this search," Devlin ended, "is that we can look in both places, the ship and our training period memories, at the same time."

But their detailed examination of the ship's cold-sleep, life-support and food dispenser systems turned up nothing suspicious. True, the information reached them through the relevant computer displays and it was possible that the computer had been programed to conceal the data they were seeking. But that would have introduced an unnecessary and highly dangerous complication into the mission, so they had to assume that the information given to them was accurate. As a check on this accuracy they returned again and again to the memories of their training, to lectures and simulations, conversational asides and wall charts, circuit diagrams and stores inventories—none of which they had thought themselves capable of remembering at the time. Their ability to remember, whatever the reason for it, was phenomenal. One important piece of information which they learned was that the ship was pushing hard against its limits of operational safety.

The next fly-by, due in just under one hundred and eighty-one years, would probably be the last with a fully functioning ship.

"I wish we hadn't found out about that," said Devlin later, while they were discussing their findings in the control center. "We're still trying to solve the cold-sleep problem, and that knowledge tends to sidetrack one's train of thought."

"Not necessarily," she replied. "The data on the next target system looks good—one of the best prospects we've had, in fact. Would it be possible for us to reprogram the computer so as not to awaken anyone at all until we go into landing orbit?"

Devlin shook his head in helplessness. "One of the things drummed into us was the necessity for mental and physical exercise at regular intervals. Besides, I wouldn't like to fool around with programs as important as that."

"But one of the things they were worried about," she argued, "was the possibility of memory loss due to the reduced temperature allowing the electro-chemical charges used for memory storage to leak away. That is not happening."

"I know, I know," said Devlin irritably. "Our problem is finding too many memories, not losing them. But you're forgetting that the period will be much longer than one hundred eighty-one years. If the fly-by shows a planet suitable for colonization we have to decelerate and return, so that it could be three times that period before we are in landing orbit. We don't know what effects that might have.

"If there were no physical or mental deterioration," he added, "I'm still not convinced that we should risk it. I mean, over three hundred years in cold-sleep. To crib from Shakespeare, what dreams might come . . . ?"

"But we must do something!"

Devlin was about to snap back at her, then stopped himself in time. They were both tired, and anxiety, as it usually did, was making him hungry. He smiled instead and said, "Let's eat."

She yawned suddenly and added, "And sleep."

Neither of them was afraid of what might happen during a warm-sleep so that they were able to relax in their couches. But perversely, sleep would not come. Devlin's mind would not leave the problem and Patricia could not stop talking about it.

"From what you've just been saying," she said, after yet another exercise in circular logic, "we can be sure, well, fairly sure, that any of the psychodrugs, whether they were hallucinogens, personality changers or whatever, would not remain active over this length of time. Despite the fact that an efficient cooldown system is supposed to halt all chemical and metabolic reactions, those particular drugs are composed of unstable material which is also highly complex structurally. As well, they had not been in existence long enough before our departure for proper long-term tests, a couple of centuries or more, to be carried out. They would not have risked the success of this project by using drugs with long-term effects which could have had unforeseen mental effects on us."

"That's what I said," Devlin replied tiredly. "But they may have taken the risk, and this is the result."

She shook her head. "If they had administered a drug with memory reinforcing capabilities, and remember that they seemed to be very concerned during training about the possibility of us *losing* our memories, then any biochemical instability would react against the original purpose of the drug—our memories would remain normal or perhaps even faded instead of becoming sharper, as has happened. More likely such instability and subsequent breakdown of the chemical structure would have caused severe and apparent brain damage and, at the very least, the type of hallucination generally encountered with derivatives of LSD. We have had nightmares, and bad ones, but they were invariably self-consistent."

"You are saying then," said Devlin, rubbing his eyes, "that they didn't administer a psychodrug, stable or otherwise?"

"No, not exactly," she replied. "They could have administered something that would not change over a long period because it was non-material. The treatment could have been hypnotic rather than biochemical."

Devlin rolled on to his side so that he could look across at her. He said excitedly, "Hypno-conditioning is affected only by the passage of biological time, and so far as our waking and conscious minds are concerned, the conditioning took place only days or weeks ago. Assuming you're right, it was probably administered at intervals during training. But that fact doesn't answer all the questions, you know."

"I know that," she said, turning toward him. "But I think we are probably close to the true explanation."

"Until we know the true explanation," he said drily, "I can't answer that. But assuming it is the right or nearly right answer, think of the work involved for the project staff. Hypnotizing us, and concealing the fact with various forms of post-hypnotic suggestion, would have been the easiest part of the job. They would have had to subject us to films, sensory impressions of all kinds, and fine psychosurgical work of the type that needs a lot of time. But my strongest objection is based on the quality and detail of the dreams themselves and the apparent duration of the dream sequences. I say apparent because I know how time can be telescoped during conditioning, but those dreams went on for years.

"Assuming your idea to be correct in every detail," Devlin ended, "how does it help us?"

"I'm not sure," she replied. "But wouldn't it be possible to search our memories of the training period for the gaps which must be present during the conditioning sessions, and try to use our improved memories to break those post-hypnotic commands. Alternatively, isn't it possible that if we go over some of those dream sequences again, the humdrum episodes as well as the more dramatic bits, we might be able to spot the joins or see some evidence of artificiality or error in the dreams.

"They must have put a lot of effort into those alleged dreams," she ended, "but no simulation is ever perfect."

Devlin sat up suddenly and swung his legs off the couch. It was a reaction to his feeling of excitement rather than a need to go anywhere. He said, "I see what you're driving at. But examining some of those dreams for technical errors will be a, well, harrowing job. What you're really saying is that if we can show that the dreams have been imposed from without, that they might be a result of hypno-conditioning gone wrong, we can communicate this fact to the others and perhaps convince them that it is possible to negate the worst effects of the dreams."

"That's it," she agreed. "Even when I dreamed of being a crustacean or a wolverine, I was still also aware of being myself. Maybe we can do or suggest something to strengthen that awareness."

Devlin nodded. "It might not be as simple as you make it sound," he said, "but where do we start? With the dreams or with the actual memories?"

"With memories," she said firmly. "I'm very reluctant to go back to some of those dreams, and we just might find what we're looking for in the real past. I realize that the actual conditioning sessions would not show because we have been ordered to forget them, but there must have been a lead-up, some prior mental preparation, by the project staff. Brother Howard might have let something slip during those early meetings—in the park, at the project building or in the rec hall. If hypno-conditioning was being used, he must have known about it."

Devlin nodded again and said, "I don't think he let anything slip in the park or during his first visit to the block. I went over that day as a memory exercise during an earlier warm-up. It was a pleasant and important day for me, except for the riot on the way home, and I remembered it in considerable detail—"

"Funny," she broke in, looking away from him as she spoke, "I picked the same day to remember."

"We'll go into the deep, dark, psychological significance of that later," Devlin went on, smiling, "because if we did it now we probably could not reamin objective about ourselves—"

"Later that evening," she broke in again, "Brother Howard was very objective about us. Objectionable, even."

"My cooldown warning came before I was able to remember into the evening," Devlin said, "and that is the time when I recall that the Brother spoke very freely. I'd like to go over that memory again, from the time when your father left us ..."

Citizen Morley had been a small man who did not try to compensate for this fact by making a lot of noise. He wore an empty belt signifying that, although he was technically safe within and among the residents of his block, he was not entirely surrounded by his own family circle. When Brother Howard and Devlin found their table and were introduced by Patricia, her father, for all his mildness and friendliness, looked quietly furious.

She had explained the presence of the Brother and the doctor by saying that her self-inflicted wound had caused them to be concerned about her mental as well as her physical well-being, and that Brother Howard was a friend of the doctor who was anxious to help her. Citizen Morley, as he handed her formally into their charge, said that he could not really blame his daughter for doing as she had done, but it was very obvious to Devlin that if the citizen ever did find someone to blame, that person's life-expectancy would be drastically shortened.

For the first few minutes at the table they had privacy of a sort. The Brother's profession was obvious from his dress and Devlin's from the ornate dress earring which he wore on semi-social occasions, but a crowd of high-spirited but essentially good youngsters—as the block sociologist, but nobody else, described them—seemed intent on harrassing these two half-sheep who had the temerity to sit with one of the best-looking girls in the building.

None of them were old enough to be citizens, which meant that theoretically anyone living in the block who had reached maturity had the right to chastize them. In actual fact, however, no one who was not a full citizen with a large number of citizen relatives could do so if he or she expected to go on living, much less working, in the block. And in any case it would have been senseless to try chastizing a group which outnumbered them five to one and whose members were wearing spiked chains with their leathers.

Devlin suggested that they go up to the roof.

The high-spirited but essentially good youngsters were not allowed on the roof lest they render it as uninhabitable for ordinary people as the Maxers did the city parks at night. But Brother Howard and Devlin were adults and responsible, theoretically, even though they were not citizens; and whether the girl and the doctor were accompanied by the Brother as a chaperone, or whether she was psychologically ill as well as facially damaged and was seeking quiet for physical and spiritual solace, both were acceptable reasons for their being there. The fact that Citizen Morley was on duty with the roof security party who searched them for weapons saved a lot of red tape.

A cold wind was blowing in from the sea, dissipating the air wastes inland and carrying away the sounds of desultory gunfire from the business districts. They found a radiant plate which both sheltered them from the wind and gave them a good view of the city through the antisuicide netting while the plate's warmth bathed their backs. Occasionally a security man came along to check on the plate's functioning in case they had been irresponsible enough to damage it or switch it off. They did not mind that because the plates were not there for the convenience of block-dwellers on cold nights, but as infrared dazzlers against high-spirited but essentially good types in other blocks who wanted to shoot at roof security men with heat-sighted or heat-seeking weapons.

But their conversation, while interesting, was not very informative regarding the project. Without making it obvious, Brother Howard was refusing to change the subject, and the subject was the Morley girl. Without ever telling her why he wanted to know, the Brother found out a great deal lot about her, and Devlin knew enough to know that she was being subjected to one of the most expert verbal probings he had ever witnessed.

After more than two hours of delving, an interruption, a sharp detonation and ground-level flash from a few miles away, stopped the interrogation long enough for Devlin to ask a question.

"Now that you know everything there is to know about Patricia," he said, "I expect it will be my turn. Then, presumably, you will decide finally whether or not we are suitable candidates for training?"

The light from the fire which had followed the explosion was still too weak to enable Devlin to read the Brother's expression, but the other sounded impatient as he replied, "I decided that you, Doctor, were suitable a few hours after meeting you for the first time. Deciding about Miss Morley is a longer and more difficult job, because no man can get inside a woman's mind and fully understand what is going on there. But don't worry, either of you—you will be on the ship. The process which you are shortly to undergo is not really training so much as a transfer of necessary information, an adult education exercise . . ."

He broke off, then said worriedly, "I'm not sure of my bearings from this block, Doctor. Was that explosion close to the project building?"

"No, nowhere near it . . ." began Devlin, when there was a second and larger explosion from the same area. Armored fire and ambulance units were already racing toward the trouble spot, their positions signaled by flashing blue lights and the strident donkey-call of their sirens. As they converged on the fire, heavy gunfire and a few armor-piercing rockets hammered at them from the surrounding darkness. The ambulance and fire-fighting units grounded themselves to protect their vulnerable undersides, unable to deploy their equipment. Then the lights and sirens of the city security heavies, a great many of them, came bounding in to their support. It was rapidly becoming impossible to hold a conversation without shouting.

Citizen Morley appeared out of the darkness beside them.

"This looks like it may be a bad one," he said, speaking slowly and clearly. "The timing and tactics indicate cooperation between a large number of protesting factions, and the incident, together with the city security reaction to it, is sure to involve a lot of uncommitted local residents. That will mean confusion and wild shooting.

"You will be safer in your room, Patricia," he ended, "and I suggest that you gentlemen will also be more comfortable below."

He could have sent them from the roof with a few

short, sharp words, Devlin thought, but Patricia's father was a citizen in the true sense of the word—firm, decisive, responsible and considerate. As they turned to go below Devlin's last view of the incident, the most serious they had had that week, was a writhing, red and many-petaled flower growing rapidly in a bed of flickering blue stars.

It had been a terrible and all too familiar beauty . . .

The control-center bulkheads took on substance behind the fading mind-picture, and Devlin said, "The initial explosion and his worry about the project building may have put the Brother off guard for a moment. Perhaps he did not mean to say what he did about training and education. I asked him about it later, at my place. If you give me a few minutes I'll recall the conversation for you."

She shook her head and said, "I'm hungry."

"So am I," said Devlin.

"I'm worried about the others," she went on. "Do we eat and sleep again or do we try to find an answer now? We were to check cold-dreams as well as our waking memories, remember?"

"I know, I know," said Devlin, wishing that she would not remind him of their duty when he had been silently engaged in reminding himself. "We'll check the dreams for faulty workmanship for a while, then I'll go back to Brother Howard talking on my surgery couch. But I suggest you begin with a pleasant episode, or one that is not too unpleasant."

She shook her head again. "We're not trying to protect them against pleasant dreams."

Angrily, Devlin said, "You can do just as you please, of course." Then he lay back in the couch and pointedly stared straight ahead. He was beginning to realize that a woman strong-willed enough to disfigure herself for wholly unselfish reasons could, at times, have mannerisms that were not entirely charming.

Very carefully he sent his memory probing back.

His biggest problem was ignorance. He did not know enough about the subject to tell whether there was a technical error in the sensory impressions or environment of a trilobite or a giant saurian, or whether the weapons and armor given to the young king by Hawn were correct for that historical period. Some of the vegetation, coloration of fur and skin, methods of making and fastening clothing were surprising but not, because of that, necessarily incorrect.

Timidly, Devlin began to move into the actively unpleasant areas, even though it was impossible to remember the finer details of environment and sensation through the floods of remembered pain. He had the feeling that such areas were crude and melodramatic, if they were in fact psychological constructs, and the people who might have implanted them might also have become a little careless.

He had no knowledge of the physiology or nervous systems of the majority of the creatures he had dreamed himself to be—with one exception. The king had been a man, a human being, and Devlin knew about human beings as only a trained medic would know them. Very carefully he recalled the assassination of the old king and how the knife had felt going in, how it felt inside the wound and how he had felt as he went rapidly into shock from loss of blood and died. He went over the incident again, with greater attention to detail, and again. He could detect no technical or physiological errors. Suddenly he sat up.

"Something's wrong," he said harshly. "Have you been going over the painful stuff, too?"

She nodded. "A very unpleasant death in childbirth in a smelly cave with—"

"You don't seem unduly bothered."

"No," she said, looking startled. "It wasn't pleasant, but it wasn't nearly as bad as the first time I remembered it. Why is that?"

Devlin was silent for a moment while he thought out

the explanation for himself before he began giving her the answer.

Simply, Patricia and he had done something that none of the others had done—they had slept. The situation was analogous to the painful post-operative period following major surgery. The patient remembered the experience for the rest of his or her life. Fortunately this memory dimmed with time, sometimes a very short time, otherwise anyone who had ever been hurt would spend the rest of his life hurting. But the mind was capable of putting up a barrier against remembered pain that allowed incidents to be recalled while filtering out the associated suffering. Even after a really bad op, patients felt much better after a good, sound sleep . . .

"I see," she said seriously, when he had finished his explanation. "It's as simple as that. When we were warmed and awakened the cold-sleep memories were too fresh, too intense—like a raw nerve. But after we slept naturally they became normal memories, unpleasant but not actually painful." She laughed suddenly. "The others will be relieved when we tell them all they have to do when they are awakened is to go back to sleep."

Devlin did not smile. He was still very frightened at the prospect of another interminable session of cold-dreaming, but this time he wanted it to be himself who reminded them of their duty—even though he knew that he was being petty and probably stupid. He said, "We have the answer to the cold-dream suicide problem, even though we still don't know how or why or when the dreams were foisted on us. But we can go on working on that problem while we are waiting to be cooled.

"Right now we should tape instructions to the others," he went on firmly, "and I see no reason for our eating while we are doing that. Unless you have a strong objection, I suggest that we go cold as quickly as possible."

She was still laughing at him with her eyes as she

said, "Before our feet get a chance to go cold before we do."

The message which they composed was as simple as possible to avoid confusing people who would be freshly awakened and very frightened.

```
URGENT MESSAGE FROM THE CREW TO BE GIVEN TO
ALL COLONISTS AT EACH AWAKENING FROM COLD-SLEEP.
MESSAGE TO BE INSERTED BETWEEN PERSONAL
GREETING AND SHIP STATUS REPORT.
MESSAGE FOLLOWS.
IT IS PROBABLE THAT SHIP'S PERSONNEL ARE
EXPERIENCING SEVERE MENTAL DISTRESS AS A
RESULT OF DREAMS ENCOUNTERED DURING COLD-SLEEP.
THE REASON FOR THE INTENSITY OF THESE DREAMS
IS NOT YET UNDERSTOOD, BUT THE DISTRESSING
AFTER-EFFECTS CAN BE REDUCED BY ONE OR MORE
PERIODS OF NORMAL SLEEP.
SINCE IT NOW SEEMS LIKELY THAT COLD-SLEEP DOES
NOT PERFORM THE PHYSIOLOGICAL AND PSYCHOLOGICAL
REPAIR FUNCTIONS OF NORMAL SLEEP, AND THAT
PHYSICAL FATIGUE IS ALSO PRESERVED INTACT DURING
COLD-SLEEP, THERE SHOULD BE NO DIFFICULTY
EXPERIENCED IN SLEEPING NORMALLY.
IF THE AWAKENING PERIOD SEEMS TOO SHORT FOR
NORMAL SLEEP, EXTEND IT WITH THE EMERGENCY
OVERRIDE FOR AS LONG AS NECESSARY. BE SPARING
IN THE USE OF CONSUMABLES.
CARRY OUT ALL OTHER PHYSICAL AND MENTAL
EXERCISES AS INSTRUCTED.
MESSAGE ENDS.
```

They agreed that that message should do it, until Patricia became anxious in case the constant use of the manual overrides would worry the computer into awakening the crew to check for possible physiological malfunctions in people who insisted on sleeping in their caskets instead of being out of them exercising. It was a valid cause for worry so they spent an additional few minutes modifying the computer instructions to cover this possibility. Then they spent several minutes more in very close contact without, however, recalling unpleasant dream memories.

As they were returning to their caskets, Patricia said sadly, "Poor Purdy. If only he hadn't managed to die in his sleep."

16

HE HAD TWO hours before cooldown. It was more than enough time, Devlin thought, to recall the details of a conversation which could only have lasted for half of that period.

Brother Howard had been tired, irritable at times and argumentative. When viewed with hindsight he might also find that the Brother had been less than careful about concealing his true intentions, whatever they were. But at that time Devlin had not known enough to ask the right questions ...

"I don't quite understand your acceptance standards, Brother," Devlin said. "You keep insisting that the colonists are nothing special. In fact, you seem to suggest that their mediocrity is almost a virtue. Surely you must be looking for some special qualifications?"

For a few seconds Devlin thought that the Brother was not going to answer. He lay on the examination couch, fully dressed except for his shoes and high, tight collar. But then he stretched, sighed and said, "These days, mediocrity is a special qualification."

"If it were as simple as that," said Devlin, irritably, "all you would need from us would be our name, age and sex before putting us into cold storage until it was time to go. I need a serious answer to a serious question."

"And I gave you a serious answer," the Brother replied. "But what you really need, perhaps, is to know if you are just a little bit above normal, or someone who is a shade more average than the others. Well, the trip requires two people aboard to observe, make a few simple decisions and, occasionally if at all, perform simple actions.

"For this reason," he added sardonically, "we have chosen carefully from our very average travelers two who will act as the ship's crew."

"But why the average people?" Devlin burst out. "What is it that you're afraid of? Surely, for the success of the project, you need an above-average crew, at least? Even in these degenerate days there must be a few stable, highly intelligent and dedicated supermen—"

"Like me?"

"If this is something I shouldn't know about, say so," said Devlin angrily. "Don't make jokes."

The couch sighed as Brother Howard raised himself on to his elbows. In a very serious voice he said, "I am too tired, and there is too little time left to me, to waste it making jokes. You would like to know why we seem so abnormally interested in normal people. Well, I must admit there are a few pieces of information that must be concealed from you, for the present, that is—but this is not one of them. Before I try to answer, I want you to think about the present society we are living and all to frequently dying in; now, where would you go to find a superman in these conditions? This is assuming that there ever was such a thing in the first place, and not just an over-trained, hyper-conditioned and force-grown human being. Then ask yourself where do we, the human race, go from here?"

This, thought Devlin impatiently, *is the sort of question I have debated many, many times.* Mostly he had argued on the side of the optimists, insisting that the combination of the arts and sciences—sensitivity with high technology—were bringing Earth's culture to the brink of a newer and even greater Renaissance. The suffering of a comparative few individuals and the excesses of others were only to be expected, just as the first Renaissance had been marred by its plagues and famines and unbalanced distribution of wealth.

He developed the argument for the Brother, insisting that in spite of the fact that so many individual and group activities were destructive, there had never in all recorded history been so much freedom of expression, so much medical care, so much food and associated comforts available to the population as a whole. Construction of mass-accommodation buildings, road systems and recreational areas—especially in cities with strong and psychologically well-trained security forces —were slowly but surely pulling ahead of the protest groups that were bent only on wrecking civilization for reasons which they themselves could not adequately explain. But then there had always been danger to the individual in a growing vital culture—carnivorous beasts prowling around the village at night, robbers and assassins infesting the highways and cities, and now protesters and Maxers and security forces . . .

"You're an oppy, then," Brother Howard broke in. "You *like* it here?"

Devlin shook his head. "You know I don't. But I want to be optimistic, mostly because I don't want to agree with the doomsters. Then I think about the drugging and killing and senseless destruction of everything that has been or is being built, chaos and ultimate doom is all that I can honestly foresee. Yet the people who realize that we are headed for trouble, and who try to rise to the top where they can do something about it, are usually too old to survive the affairs needed to get there. And the ones who do get to the top without fighting are the ones who do what the people at the bottom want them to—which is nothing, because the people at the bottom don't know what they want.

"Even so, there must be a few who reach the top without losing their ideals, their sensitivity, their feeling of responsibility for the long-term welfare of the people below them," Devlin went on. "These are the kind of people you should send to the stars. I know that I seem to be arguing myself out of a berth on the ship, and I don't want to do that, but I don't think that I'm really fitted for this job. I don't know who *is* fitted or even—"

"Nobody is really fitted for this job," said the Brother dryly, "because it is a brand new one. But you could be right. There are probably a few altruists and farseeing types around, but they are much rarer than you realize. The majority of the people from the middle levels to the top, even within the starship project, are motivated by intelligent—sometimes highly intelligent—self-interest. They do very valuable and necessary work, all of them, and very often display compassion and other noble qualities. But when you probe deeply enough, you find that they want power over people, even if it is the power to do only good. That, naturally, is an absolute bar as far as I am concerned."

"But why?" asked Devlin. "Surely we need leaders where we're going? And what about you, Brother? Why aren't you a suitable candidate?"

"Because," said the Brother, "my self-interest, intelligent or otherwise, impels me to stay at home and exert pressure." He smiled wryly, held up one hand and pressed the index finger and thumb together until both nails were rimmed with white, then added, "You could say that I want to give someone, somewhere, the pip."

Devlin shut his mouth firmly so as not to express his anger verbally, but he could not clamp down on the expression on his face.

"Before you accuse me of joking again," the Brother went on, "or you run to a citizen neighbor to borrow his belt, let me tell you that I am giving you the sober truth even if it is, at times, couched in non-serious language. I am a completely unsuitable candidate. Before I became a Brother I was the kind of person that you think is needed for this project—highly trained, highly intelligent, emotionally stable and possessing all the qualities that you seem to think are desirable for the job. But then I had a revelation—a quasi-religious experience, you might say—which made me a fanatic. As such I had time and energy for only one form of activity ..."

Once again he held up his tightly pressed thumb and index finger.

Before Devlin could reply there was a triple shock which jerked his fold-away bed on its supports and made the room's walls creak. The emergency PA began calling for all block security personnel, regardless of status, to evacuate the roof in preparation for a landing by city security forces.

Obviously the protest was turning into a big one and, judging by the shocks to the block's structure, limited mass-destruction weapons were being brought into use. This was only the third time in a year that such a thing had happened in the city, but it could mean serious damage and perhaps destruction of the block's sheltering, albeit unwillingly, the protector force. A large number of bystander casualties might result. Devlin sighed and tried not to think about it while he was waiting for the Brother to start making sense.

"My view of the future is both oppy and doomster," the Brother went on, raising his voice above the sound of the PA. "Earth, our present high level of science and culture, the vast majority, if not all, of the people who live on it, will be gone within a century at most, and it could fall apart within the next decade. To me, and remember that you had the same idea, Earth is like a large, overripe but not quite rotten fruit.

"I arrived at this idea before my, well, revelation, when I was still a sane and well-integrated superman," he went on, without smiling. "The analogy is a reasonably good one. Initially the fruit is small and bitter and not at all pleasant. There is no subtlety of feeling in such a society, no freedom, little happiness for even the very few who grasp power because of the violence which brings them down. But later the fruit begins to grow and ripen. Order is imposed on the earlier chaos;

laws and community cooperation replace continual war and give much more individual freedom, which in turn sends minds questing inward toward philosophy and outward into science. The fruit continues to ripen, becomes mature. No longer is anyone forced to labor mindlessly for two-thirds of his or her waking life. There is time to develop new and subtle tastes and forms of pleasant or painful activity. Everyone feels free to indulge in any pursuit he fancies and to go to Hell if that is what he wants to do. Many people, unfortunately, feel free to take the others to Hell with them. So the fruit becomes overripe and the next stage is dissolution and decay . . ."

"So endeth the parable," said Devlin patiently.

"So beginneth the parable," the Brother replied firmly, "because here the analogy breaks down. Our growing, ripening fruit is not free to expand indefinitely, you see. It is growing within a thick, strong skin which produces compression effects. Population pressure, diminishing resources, pollution as well as various psychological and social ills are together squeezing a culture which is rotten to the point of fermentation. One, and the most important result of this pressure will be that the seedling or pip of our overripe fruit will be squeezed out."

He brought his index finger and thumb together again, then added very seriously, "The pip has to be directed toward fallow ground."

"Yes," said Devlin, "but . . ."

"But the composition of the pip is important," the Brother went on. "There are philosophical aspects that I will not worry you with just yet. However, we at the project think that the whole process is a natural one and that our planetary fruit will emit its seed as naturally and inevitably as a caterpillar becomes a butterfly. But even so, we worry. Not only must we guide our pip toward an area where it will stand the best possible chance of taking root, we must also decide on the type of seed it must be so that it will survive into the indefinite future, because we may not have enough time or resources to squeeze out another pip.

"So we are faced with a hard decision," he continued. "Should we squeeze out a highly intelligent and technically trained pip, which might find its intelligence and training wasted if there should be a forced devolution into a primitive agricultural society? Or should we send hardy, thrusting, aggressive seeds which will survive and spread rapidly and perhaps choke themselves to death as we are doing now, or be destroyed by someone because they have become an obnoxious form of weed? Many times we have asked ourselves these questions, trying to find a seedling whose composition best represented our race.

"The more deeply we went into the questions, the more frightened we became of making a mistake," he went on, rubbing the back of his hand across a suddenly sweating forehead. "In the end we succumbed to moral cowardice and decided, if you could call it a decision, to select for mediocrity . . . It can't be my imagination. What is happening to your cooling system?"

"Probably the security forces on the roof are drawing power from this area for their equipment," Devlin replied. "It won't become unlivable, but you'll feel more comfortable without your blouse—that is, if your belief allows you to . . ."

"Thank you, no problem," said the Brother. While he was unfastening his black garment he went on, "So you will find no citizens or ex-citizens traveling in the ship. There is nothing at all special about the colonists, other than they are only moderately good, moderately intelligent, neither too idealistic nor too cynical, not too lazy or too energetic and, well, average.

"You see," he continued seriously, "when we really began to look into the situation we found that the ordinary non-aggressive, non-violent, moderate and average people have always been with us, and they have always been in the majority. They have always been here—a great, inert mass of humanity that refused to make anything but the smallest change in their thinking and life-styles when our flashy supermen and world conquerors tried to change, for good or bad, their world. Throughout history they have been like a great mass of sheep, slowly evolving—sometimes because of, sometimes in spite of, the scientific and cultural predators in their midst. They have grown slowly but they have survived as a type even to the present day ..."

He broke off as he pulled the blouse over his head, folded it carefully and placed it on the floor.

"And that is why," he added, "the meek will inherit the new Earth."

Devlin tried hard not to stare at the upper torso which the Brother had revealed. The other was in his middle or late fifties, but the muscle tone was still good. However, the onset of the degenerative processes had caused the scars, which had been left by the removal of a large number of surgically implanted bio-sensors, to show clearly. Devlin had seen pictures of such scarring in the textbooks but until now had never met, or ever expected to meet, such a case. Until now he had not believed that stellar astronauts really existed.

"If supermen are excluded," he said, clearing his throat and trying not to stare at the ghostly scars, "surely the ordinary people must be given training to prepare them for ... I mean, we could meet anything out there."

"What training could we possibly give to an average, normal individual," Brother Howard replied, "that would prepare him to meet the completely unimaginable? No, training as you understand the term is out. It might cause our carefully selected average people to warp or break, and we can't risk that happening. No, Doctor, the process does not involve training, but education ..."

Suddenly the picture and sound of the Brother began to dissolve as a change in the lighting beyond Devlin's closed eyelids brought him back to present time. He opened his eyes to look at the cubicle display.

GOODNIGHT DEVLIN.

The fear of what the next frigid sleep might bring came rushing back to him as he realized that the cold explosion was only seconds away. But there was still a large portion of his mind that remembered only the feeling of awe at speaking to a stellar astronaut who, it had been rumored, had been one of the first to test hibernation anaesthesia in space conditions, and the Brother's enigmatic closing remark before he, too, had wished Devlin goodnight.

"... Before you can understand the people you may meet, you must first fully understand yourself."

17

THE DREAM BEGAN very badly, with a long and rapid succession of deaths. Like an endless deck of playing cards dealt face upward, they were presented briefly and with all the details clear before being replaced by another face of death with a greater or smaller value of fear, violence or pain.

There was a card for the brontosaurus and the trilobite and the cave-dweller and the old king and many, many others whose deaths he had not experienced before. There was the instant barbecue of an old schoolteacher, the drunken agony of a salesman spitted on his car's steering column, the frantic coughing of a soldier drowning in the blood from his throat wound and an airline pilot who had his third cervical vertebra and a large section of his lower jaw blasted away by a hijacker's bullet.

Some of the deaths were much worse than the others and a few were almost pleasant. These were the slow, comfortable deaths from wasting diseases or exposure when the breakdown of circulation brought drowsiness and a feeling of warmth. But even those cards, although free of the symbols of violence and pain, were often stamped with the dark and dreadful markings of fear of death itself and of what might come after.

Only gradually did he become aware that he was able to make comparisons between these terrible or merely unpleasant deaths and, much later, that he was an individual called Devlin who suffered it all but was at the same time detached from everything that was happening to him.

Devlin did not know how long it was and how often he died before he discovered that he could exercise a small measure of control over the process.

He began by trying to hold on to the less unpleasant dyings for as long as possible—those which were comparatively painless, or those which had pain associated with them but where the fear of death was absent or of secondary importance because of anxiety for or pleasant memories of loved ones. Then he learned how to push away from the death instants, to go farther and farther backward in time into the period preceding the continual and fearfully detailed dyings.

The deaths were not banished or forgotten. They were still the most intense and painful episodes in the dream lives. But now he could be selective, he could tune for the less savage and painful experiences leading up to death in the hope of going even further back to times when there was only life and pleasure instead of death and pain.

A few of the cards Devlin had already seen, but very briefly ...

He was a good salesman and always had been since he had joined the organization at the age of twenty-two. Section heads, supervisors and sales directors of increasing seniority had commended him for his youthful enthusiasm and complete faith in the product of the moment. He had always given every sales pitch everything he had, and he had had a lot to give.

Offers of promotion had come early, but less and less often. Customers were so much wax in his hands, but for some reason he was unable to inspire fellow salesmen to anything like the same degree of enthusiasm. They were a cynical bunch, in general, who refused to share in his act of faith in their product. So he was given selling assignments of increasing importance because, it was said, his talents should not be wasted on a purely supervisory job, and his commission and expenses were the envy of all except his mother.

She did not like the way he worried about his work at night—that was in the early days, of course, when he spent most of his spare time at home. She was also fond of telling him that he did not have to be successful at everything to be happy, that she had stopped being taken in by his sales pitch shortly after his tenth birthday, and that if his father had been alive he would have told him to change his job.

Talk about his father always made him uncomfortable because her voice reminded him, just a little, of the tone he used while referring to his merchandise. When his father had died he had been too young to feel any sense of loss or grief, and the pictures he had seen had shown a pretty average person of the kind who could be talked into buying anything.

But somehow this colorless individual had sold himself to his mother so successfully that, even twenty years after his death, she remained faithful to the original product to such an extent that talking about him made her almost happy. He had never been able to understand how his father had been able to achieve this effect, but the reason was probably that he had been unwilling to spend the time and effort necessary for such a long-term sales project by marrying a girl himself.

But then a good salesman did not need to be married to get a girl.

Nowadays he could not get girls so easily, and sometimes not at all. His boyish enthusiasm did not sit well on a face whose red-veined nose and deep-etched wrinkles were anything but boyish. He had almost lost today's client despite the half bottle he had killed at breakfast to fortify himself for the fray.

It had been a tough fight at that, lasting most of the morning and through a three-hour working lunch, and he had won it by sheer, dogged persistence that had been close to desperation. Having won he had celebrated, mostly because he liked celebrating and to dismiss any lingering self-doubts that might trouble him. His desperation, he was sure, had not been apparent to the client, and the sale had not been won because the client had felt sorry for him. He would continue the celebration as soon as he got back to his hotel.

He was into the parked truck with its muddied rear lights so suddenly that he had only time to pull down hard on his steering.

A fast, relaxed and accurate driver, he was fond of telling people, had no need of a safety belt. Instead of burrowing under the truck's overhang and hitting the differential, he ran into the tires of the enormous double wheels, and he did not bounce because he was stuck fast on the steering column . . .

And another familiar card came up.

The large, cold drops of rain slapped at the canvas cover with a sound like distant gunfire, and the vehicle's slow lurching progress along the dark street made his head roll from side to side and allowed the droplets running down his face to collect inside his collar. Facing forward as he was, with his elbows hooked over the support rail and his weapon at the ready, all he could see was a stretch of shining black road surface pitted and wrinkled by past gasoline bombs and carpeted with half-bricks, broken bottles and pieces of smashed pavement. The houses on each side of him moved past, their downstairs windows glowing or flickering as the living-room lights or a TV screen source tried to fight its way through the heavy drapes, while the dripping hedges and front garden, some shaggy and some neat, could have been hiding anything.

He felt too cold and wet and miserable, he realized suddenly, to have any room left for fear. No terrorist, he was sure, would risk pneumonia by setting up an ambush in these conditions. They would probably be watching television like normal people—especially the news coverage of their shootings and bombings, or the mouthings of the pundits discussing the possible political ramifications of the latest blast. Or they might be plotting around the fireside, or up in bedrooms with their wives or girlfriends, engaged in seduction rather than sedition. Which made him wonder if the women concerned were bothered by the fact that the hands caressing them had, a few hours or days earlier, been responsible for killing a buddy or an uncommitted civilian with a bomb or a rifle or a rocket launcher. He wondered if, sometimes during this tour of duty, he would kill someone and would be foolish enough to tell her about it. The circumstances were completely different, of course, but when he got on to this particularly uncomfortable line of thought he sometimes wondered if he was in the wrong job.

Tonight he was so cold and miserable he *knew* he was in the wrong job.

The unlighted or heavily curtained windows paraded past. Sometimes he imagined that the curtains moved or that the venetian blinds twitched. Possibly a gunman was drawing a bead on him, or a terrorist sympathizer was keeping him under observation, or he was being watched by a curious youngster who couldn't sleep. The rain was beginning to trickle down his back.

They were rounding a curve in the street and were passing under a lamppost when the firing started—a couple of rifles, it sounded like, and a Thompson to make them keep their heads down while the sharp-

shooters tried to pick them off. He was out of the vehicle and flat on the ground with the others before he
actually thought about doing anything—a reaction, the
corporal was fond of saying, that demonstrated the
trained reflexes of the professional soldier—while the
bullets whanged off the body-work or punched holes
through it. He rolled through a shallow puddle until he
was partly under a garden hedge. The noise made it
hard to think. Despite the heavy terrorist fire he could
not spot any of the flashes from his position. Suddenly
his foot was gripped and shaken roughly.

"Get that damned light!" said the corporal. "We'll
cover you."

He rolled away from the hedge and onto his back,
took careful aim at the center of the fluorescent lamp
and did as he had been told, losing what remained of
his night vision in the process. He blinked rain out of
his eyes and returned to the shelter of the hedge again
as the shooting became less accurate and began to die
away. He could hear the whine of a couple of heavy
APC's tearing along the street which paralleled this
one, trying to cut off the gunmen's retreat. Beside him
someone loosed off a shot, but all he could see were the
floating green blotches left by the street lamp.

The hedge was not an effective shelter. Not only did
it allow bullets to whip past unimpeded, its leaves saved
up the rain and dropped it on him in small, irregular
torrents. But the dripping hedge reminded him of another wet evening many years ago, and he decided that
he could tell Jean about this evening because she would
enjoy the joke.

Long before they had been married there had been
another hedge in a very secluded spot near the road
where Jean lived. The first couple of times he had been
out with her they had not stopped at the place, but on
the third occasion it had been Jean's birthday and he
had put a lot of thought and effort into showing her a
good time, and they had stopped. A few minutes later
the great granddaddy of all cloudbursts not only damp-

ened their ardor but washed out his main plan of attack.

There had been other secluded spots and hedges when his strategy had gone very well and the final assaults had met only token resistance, and after every one of them they had always remembered and laughed over that first wet hedge. Now David was four years old, and there was a boy or a girl at minus two months, and they could not make up their minds which they really wanted. It was a very permissive society, these days, and it seemed to be getting sick and violent with it. He had enjoyed his permissive society, but for a girl-child growing up in the sort of place the world was becoming, it might not be so good. Parents of girls had a lot to worry about ...

The bullet ricocheted off the curbstone and tore a large uneven hole through his neck, rupturing the left carotid and opening a passage into the trachea. The sudden, burning pain made him want to scream, but when he drew in his breath a thick, bloody froth flooded into his lungs, strangling him. He grabbed at his throat with both hands, coughing to clear the obstruction, and felt air and warm bubbles squeezing between his fingers from the entrance and exit wounds; but when he tried to breathe in there was no air, only the warm spurting wetness.

Very soon he was dead. But for him, not nearly soon enough ...

Another life-card ...

"Airfield Two this is Golf Alpha November Mike Zulu," he said with quiet fury. "I am approaching the coast on a bearing of two eight seven at flight level seven five zero. Landing instructions, please."

"*Mike Zulu, Airfield Two. Remain on present heading. Reduce to flight level six zero. You have twenty-eight miles to run to touchdown. Visibility is ten miles.*

Wind gusting to twenty knots. Request aircraft type and passenger details."

The voice was devoid of emotion, the diction was good and there was no indication that the man was gloating over their misfortune.

"Nimbus Five Transonic," he said. "Seventy-five percent load. Six hundred and twelve adults, fifteen children plus crew."

"A Nimbus yet! The only suitable runway is zero four. It is barely long enough and a bit rough and you will have an eighty-degree crosswind port side. We suggest you divert."

Before he could reply the edge of a very hard hand was rubbed painfully along the side of his neck, and the man standing behind him said, "No."

"I have been requested to land at Two," he said.

"Understood. But remind your friends that we have a profit-sharing arrangement with the other two airfields, and if you crash that aircraft there will be nothing or nobody to ransom."

The hand rubbed his neck even harder.

"My friends are impatient as well as greedy," he said. "A diversion is not possible."

"Your funeral. Reduce flight level to five zero. Maintain present heading."

"Five zero on present heading," he said, then furiously to the man behind him, "I don't give a damn if you commit suicide, but there are others involved."

The man behind him laughed softly, then asked, "Can your co-pilot land this thing?"

He wanted to say "No" because it was the truth, and his second officer knew that as well as he did, but being young and inexperienced was something that happened to everyone at some stage in his life. Instead he said quietly, "In these conditions we will both be required to land this thing. You must understand that these supersonic jobs have to put down an awful lot of flap to slow us sufficiently for a landing, and during the last half-minute we will be holding on to the sky with our fingernails in an attitude which is dangerous if the wind velocity and direction is not right. With gusting conditions and maximum flap we could fall out of the sky, or the ground effect could—"

The edge of the hijacker's hand struck the side of his head just above the ear. It was not a hard blow, not painful, but it was a conversation stopper.

For the next few minutes he maintained an angry and helpless silence. This had been no ordinary hijack operation or the security guards—traveling incognito even to the crew, and numbering one to every fifty passengers—would have been able to stamp on it. The disguised guards had picked up their weapons inside the aircraft, and the loading tube detection system would have insured that nobody else carried a weapon on board. He was still not sure what had happened exactly, but his senior hostess had been able to reach the flight deck and tell him something about it during the minute or so before the man behind him had arrived and broken her neck.

Apparently they had staged an incident during which one of their number caused a near-panic in his immediate area by producing a shaver with a black plastic casing that looked like a weapon. This had caused two of the guards in the vicinity to break cover and several others to tense up sufficiently for them, also, to be spotted. During the milling around which followed, hijackers had disarmed these guards using killer karate. Not all of them had been successful, but enough of them had been able to get weapons to shoot it out with the remaining guards who had, of course, been hampered by trying to avoid hitting innocent passengers—a disadvantage which the hijackers did not have.

During the ten-minute gun battle the great tubular barn that was the main passenger cabin had suffered a sharp pressure drop. But as all the guards, four hijackers and seventeen others had died, the remaining passengers thought themselves lucky to have only bleeding noses and earaches. He still did not know why his senior hostess had had to die simply for giving him a situation report.

He liked to understand people even if he did not agree with their points of view, and he knew some of the reasons why this intelligent, highly trained and resourceful team of hijackers had taken his aircraft. But the senseless display of violence in killing Nancy, a completely unnecessary murder performed with an utter lack of feeling, made him so angry that he felt physically ill.

"*Maintain present heading, Mike Zulu. Reduce to flight level four five zero. Twenty-three miles to run.*"

"Mike Zulu," he acknowledged, then tried again.

"One of these days," he went on quietly, "the governments are going to stop paying ransom money for hijacked aircraft and passengers, and then you will be out of a job. And this green and pleasant land below us, with its thriving pirate economy, will feel the pinch. No government wants to be the first to throw three or four aircraft and a couple of thousand passengers to the wolves, of course, but there are a couple of administrations on the point of doing just that. It will take just one to make the decision and the rest will follow.

"When that happens, you, and the people below, will not have the benefit of consumer goods smuggled in at top prices," he continued, "because you will have no money. You will have no money because your currency will be declared valueless, and any you nay have salted away on the continent will be frozen—the measures are already being planned. You, assuming that you are the brain behind this hijack, should be intelligent enough to realize that you can't possibly continue to . . ."

He broke off as one of the hostesses, looking pale but with her voice steady enough, excused herself and asked for instructions.

"We shall be landing on a runway which is a rather tight fit," he replied easily, and smiled at her. "This means that I shall be making a steep approach, shoving on reverse thrust a few seconds after touchdown and stepping hard on the brakes. Make sure the passengers' straps are tight and check the tables for loose objects. Right?"

"If the runway is short, sir, how will we get off again?"

He smiled reassuringly, thinking that the girl was too intelligent for her own peace of mind, and said, "This situation has happened to me before. The ransom covers the passengers, aircraft and crew but not the baggage and freight. We will be much lighter at takeoff."

"Yes, indeed," said the man standing behind him. Perhaps he was irritated at being left out of the conversation, in which case he had displayed his first human feeling.

When the girl had gone he went on, "I am not probing for information useful to our security people, and it doesn't matter to me whether you are freelance or employed by the government of this country. Officially, the people down there do not boost their own hijack trade, and you would never admit that you had been smuggled out as refugees to set up this operation.

"And you could be telling the truth," he continued, "because if you had come from this country you would do as Airfield Two suggests and divert. So you must be a freelance group hoping to set yourselves up here with your share of the ransom. Fair enough—but there will be no ransom for anyone if we flop over and burn on Two's runway, will there? And I hate to say anything complimentary about an operation which places so many people in jeopardy, but this job showed planning of a high order and considerable intelligence. Surely the same degree of intelligence and forethought will tell you that—"

"Turn three degrees on to a heading of three zero one, Mike Zulu. Descend to flight level three zero. Eight miles to run. Have you the airfield in sight?"

"Mike Zulu. Descend to three zero on three zero one. I see you, Two."

Behind him the man changed his captured gun from

one hand to the other, but made no attempt to answer any of the questions.

Angrily, he said, "This is the most beautiful, unpolluted and under-populated country in the world. It has always been beautiful, of course, and in the past it was very popular with tourists. But it is free of pollution because there is virtually no industry and its technical skills have gone with its people—those who were lucky enough to get away before immigration was forbidden. Now no one wants to come here except people like yourself, and the lower orders of farmer and laborer are also trying to leave, many of them dying in the attempt. The country imports everything except a small proportion of its food and exports nothing at all, and this beautiful and dangerously unstable country is where you want to spend the rest of your lives. Can't you see how stupid that is?"

The man sighed faintly but did not speak.

Ahead of them the airfield was a tiny, flattened plus sign, pale gray against the hazy green patchwork of the surrounding fields. He made a last desperate appeal to the man's humanity as well as his reason.

"You are not trying to right a political wrong or serving the cause of any minority group by coming here," he said. "You come to this place only if you are in it for the money. Fair enough—greed I can understand. But why gamble on losing so much when a twenty-minute diversion would make it a certain win? Is it feeling of power that you need? Or the feeling that you are so much more vital and important than the majority of poor, hard-working, dull sheep inhabiting the world—that their suffering is too small a matter to affect you? Or maybe this time you want to share their feelings! Are you, then, so terribly bored with life that you want to know what it feels like to be broken and torn apart and breathe in the fire of burning fuel . . . ?

He broke off, then added coldly, "I'm going to be busy for a few minutes. Your answers can wait until after we land."

Two's main runway was opening out below him like a gray isosceles triangle, spotty with clumps of weeds and cow droppings. The grass had not been trimmed for many years and the wind sent broad, green ripples hurrying across it. With maximum flap and barely enough power to hold them in the air, he aimed at putting her down on the runway short of the threshold markings, because for this landing every yard would count.

As well as catching the fully extended flaps like a sail and pushing up the port wing, the crosswind necessitated a crabwise approach which would have to be corrected at the latest possible instant before touchdown if he wasn't to burst all the tires and probably rip off the undercarriage bogeys. He rounded out over a patch of swamp about a quarter of a mile from threshold, with the stall warning having hysterics and his wings dipping first to one side and then the other as he compensated and overcompensated for the gusting. During the last few seconds before touchdown he found that he could anticipate the gust effects by watching approaching wind ripples in the grass, and as she began to sink he brought the nose onto the center line of the runway.

He felt two tires go and checked a slew to starboard while he dumped lift by running out the spoilers and calling up full reverse thrust. He would stick to the ground, now, but the other end of the runway was rushing toward him at an incredible rate. He applied the brakes much harder than recommended for the present ground speed, then harder still. He felt another tire go, then three in rapid succession. Among them the landing bogeys had thirty-six tires and if the bursts were fairly evenly distributed among the three bogeys he might be all right. But apparently they weren't and the plane began a slow, inexorable yaw to port.

He was sure the port wheels were about to go off the runway by the time he checked the yaw, and he had a glimpse of a man writhing about in the grass with his hands pressed against his ears, and a noise-maddened cow running across the verge, but he did not feel the aircraft hit either. For an instant he thought cynically that a pirate airfield with a too-short runway did not deserve a minimum-noise approach and landing, and that in any case they would probably add the broken windows and curdled milk to the ransom amount, just as they would insist on an extra ransom for the aircraft and maintenance crew needed to fly in and fit the spare wheels to this brute before she could take off again.

Another tire blew as the forward bogey stopped within a few yards of the boundary fence. He shut down everything except the auxiliary power unit serving the flight deck and cabin systems, and settled back in his seat.

"A very nice landing, Mike Zulu."

"Thank you, Two."

Behind him the man laughed softly and said, "I don't think that a highly trained, hard-working sheep like you will appreciate it, but this is the only answer I've got."

Something crashed through his head so fast that neither the pain nor the sound of the shot had time to register before a terrible darkness swallowed everything.

But the darkness was not permanent. It became an infinite area of black velvet on which cards were displayed briefly before being replaced or covered with other cards. Some of the cards were closely linked, such as the one for the co-pilot, whose skipper had been killed before his eyes and who had crashed one of the world's largest jets on takeoff, or the one of the hijack team leader whose action in killing the aircraft's captain had led to the deaths of all the passengers and crew a few days later, and in turn precipitated a crisis which wrecked the pirate economy of his adopted country.

That hijacker, too, suffered briefly but intensely before he died. But his life-card was difficult to scan, the lines of cause and effect were tangled and his emotions and drives needed too much effort to understand, if they could be understood at all. There were not many lives like his. The majority, although painful in places, were very easy to understand. Some of them were surprisingly rich and pleasant, and many of these belonged to people whose lives, measured against the yardstick of Devlin's now vast and varied experience, should have been utterly miserable from the moment they had been born.

Devlin had learned how to hold a life long enough to examine part of it, usually the last part, in detail . . .

Lit by the laser light of sunset, the great cranes of the long-abandoned docks and shipyard stood out against the darkening sky like a sketch executed in blood. In more than fifty years of disuse they had rusted but they had not fallen down, just as the ships along the dockside had rusted and sunk at their moorings but had not gone away and had, instead, grown outward as their hulls silted up and provided greenery for nesting swans and sea birds. One of the swans, deep pink in the fading light, drifted in mid-river as if it had nowhere to go.

Like all the rest of us, he thought.

Aloud, he said, "This kind of approach has been made to me before. I don't want to listen to you naming names in high places, or to your plans for overthrowing the Council, or to your extolling the virtues of the cause which is driving you to do these things. I am utterly disinterested in anything you want to say or do. I have heard it all before."

"Yes," said the young man, "and you've done it all before."

He leaned his elbows on the parapet of the bridge and sighed, unable to make a negative answer.

"You are going to listen because this will interest you," the other said fiercely. "We know you were a master tactician once, that you planned and carried through one of the neatest coups in recent history, and that you could have had a high place in the Council if you hadn't dropped out of sight and become a school-teacher."

"That," he said dryly, "was a tactic of survival. Considering the number of times that the Council has been replaced since then—"

"They'll be replaced again, and soon if—"

"I'm not interested in listening to treason, either," he said tiredly.

He could feel the intensity of the young man's gaze on the side of his face as he continued to watch the swan. Then the other said, "I agree, you are the survivor type. But there are times when one must take risks to go on surviving, and right now we want you to take a very small risk. What we need is your advice, the benefit of your early studies and experience, for a small and not very bloody revolution."

"I've had my revolution and seen the results," he replied, still without turning. "No."

The young man gripped his shoulder and pulled him around until they were face to face. He said, "Listen to me, you soft old man! This country is dying on its feet, the Council members are growing fat in their keeps and the local commanders in their fortified farms are not much better; even the sheep have ceased to care that we are drifting into a feudal economy even though one of the most technically advanced countries in the world can be seen from where we're standing on a clear day. You had the good of your country at heart, once. You had ideals that you were willing to die for—but you did not die. Your wife did, and you ran away from everything and ended up teaching children—sheep children, at that. You were good, the best, but not intelligent enough to realize that people must suffer and die for every advance."

What advance? he asked sardonically. But he spoke under his breath because he was, after all, still trying to survive.

"Naturally we will handle the execution of the present Council and any local commanders unwilling to

support us," the young man went on. "But there are a
lot of important people who want to play safe and who
will not back us unless they think the takeover has
popular support. This is where you come in. Specifi-
cally, we need your expertise in setting up a popular
rebellion situation. Something that will waken the
sheep, make martyrs of as many of them as seems
necessary, and get them personally involved in—"

"The sheep won't get involved any more," he said,
and looked at the other's hand on his shoulder until it
was taken away, then went on. "The less sheepish ones
have either left the country or become lower-grade supporters of the Council. The rest are patient, long suffering and very cynical sheep."

The young man shook his head angrily and said,
"We really are trying to better conditions for everybody
this time, even for the sheep. We have ideas for re-start-
ing trade with the mainland, legitimate trade that will
enable us to build up some foreign credit. Instead of a
subsistence-level economy we'll be able to afford a few
comforts again, and we'll be able to rise once more to
become—"

"What exactly will you trade?"

"I see you're becoming less disinterested, old man,"
said the other, smiling. "We trade something which
those soft, bored, overcrowded and polluted foreigners
do not have—space, clean air, scenic grandeur and,
most of all, excitement. We invite parties to join safaris
into what used to be, and to them still is, the most dangerous country in the world. We will take them to the
historic places where it all happened fifty years ago,
and we'll put on a show for them with bombings, am-
bushes and general aggravation. Some of them may
even get hurt from time to time, but not badly. They
will probably want to bring their own medics with
them, and pay us well for the privilege. But right now
we need two things, and one of them is you.

"We need you because you have done this before,
and very successfully," the young man went on ex-

citedly. "We are willing to pay a high price because we want it to be obvious that this is not simply another change of Council faces, but something different and much, much better. Instead of a Council composed entirely of people in their twenties and late 'teens, the new one will be led by an older and wiser head, someone with intelligence, judgment and experience, someone the foreigners will be more inclined to trust.

"Now you are interested, old man," he ended triumphantly, "because we are offering you the top job!"

He was silent for a moment, thinking about his experience and qualifications for the job. Because of one experience his qualifications were gone.

In those days he had been young, self-confident, idealistic and able to effectively compartmentalize his mind so that the necessarily evil acts which he planned, and which others carried out, did not trouble him because everyone knew that a greater good would come of them. He was very sorry, in a clinical fashion, for the innocent sheep who died or were maimed, but he had thought of them as statistics and always had tried very hard to keep their number as low as possible. His wife was, of course, far too sympathetic in her nature to be told of the work he had been doing, even if he had been allowed to tell her of it. But then one sunny afternoon outside a supermarket she had become a statistic.

He remembered her beauty and warmth and the concern she felt for everything and everyone who suffered. He remembered the peace he felt when he was with her just watching her movements and expression, and he recalled the incredible passion, so slow to kindle, with which she loved him. For many years he had forced to the back of his mind and locked up in its compartment the picture of the torn and dismembered thing he had had to identify, but now the door was open again.

He swallowed and said, "The top job, eh? But you mentioned needing two things."

"The other is money," said the young man. "Money for arms and to pay off the local commanders whose estates will be used during the initial safaris. But the money is coming in nicely as a result of some minor-key hijacking of private aircraft—"

"That is insane!" he burst out. "We were warned what would happen if we ever tried that again!"

"Bluff," said the others, laughing, "sheer bluff. Too many governments would like to move in here, and we can play them off against one another. They need this underpopulated piece of real estate, they each need it so badly that none of them will let another take it. So relax. All but one of the aircraft were small, they were brought down in ordinary fields close to our supporters' keeps, and the ransoms were ridiculously low by former standards. The reason for that was that we were also testing the hostages—they were private plane owners and their rich friends, remember—with the safari idea, and they all seemed keen. There was nothing in the foreign newspapers or TV about the incidents, so obviously everyone is keeping quiet and playing ball. And with the latest job, a two-hundred-seat VTOL, they paid up promptly and with even less fuss than with the private aircraft.

"This idea is going to work, old man," he ended, with great certainty in his voice. "We have something to sell, something they want badly enough to ignore a petty irritation like a few hijackings which will, in any case, stop as soon as the safari trade gets going. Well, what do you think?"

All at once he felt deathly tired and, surprisingly, not at all afraid. He said, "We have sold, or at least exported, ideas and methods that have wrecked cities and countries all over the world, and for that we have been insolated like a sociological disease. Now you have developed a mutated strain which might possibly allow the disease to spread once again. Haven't you considered the possibility—no, the virtual certainty, dammit!—that if one of them can't have us they will make sure that nobody else can?"

He turned once again to face the river mouth and the sea. A few minutes ago he had opened a frightful compartment in his mind, but there were many other compartments in which his wife was alive and beautiful and loving, and he wanted to open all of them while there was still time. The light had almost gone so that the swam drifted in the black water like a graceful ghost, and one bright star, or perhaps it was Jupiter, lit the darkening sky.

> And then she came homeward,
> With one star awake,
> As the swan in the evening,
> Moves over the lake.

"What?" said the young man irritably, making him realize that he had been thinking aloud.

"I was remembering an old song that my wife liked to sing."

"That's sheep thinking!" the other said angrily. "We're offering you the number one spot and all you can think of is—" He broke off and swung around to stare across the city and beyond.

The sky had lightened again in the west and suns were rising in all the wrong places. But before he could even feel afraid, and long before the sound of the nuclear explosions reached him, the sun aimed at this particular city burst above his head with a flash of impossibly bright light that was followed by absolute darkness.

18

OTHER LIVES PRESSED in to fill the darkness, in uncountable numbers and all clamoring, it seemed to Devlin, to be remembered. Most of them were very ordinary lives at first feel, but even the mundane ones had their moments of glory which made them unique and, in the majority of cases, the equal of the brilliant, hypersensitive individuals who sometimes created without control, who sought power without responsibility and who were flawed without ever having tried to correct their flaws.

Some of the flaws he observed were minor and easily overcome. Others were major and overcome with extreme difficulty, and many were impossible to overcome no matter how hard the individual tried. The flaws ranged from petty dishonesty, selfishness, minor-key destructiveness and character assassination in otherwise normal individuals up to the bright, fuzzy, helpless struggles of a short-lived Mongoloid and the perverted intensity of feeling experienced by men deeply and emotionally involved with other homosexuals.

When viewed with complete knowledge, Devlin could no longer be sure what, if anything, was a perversion—to understand all was to forgive almost everything. But he still felt repulsed by some of them, principally the perversions which depended for their pleasure on the sufferings of others. To him it seemed basically wrong that one person's pleasure should cost others so much pain. As a result, these lives as a whole were highly unpleasant to recall, save only for a few youthful incidents, so that they hung in the dark outer fringes of his memory like books in a corner of a library which was rarely visited.

Death, suffering and sex left the strongest impressions in every life, which was probably the reason why Devlin had been driven almost to suicide by the earlier cold-dreams. But now he could be selective in his choice of individuals and incidents, and he was beginning to enjoy the process when a gradual diminution of sensation made him realize that he was coming out of cold-sleep.

He tried to fight it for as long as possible by holding on to his most recent selection, an incident following a domestic quarrel when both parties were pretending that it had never happened but had not yet reached the stage of kissing and making up. The period was contemporary, or perhaps a decade or two in Devlin's Earth past, and the rather one-sided discussion was taking a philosophical turn which gave it applicability to the present ...

Their house had always been too small, and the area of the tiny back garden was further reduced by the thickness of the tall hedge on three sides which gave privacy and a feeling—only a feeling—of security. Caught in that sun-trap and sandwiched between the hot, dry grass and the nuclear-powered heater in the sky, he felt himself begin to relax enough to start apologizing.

"You're right, dear," he said, staring sunward through the bright redness of his closed eyelids. "This place is no longer safe. It is also becoming too expensive. I was hoping that it wouldn't be, and trying to keep it going, which is why I accused you of being ungrateful and never satisfied ... Well, anyway, living in a block will be much less expensive and, even though the sunshine will be artificial, they have effective group security and we won't have to worry about—"

"I know that what you said about the statistical element is true," she broke in. "There are far too many people like ourselves for us, this house, to stand much chance of being hit. But yesterday was the first time that I actually *saw* Maxers in action. She ... she was a shoplifter the store detective had caught outside the main entrance. The Maxers pushed the detective away and cut off her hand. They *enjoyed* doing it ..."

Her hand crept into his and he squeezed it reassuringly as he said, "Maximum response looked like the answer a few years ago. The soft approach of the psychologists and sociologists wasn't working, so they brought back corporal punishment administered, if necessary, by citizens on the spot. But now we have so-called citizens going around searching for crimes to punish, and the idea of maximum response to minimum offenses, while it sorted out our crime problem in very short order, has been twisted out of shape like all the other good ideas. Now we're getting Maxer gangs setting up minor incidents for them to react to, or even delivering a maximum and downright murderous response to the mere rumor of an offense—and they start the rumor!"

"It isn't just the Maxers," she said, moving so that her sun-warmed arm and leg were pressing against his. "I read last week that four hundred violent deaths per day—that includes nights, too, of course—is now considered to be an acceptable figure for a medium-sized city like ours. What is the matter with people? We have enough to eat, there is plenty of entertainment, lots of interesting things to do with one's spare time, and there would be no sickness if the hospitals weren't so overcrowded with nut cases who tried unsuccessfully to carve one another up or botched the job on an innocent bystander. Scientifically and culturally we should be living in a golden age, so why are so many of them bored and angry and violent?

"I'm not really asking questions," she went on before he could speak, "just complaining. I know that you would say that different and often unlikeable people have always been responsible for the world's advances in art and science—they prod us ahead more quickly, like dogs snapping at the heels of sheep. Maybe that's what is wrong. The sheep should have been allowed to wander forward at their own pace, getting where they were supposed to go with shepherds leading them instead of sheepdogs and wolves driving them.

"I grant you," she continued quickly, "that we have a few responsible people trying to push us in the right direction. But their attitude of mind is never to consider individuals, only the big picture, and to consider females as mere statistics and unworthy of serious male attention once they pass the age of thirty. It is no coincidence that the proportion of female suicides in this age-group is—"

"You," he broke in firmly, "will always have my serious attention, even when you are old and gray and your statistics have changed out of all recognition."

"In ten years," she said more quietly, "I wonder if you will still say that."

Reassurance given too often loses its effect, he thought, and tried to move the conversation on to a less sensitive area.

"Of course I will," he said. "But to go back to something you said earlier about boredom and violence coupled with high technology and culture—I've been trying to make sense out of the present situation, too. It seems purposeless and stupid, and I certainly don't approve of it, but suppose there is, in fact, a reason behind it—perhaps an evolutionary process that went wrong. Suppose the wolves were intended to inherit the Earth and do something constructive with it. But they were hampered by too many sheep getting underfoot and practically begging to be eaten or beaten or enslaved or used in some other fashion. So, instead of having to fight against something hard and dangerous that would have kept them in top condition, they are punching at pillows and feeling frustrated."

"I'm very sorry for them," she said in an insincere voice.

"Seriously," he went on, "let us assume that the present mess the world is in presages the next step up the evolutionary ladder. The cultural level is sufficiently high, as is the technical ability, and there is certainly enough population pressure to force people off the planet. Evolutionary changes are never pleasant and the next one could be the most unpleasant of all, because it might take us to the stars ..."

"It might take *them* to the stars," she broke in, laughing, "and good riddance."

"Every time I start by saying 'seriously' you end by laughing," he said, shaking his head. "I simply wanted to discuss the idea that, if and when the human race gets out among the stars, it might not meet benevolent bug-eyed monsters belonging to beautiful and benign cultures, but instead will be faced with greater dangers from beings so vicious that, by comparison, an Earth tiger would look like a sheep. And if the race managed to survive that contact, and even win, there might be something even more terrible waiting for us on the next rung. In short, I'm suggesting that the universe might not be a pleasant place, and that us pacifists, by insisting that it should be, are seducing the race from its rightful path and destroying its chance of future—"

"But surely," she broke in, "they couldn't have reached the level of technology necessary to leave Earth if we hadn't gone in for cooperation instead of conflict. These people only want to destroy things and hurt others."

"Only because they are frustrated by having too many sheep telling them they are wrong," he replied. "You must try to think of a pure, highly moral, violent type with the power to use the world's sheep effectively—"

"Power corrupts, and absolute ..." she began.

"Highly moral and incorruptible, then," he said. "A sublime, violent type."

"Causing sublime and character-building suffering, no doubt," she said witheringly. "That is ridiculous and you know it—and you know I know you know it! You were always pulling that trick at school—starting a major debate to effect a minor change of subject—and you're still doing it."

She laughed suddenly and went on, "It worked then when I got too involved in something unpleasant, and it still seems to be working. But before we leave the Maxers, I've heard that their latest excuse for turning loose with everything is in defense of a lady's honor. They feel quite noble about defending the honor of a helpless woman to the death—the other person's death, of course, even if the poor man happens to be a slightly impolite husband."

"As I remember," he said, "you were pretty good at defending your own honor. But I'll be careful not to insult you in public."

She was silent for a moment, then she loosed his hand and he heard her roll on to her side and prop herself up on one elbow. Her other hand rested lightly on his chest, then more heavily as she leaned across him. The movement of her head shadowed his face from the sun, and he opened his eyes.

He said, "I'll try not to insult you in private, either, or have any more stupid fights. But let's change the subject, eh?"

The pressure of her hand lightened again until its touch became the beginning of a caress, and her face moved closer to his. She shook her head and said softly, "Not yet, dear. Let's find out if you are capable of a . . . a maximum response."

The dream became very pleasant after that, even though the sensations became rapidly less intense as the process of resuscitation was completed. But he was glad rather than sorry about that because, considering the depraved period in which he had spent his formative years his upbringing had been fairly strict, and the increasingly ecstatic face above him was familiar.

It was much more youthful and beautiful and relaxed than he had ever remembered it, but there could be no doubt that it was his mother . . .

GOOD MORNING DEVLIN.

He signaled that he was fully awake and in possession of all his faculties by looking around his cubicle, putting one hand on the edge of the open casket and saying, "Good Morning, Ship."

Devlin was feeling relieved and a bit light-hearted because this time he had been warmed without feeling that the cold-dreams had driven him to the verge of madness or suicide. He wondered if Patricia and the others had been equally fortunate.

SHIP STATUS NINE HUNDRED AND TWENTY YEARS INTO MISSION. MAJORITY OF SHIP SYSTEMS AND/OR BACKUP SYSTEMS FUNCTIONING. DETAILS OF EXCEPTIONS AVAILABLE IN CONTROL CENTER. SHIP PERSONNEL CURRENTLY AWAKE—TWO. IDENTITIES PATRICIA MORLEY AND JOHN DEVLIN.

After more than nine centuries, he thought, some of the ship's systems were bound to have failed. But he was looking forward too eagerly to comparing mental notes with Patricia to give this information the amount of worry it deserved.

IT IS PROBABLE THAT SHIP'S PERSONNEL ARE EXPERIENCING SEVERE MENTAL DISTRESS AS THE RESULT OF DREAMS ENCOUNTERED DURING COLD-SLEEP . . .

"Not this time," said Devlin. But the computer ignored him, naturally, and continued spelling out the advice and instructions programed into it what seemed like only a few hours ago. His advice was still good and he ought to take it, ought to show a little self-control by forcing himself to sleep normally before rushing out to see Patricia. With luck, she might grow impatient and come in and waken him . . .

REASONS FOR AWAKENING. ONE—MISSION TERMINATION DECISION REQUIRED. TWO—TO CHECK FUNCTIONING

```
OF MORLEY/DEVLIN MUSCLE SYSTEMS, CIRCULATION,
SPEECH ORGAN AND MEMORY. PERIOD OF AWAKENING
DICTATED BY DECISION TIME NECESSARY FOR
REASON ONE.
INSTRUCTIONS HELD UNTIL END OF MORLEY/DEVLIN
PERIOD OF NORMAL SLEEP AND ACTIVATION OF MANUAL
GO INSTRUCTION.
```

"You expect me to sleep after hearing news like *that!*" said Devlin, jabbing at the Go button.

Mission termination decision required. That could only mean one thing—Journey's End! But the display was not being very informative.

```
PROCEED TO CONTROL CENTER WHEN CONVENIENT, it
said.
```

He hurried through the post-awakening exercises and dashed into the corridor, where he met Patricia coming out of her cubicle. There was no need for them to rush to the control center, but they did. The main display was more forthcoming.

```
SITUATION REPORT. SHIP IS CLOSING ON NINTH
SOLAR SYSTEM TO BE VISITED. OTHERS NOT SUITABLE
FOR SEEDING AND BYPASSED WITHOUT CREW
CONSULTATION WITH THE EXCEPTIONS OF PASSES
THREE AND FIVE WHICH WERE AUTHORIZED BY
JOHN DEVLIN.
LONG-RANGE SCAN INDICATES TARGET NINE MARGINALLY
SUITABLE FOR HUMAN COLONIZATION. EQUATORIAL
DIAMETER 9,740 MILES. ROTATIONAL PERIOD
TWENTY-SEVEN POINT THREE HOURS. GRAVITY ONE
POINT THREE TWO EARTH NORMAL. ATMOSPHERIC
PRESSURE NINETEEN POINT TWO POUNDS/SQUARE INCH.
TOXIC TRACE ELEMENTS PRESENT IN ATMOSPHERE
IN ACCEPTABLE QUANTITIES. INDICATION OF MINOR
POLLUTION AND RADIATION SUGGESTING PRESENCE
OF INTELLIGENT LIFE-FORM POSSESSING RESTRICTED
NUCLEAR TECHNOLOGY.
COMPUTER DECISION TAKEN TO LAUNCH HIGH-VELOCITY
PROBE FOR CLOSER INVESTIGATION. COMPUTER
DECISION TAKEN TO AWAKEN CREW-MEMBERS MORLEY
AND DEVLIN.
```

"I suppose we could adapt to the higher gravity and pressure," said Patricia worriedly, "but . . ."

"But there are people there already," Devlin finished for her. "And if they should be disposed to be nasty, they'll have the muscle already available to back it up."

BEFORE EVALUATION OF PROBE DATA AND YES/NO DECISION ON MISSION TERMINATION, CAREFUL STUDY AND EVALUATION OF SHIP LIFE-SUPPORT AND ASSOCIATED SYSTEMS ARE IMPERATIVE REPEAT IMPERATIVE.

"I don't like the look of that," said Devlin.

Patricia nodded without speaking, then pressed the recall button and tapped for data replay at half speed. They were, after all, supposed to study it carefully. But as the minutes and the bright, sharp data presentations unrolled before them they saw nothing to make either of them feel any better.

The personnel status display gave them the first shock. They had been expecting the telltales of the cubicles containing Yvonne Caldwell and Thomas Purdy to be dark, but not the twenty-three others. The people concerned were not actually dead because they were still safely in cold-sleep. But the cubicles concerned had flagging mechanical and/or power malfunctions which would make it impossible for them to be revived.

Patricia looked as sick as Devlin felt.

He was suddenly aware that the bright, clean control center with its gleaming instrumentation, spotless trim and virtually unused upholstery was no longer new even though it appeared unchanged from the first time he had seen it, less than two weeks or over nine hundred years ago. Despite the surface cosmetics of rustless metal and bright plastic, the control center and the ship built around it were *old*.

Devlin shrugged involuntarily as the sheer wonder of it tightened the skin at the back of his scalp. For nine centuries the ship had been picking its way among the stars, a fragil metal pod protecting its human seedlings. The men and women who had designed and built the ship, the programers who had given it the ability to follow its complex instructions while maintaining the lives of its utterly vulnerable charges and the countless other people who had helped unknowingly or unwillingly or who had not helped at all, were long since gone. Even though he could still remember them and the society to which they belonged as if it were last week, they, and probably it, were dead.

The realization so frightened him that he tried hard to be optimistic. But the very most he could hope for was that a sick but surviving remnant of humanity was still living in the polluted wreckage of a once-great culture, on a world so impoverished in material resources that they would never be able to pull themselves up, and into space, again. Nor would they ever again be capable of expelling another seedpod among the stars.

Even the seedpod which it had expelled—and perhaps it had managed to shoot out two or three—was beginning to weaken, to lose its initial impetus and suffer from a withered casing. Very soon it had to find fallow ground.

Or any ground.

Devlin gestured toward the status board and said, "Do you want to go over it again?"

"I've got a good memory," she replied, then added, "now."

He nodded and began tapping for a rundown on the ship systems, insisting on a slow playback. His memory, like Patricia's, was well-nigh perfect—but he was not a superman. He still felt like himself even though he could remember every single thing that had ever happened to him and to a countless number of other people. He still felt afraid and stupid and baffled by the complexity of the data that was being presented on the screen.

Or was he?

"I have the feeling," he said, "that I understand what is going on a little better."

"Yes," said Patricia. "I have the same feeling. That instructor—the small, blonde one, remember?—knew a lot about the ship's computer even though she didn't tell us anything more than which buttons to push. I'm remembering some of the things she knew."

"I see," said Devlin. "During the attack from Target Five I had a funny feeling that I knew more about the ship's control and guidance systems than I'd ever been taught. I take it that you dreamed about this girl's lifetime and now you're remembering it?"

"No," said Patricia firmly. "I did not dream about her, but I'm getting her memories anyway. She must have spent a lot of time in here, so maybe she is haunting the place." She shook her head in obvious self-irritation, then went on, "That last cold-sleep wasn't as bad as the one before, but I seemed to be every woman who was ever born—with the exception of a few twisted and horrible ones that were too difficult or unpleasant to remember. But what is happening to us? And why do I always dream of being a woman?"

"I'm always a man," said Devlin, "or a male something, at least. I don't know what is happening to us, either." He stopped as a clear, sharp picture of Brother Howard was thrown on to his mental display screen. It was the picture in which the Brother looked concerned and spoke without sound. Feeling afraid for some reason he could not understand, Devlin went on, "But let's not get sidetracked into a philosophical debate. At least, not just yet."

"I need a philosophical debate," said Patricia seriously, "before I go mad. I need some answers."

"Me, too," said Devlin in a matching tone. "But right now let's concentrate on the patient—I mean the ship."

She smiled and said dryly, "Was one of your dream lifetimes a man called Freud?"

As the displays presented their data, it became apparent that the patient was in good physical and mental condition, considering its advanced age. The heart was sound—power was available for the decades-long deceleration and just enough fuel for a landing—and capable of at least one burst of sustained activity without failure, provided the effort was called for before the patient became much older. Peripheral circulation and sensitivity were not good, but, again, adequate for a few decades to come. The ship's long- and close-range sensors had suffered from multiple component failures, but it could still see and hear in a short-sighted and dull fashion, which was the reason why they had not been awakened until the ship was passing within the orbit of the outermost planet of the system. The patient needed to hold things close to his eyes.

Not sick, Devlin thought, just senility rearing its toothless, graying head. What he needed now was an accurate prognosis before the brain, too, began to succumb to the ageing processes.

He did not realize that he had been thinking aloud until Patricia, with her new-found expertise, called up the required data.

According to the display, if the system they were entering was bypassed, the chances of reaching the next target sun were ninety-three percent. The power needed to decelerate and return to Target Ten would be available. Data gathering systems would be less than sixty percent operational. Life-support and resuscitation systems had a predicted failure of thirty-seven percent. Personnel consumables would remain adequate due to the projected death rate caused by life-support and resuscitation system failures.

The display went on, SHOULD BOTH TARGET NINE AND TEN BE BYPASSED THE PROBABILITY OF REACHING TARGET ELEVEN IS SIXTY-ONE POINT THREE PERCENT. PROBABILITIES OF SHIP SYSTEMS DETERIORATION FOLLOW.

EXTERIOR SENSORS SIXTY-FIVE PERCENT. CONTROL AND GUIDANCE FORTY-THREE PERCENT. COLD-SLEEP

MONITORING AND RESUSCITATION SYSTEMS SEVENTY-ON PERCENT . . .

"That's enough!" said Devlin angrily, hitting the Cancel button. To go on would be virtual suicide. More quietly he added, "We don't have much choice, so let's have a look at our new home . . ."

The pictures from the orbiting probe showed a world which appeared to be two-thirds ocean and whose continental outlines were obscured by dazzling weather systems and a thick atmospheric haze. On the adjacent display appeared the figures for the atmospheric pressure and spectro-analysis, gravity, analyses of supended water vapor and surface liquid from the ocean and inland lakes, measurements of radio and nuclear radiation, pollution levels in areas around the few small cities and towns . . .

"We'll be able to live there," said Devlin quietly. "It won't be easy at first. We'll have trouble with strained backs and varicose veins. But in a couple of generations we'll grow the muscles to cope, and if the natives are friendly . . ."

He broke off, his mind racing too fast for coherent verbalization, then he went on excitedly. "A planet like this should have a much larger population. Considering the level of technology here it should be densely populated, in fact. I wonder . . ."

He halted the playback where it showed the gray cross-hatching of a small coastal town and stepped up the magnification. Distortion caused by the turbulent but very clean air made it difficult to resolve fine details, but he could see a number of parks, the largest containing a silvery dome-like structure, an airfield and a river bisecting the town. He saw no evidence of railways or large ocean-going ships or dockyard facilities. For a town, the place looked curiously fresh and clean.

"You wonder what?" said Patricia when the silence had begun to drag.

"I wonder why there are no large ships, railheads or major road systems linking those towns, which are so small and widely separated that air travel is the only convenient way of getting around," Devlin said, still looking at the display. "I wonder why the place looks so self-sufficient and why, on the long road up to a nuclear technology, it didn't pick up a few industrial ruins and sooty factory chimneys. In short, I wonder if we were the first ship to come along, and if we are not looking at a well-established colony."

"Yes, of course!" said Patricia excitedly, then, "But would they send two ships like this on exactly the same course? And surely the computer would have told us if the radio signals were intelligible?"

Devlin's elation faded. She was right. The world below, he was still sure, was a colony fairly recently set up—say five or six generations ago at most. But it was not a human colony.

Patricia was already calling up the data from the soft-landing probe.

By a process of electronic analysis, chemical and biochemical, examination and the sampling of plant and animal life in the vicinity, the probe was turning a remote-controlled microscope on one tiny piece of the world, and from its observations it was deducing the makeup of the planet as a whole. For the most part the results reported were negative.

There was no evidence of harmful organisms. There was a wide range of plant and animal life, but the sizes were relatively small due to the heavier gravity and, while there were strong indications that some of the larger animals were carnivorous, most varieties of animal and plant tissue were suitable for human consumption and would augment or eventually replace the Earth grains they had brought along. There was nothing in the report to frighten, or even seriously worry, any would-be colonist.

"Let's have the visuals," said Devlin.

On the main screen appeared an unsteady picture of the planetary surface from an altitude of fifty thousand feet. The probe's vision pickup was directed forward, so that the picture showed half-black and half the dazzling white of the cloud carpet.

The vehicle was losing height rapidly, and the cloud layer began to show graduations of light and shade to take on a three-dimensional aspect. Individual clouds were sliding over the horizon and whipping past the probe, and suddenly it was through and over the sea at three thousand feet and approaching the largest coastal town. They had a glimpse of buildings and a park rushing past below; then they were close to the ground and crossing above a road with a moving vehicle in it. They had a glimpse of small animals running, vegetation which was beautifully formed and colored and hugging the ground for protection against the high winds, and the screen went blank.

MINOR MALFUNCTION IN PROBE CONTROL SYSTEM
DURING LANDING, said the display. MAJOR
MALFUNCTION IN VISION PICKUP CAUSED BY HEAVY
LANDING. OTHER SENSORY SAMPLING AND
COMMUNICATIONS SYSTEMS REMAIN OPERATIONAL.

Without being asked, Patricia tapped for a slow playback of the sequence covering the flight over the town and the close approach to the ground. As the images were crawling slowly across the screen she gave an uncomfortable laugh and said, "I know how this thing works—I could almost build it. That instructor's knowledge is in my mind. Is there such a thing as retroactive telepathy?"

"Maybe," said Devlin dryly, "she is haunting the place."

"Maybe," Patricia replied with a shiver, "she is haunting me. Is it possible that . . . ?"

"Let's not get sidetracked," said Devlin firmly. "Concentrate on the display and freeze the picture if you see something you think is important. Look, it's above the town now and crossing the park."

The streets were broad, well-planned and pleasantly decorated with vegetation. Architecture tended to be functional, squat and with a firm grip on the ground. Nothing seemed to be higher than four storys, and the small, shutter-fitted windows and curved roofing were protection against high winds. In the center of the park the object which from space had looked like a silvery dome was now revealed as a gigantic sphere, tarnished by time and weather and the heat-discoloration of re-entry. Devlin wondered if the descendants of the Earth colonists would put a park around their ship in memory of where they had come from, if things worked out right and they were able to take root here.

Even with maximum magnification they could not resolve the images of the people in the streets.

"It's a nice place," said Patricia as the probe dropped lower above the wooded country beyond the town. "We could do much worse. And we can always land well away from the other colonists' towns. The planet is almost empty, and by the time they discover us we may have discovered a way of making friends with them."

"That's true," said Devlin. "Unless they find the probe and deduce its purpose and organize some kind of defense. We'll need a long time to decelerate and return here, remember—seventy, maybe, eighty years— and they'll have plenty of time to prepare, and to fill some of the empty spaces with their people."

"Defense? But we're not attacking."

"They don't know that."

She was silent for a moment, her expression troubled, then she said, "Maybe they won't find the probe. But I'm worried about the driver of the vehicle it passed over . . . Here's that view now."

The road was a gray diagonal bisecting the screen with the wheeled vehicle hurrying along it and away from the probe, which was overtaking but increasing its lateral distance as it dropped lower. Their view moved from the three-quarters rear aspect to almost a side elevation before intervening trees threatened to hide the vehicle from sight. Simultaneously their fingers stabbed toward the Hold button and collided above it. They began to laugh and Devlin tapped for full magnification.

They stopped laughing.

The image was quite sharp. It showed a sturdy four-wheeled vehicle with a transparent canopy with three beings—two adults and a child—inside. There was more than enough of their bodies visible to make identification positive.

They belonged to the same species which, during Pass Five, had made three attempts to blow the Earth ship out of the sky.

19

"I KNOW ENOUGH, at least I remember enough, to be sure that we won't survive at all if we go on," said Patricia angrily. "We've got no guarantee that Target Ten's system will even be habitable, and by the time we get to Eleven, if we even get to Eleven, the ship will be three-quarters dead and so will half the people in it.

"I do know enough," she raged on, "to know that I don't know enough to carry out effective repairs on anything but the simplest systems. That woman was a programer, not a team of technicians!"

She was very angry because they had spent several hours arguing in circles, and now they were going around the same old circuit yet again.

"I still think this is too important a decision for two people to take," said Devlin stubbornly. "Some of the others should be consulted."

Shaking her head impatiently she said, "I've already explained why they shouldn't be. If we choose to make this decision by democratic process then we will have to awaken everyone whose cold-sleep resuscitation systems are still operational, explain everything to them, then wait while everyone tries to make up his or her mind. It is hard enough making two people make up their minds. Well, isn't it?"

Devlin did not reply and she went on, "As things are now, we have two choices. To go for Target Ten or decelerate for a return here. We have a pretty good chance of making a successful landing here, and a much poorer chance of landing at Ten even if it has a suitable planet. But if we waken everybody, think of the power demand, the increased chances of system failure, the drain of consumables while everyone is arguing and trying to decide what to do. If we waken everyone there won't be a choice, because the power drain caused by a general warming up—something which is only supposed to happen once during the voyage, during the pre-landing orbit—will make a trip to Ten impossible."

She gestured toward the main display, then added, "We've seen the figures and we know what will happen. At least, *I* know."

Patricia was convinced that she was right, Devlin thought angrily, and he already had proof of how far she would go once her mind had been made up about something—the wound in her cheek, six weeks or nine centuries old, was only beginning to form scar tissue. But his own anger, he realized suddenly, was chiefly due to the fact that he himself knew that she was right.

"At least," he said, "let us sleep on it."

"And have the same decision to make when we awaken," she said, with a note of desperation creeping into her voice. "I don't think I could stand that. We won't be any better informed than we are now. I think that we have no choice at all but to decelerate and return for a landing here, and you know it!"

"I know it," said Devlin. "I always have."

But his strongest feeling as he depressed the big red Mission Termination button was not of anger at being bested in an argument, or fear of the consequences—it was simply one of relief followed by a feeling of complete anti-climax.

Possibly the highly complex brain of the ship was aware of the drama of the situation. Perhaps that inhuman mind and cold, metallic and aging body felt a sense of exhilaration knowing that Journey's End was such a relatively short time away. But the only outward indication was the constantly changing data displays on the main screen telling of new systems being checked out, predictions regarding power consumption during the decades of deceleration which stretched ahead of them. Gradually their eyes and minds grew tired of watching displays and began to wander toward each other.

"I'm sorry for being nasty to you back there," Patricia said after a long and obviously worried silence. "It was just that you seemed to be so . . ."

"Stupid?" asked Devlin, smiling. He went on, "Don't worry about it. If you had been the one who was dithering I would probably have hit you with the same arguments. It's just that I'm the worrying type who likes to be as sure of things as possible.

"For instance," he continued, "right now I'm thinking about the cold-sleep cubicles and the number of exercise-only awakenings that are scheduled, before we return here—especially of the power drain and the increased probability of casualties through component failure which even a small and periodic power demand could cause. We are now pretty sure that no physiological or memory damage will occur during an extended period of cold-sleep, so I was wondering if it was possible for you to re-program, for just one, the final awakening?"

She nodded and smiled, yet somehow managed to look even more miserable. Devlin released his straps and moved to the edge of her couch. He said, "What's really bothering you?"

She gripped his hands tightly, but refused to meet his eyes as she said, "My . . . my memories are bothering me, and I'm afraid of what will happen after we land. But right now it is my memories. I . . . I can remember being some very bad people, and being in a lot of bad situations. I'm afraid that I may have experienced too much, that I'll be all used up emotionally, and that nothing will be new anymore . . ."

She broke off and Devlin thought that she was going to cry.

Reassuringly, he said, "You experienced nothing—at least, not during cold-sleep, and your memories in biological time are your own business. What you have are simply memories. I have some pretty hectic memories myself, no doubt concerning the kind of woman that you remembered being. But these are memories, the product of an intensive education program, if you like. Our mental notebooks are full to bursting. We are hot on theory and in a very short time, say four hour's normal sleep and a couple of days in pre-landing orbit, we will be able to get together and compare notes."

Gently he lifted her hands and put them behind his neck, then forced her to look at him. He added, "We are exactly the same people, you know, only more so."

He thought of Brother Howard and the things they had been told about the colonization project, and about the things he must have been told but could not now remember. The dream of the Brother talking seriously to them without making a sound—that, surely, had been his subconscious trying to break a post-hypnotic command not to remember when he awakened.

But the command had not forbidden him to remember the incident when he was asleep, and now Devlin had developed a highly retentive memory regarding his dreams . . .

He said abruptly, "When next we take our normal sleep, I don't think we should meet again before cooldown. I want to concentrate all my thinking on the Brother, because we still have an awful lot of questions and that way I may be able to dream the answers.

"Remember how he talked, in broad, philosophical

terms, about seeding the stars?" he went on. "Could it be that the reason why the females remember only feminine dreams and the males masculine is to make sure that when we arrive the seeds will germinate properly?"

As she nodded up at him he remembered something else the Brother had told him—an old parable about seeds, some of which had fallen onto stony ground, others among thorns and the rest on to fallow soil. In that parable there had been three options, but here there was only the stony and perhaps non-existent ground of Targets Ten and Eleven, which they might never reach, and the thorns of Nine. Among the thorns they could at least take root for a while before being choked off. Among the thorns they stood a fighting chance.

Except that the ship's personnel had been carefully chosen from the Earth's sheep, not from among the wolves. Sheep did not know how to fight.

She must have seen his sudden change of expression because her fingers curled gently around the back of his neck and she began caressing the area behind his ear. "Don't worry about it," she murmured. "We've made the decision and now there is no point in worrying." Slowly but firmly she pulled his face closer to hers, and went on, "I'm trying to reach another decision about whether or not to break a very strict ship's regulation . . ."

They took a long time considering that regulation, which they seriously bent but did not actually break. When they finally forced themselves apart the main screen had ceased its continuous data presentations and was displaying one message only.

ESTIMATED TIME REQUIRED TO PRE-LANDING ORBIT INSERTION AROUND PLANET THREE OF TARGET SUN NINE IS EIGHTY-SEVEN YEARS SIXTEEN DAYS THREE HOURS APPROXIMATELY. ALL CONTROL, GUIDANCE AND NAVIGATIONS SYSTEMS OR BACK-UP SYSTEMS FUNCTIONING. REACTION MASS FOR PLANETARY LANDING SUFFICIENT FOR DIRECT DESCENT ONLY. INSUFFICIENT FOR MANEUVERING IN ATMOSPHERE.

Deliberately they did not discuss the data or say anything at all until they parted at Patricia's cubicle, and then they simply kissed and wished each other good night.

Devlin found it difficult to focus all of his mind on Brother Howard while he composed himself for sleep. Even when his fitful dozing gave way to the shallows preceding deep slumber, the wish-fulfillment dreams with the image and sound and feel of Patricia as she demonstrated various delightful ways of breaking that ship's regulation kept getting in the way. In spite of these interruptions he finally did begin to dream about the Brother, then about Patricia and himself in a room with the Brother, who was seated beside the old pyschologist's wheel chair.

The psychologist was also talking to them silently, but suddenly the sound came through . . .

". . . You will be given a strong, drug-reinforced post-hypnotic command to forget everything you will be told during this session," said the frail old man in his tremendously deep voice. "Whether the command will hold over the time-scale we will be dealing with is another matter. We sincerely hope that it will hold long enough, at least, to protect you from serious mental disorientation, because tied to this command is an even more important one designed to force you to recall your cold-sleep dreams in chronological order. You will have enough to contend with, psychologically speaking, without having to handle an intensely vivid dream life that is apparently running backward.

"But before the Brother tries to explain what is likely to happen to you," he went on, "let me assure you that the hypno-conditioning is not intended merely to hide the truth from you. We are trying to protect your minds from we are not sure what and to prepare them for the same thing. Perhaps there is no need to do this. Perhaps these processes will happen to us as naturally, when the time comes, as reproduction. Perhaps we are wasting our time by trying to teach caterpillars to think like butterflies. The truth is that we just are not sure what the truth is, and we are trying to hedge our bets.

"Too much talking tires me," the old man continued. He was tapping the control studs on his wheel chair and moving toward the door as he added, "The Brother will try to explain it all to you, without becoming too philosophical or religious, I hope. When he is finished I shall return to reinforce the hypnotic commands and, of course, to wish you good luck."

When Brother Howard began to speak it seemed as if he were simply going to repeat their first project orientation lecture. Still without telling them whether theirs was the first, forty-second or only interstellar colonization vessel, he briefly described the ship and its systems, its capabilities and its projected course. The ship would be powered by a low-thrust drive which would accelerate it over the space of several decades to a velocity roughly one-quarter that of light. The more powerful reaction engines would be used only once, to land on the target world. Maximum safe duration for the voyage would be one thousand years so that their effective range was approximately two hundred and fifty light-years . . . .

It was a dream, Devlin knew, but he could not stop himself dreaming again the shiver of awe and wonder that he had felt then, and his feeling of sympathy for the Brother, who, for some reason not yet plain, was unable to accompany them.

Their course, according to the Brother, had been selected so as to make a close pass of ten target stars that were approximately in a straight line within their two hundred and fifty light-year range. The majority of the solar systems concerned were thought to contain habitable planets, but the optical range was extreme and only a few might do so. Should the ship approach an unsuitable solar system it would use the gravity of the system's sun to warp its course so as to direct it toward the next target system with no wastage of fuel. When a system with a suitable planet was found, the Mission-Termination button would be pressed and the ship's computer would take them into pre-landing orbit and ultimately touchdown.

It was at that point that Brother Howard diverged sharply from the early and more familiar lectures ...

20

"I HAVE DESCRIBED, not for the first time, how you will go," Brother Howard said briskly. "The reason why you are going is not so simple, and the reason why you people in particular are going is the most complicated part of all.

"To you the reason for leaving this place must seem obvious," he went on, dividing his attention between Patricia and Devlin. "This is a rotten, violent and over-crowded place, and no sane person with a choice would want to live in it. The not so obvious reason is that you, and all the rest of us, are being acted on by steadily increasing sociological, cultural, moral and economic pressures—you name it and I can tell you exactly how you are being squeezed. It is therefore highly probable that the reason you are leaving *is because you have no choice!*"

His voice had risen steadily in volume and his eyes, Devlin thought, seemed to reflect a mixture of anger and confusion. The Brother had never looked or sounded as wild as this before, and Devlin reminded himself that not all the city's madmen were Maxers or teenage citizens.

"Let us go back to your analogy of the fruit-bearing planet," Brother Howard continued in a quieter voice. "The analogy is not perfect, as you know, because this planet-sized rotten fruit has nowhere to fall in order to germinate and restart the growth cycle. Instead it is being compressed on one side by rapidly diminishing resources and by an exploding population on the other. The result will be that the seed contained within it will be expelled, like a stone from a rotten plum, and the purpose of this project is to direct the seed toward fallow ground."

He took a deep breath, then went on quietly, "Naturally we are making a big effort to insure the success of our project. But we can never be sure whether the effort and sacrifices are necessary or whether, if our particular group of talented people had stayed at home and enjoyed the various pleasures of our society, the project would have been launched by a completely different set of people using entirely different methods. However, I am fully convinced that if something is destined to happen then happen it will. Seeding must occur, and soon. I have special knowledge, you see, which makes me absolutely sure of this. As well, I am convinced, as are most of the others connected with the project, that God or Fate or the evolutionary process helps those who help themselves.

"Our main worry," he added, and the worry was evident in his voice as well as in his expression, "is that we cannot know for sure whether we are helping or hindering."

Devlin looked at Patricia, but all of her attention was on the Brother and there was no way of telling what she thought about this peculiar confession.

"I wouldn't dream of confusing and frightening you like this," he continued, "if you were intended to remember this interview. However, there is no need to be afraid for your physical well-being. The danger, the real suffering and confusion, will be mental rather than physical, and there is very little that we have been able to do to prepare you for it.

"But before I go into the details of what we have done, and why, I shall try to dispel some of your present confusion by telling you how I became involved with the project."

According to the Brother the project had its real beginning about a century and a half earlier when mankind, having slammed the door into space some forty years previously, was beginning to open it again and look outside. Scientific advances in the interim had provided methods of space travel that were much more economic than those of the first space age; science and technology had opened up the possibility of interstellar flight through the development of hibernation anaesthesia techniques.

One of the projects initiated at that time was aimed at sending a low-impulse drive ship containing a volunteer astronaut in cold-sleep on a cometary orbit that would return the ship to the vicinity of Earth in one hundred and three years.

But once again the public lost interest in space flight and in hibernation anaesthesia, because even then the future promised to be an unpleasantly crowded and polluted and vicious place. Sensible people preferred to live out their lives in the present rather than transferring a large portion of their population into this rather frightening future. But the volunteer astronaut, like most people who volunteered, was not very sensible and did not really think about the kind of Earth he would be returning to. Nor did he realize that, while his physical condition upon resuscitation would be perfect, his mind would never be the same again.

"... A lot of time and effort and money had gone into the project, however," Brother Howard went on cynically, "and one of the project psychologists, Dr. Martin, was so interested that he undertood a longevity treatment in order to be around to see the end result. The treatment, although still experimental, was effective in that it conferred long life but not eternal youth.

"Because Doctor Martin was not a normal person," the Brother continued, "and because he was brilliant, dedicated and incredibly patient, he did not give up on the only cold-sleeper to return after an extended period in space, and gradually he coaxed him back to sanity. It required many, many years of constant attention because the returned astronaut, by the generally accepted standards of the day, was hopelessly insane. In the long process of effecting a cure Doctor Martin discovered what exactly had been going on in the man's mind while all of his bodily processes—except those of mentation, obviously—had been halted, and together with his patient they formulated theories to explain it.

"But my return to sanity was not one hundred percent complete," the Brother added dryly. "As a result of those cold-sleep experiences I became convinced that I had had my nose rubbed very firmly in a form of afterlife, and I'm afraid that I caught a severe dose of religion."

He looked from Patricia to Devlin, studying their expressions, then he said, "Relax, I'm still not trying to convert you. But I must give you some idea of what to expect, so listen carefully ..."

The Brother's experience in cold-sleep had been frightening, painful, stimulating and confusing, with confusion predominating. He had been assured that nothing at all would happen during cold-sleep and that he would be awakened without any apparent passage of time. Neither he nor the project medics had expected him to dream, continuously and vividly, throughout his century-long voyage.

Even the pleasant dreams had been frightening because of the confusion and disorientation caused by them apparently running backward. Incidents were experienced normally, but when he dreamed a person's lifetime the incidents were not in chronological order. He would dream a person's entire life history, complete in every thought and detail and feeling and then, without warning, find himself the same person's infant father an instant after the aged son had died.

He kept dreaming farther and farther back in time, of people and places about which he could not possibly have had knowledge. The dream lives became shorter and more violent. Some of them did not even involve human beings. And when he was resuscitated his mind was filled with the pains, pleasures, and confusion of countless lifetimes and he was incapable of forgetting any of them.

All of the lives and, more important, all of the deaths were there as fresh in his memory as if they had happened only a few minutes earlier.

It was a miracle that old Dr. Martin, who had been a very young Dr. Martin when Howard had been cooled for the trip, had been able to return him to any semblance of sanity. But the psychologist had managed it, in part, by providing an explanation for what had happened to him.

Martin had suggested that when a man or men and/or women were removed from their home planet for extended periods of time while being subjected to reduced temperatures, a process occurred that had the effect of making these space travelers seeds, or potential seeds, of their race. The process was psychophilosophical rather than physical.

Like certain plant seeds and bacteria that were capable of surviving for extended periods in Arctic conditions and then reproducing themselves, the human equivalents were perfectly preserved in cold-sleep with none of their functions impaired. A major difference was that the human seedlings possessed minds and these, apparently, were even more important and deserving of preservation. But it was not simply the minds of the individuals concerned which were preserved, the process triggered off by time and reduced temperatures had the effect of stimulating what amounted to the racial memory.

The cold-sleepers became the seeds of humanity—retaining all its knowledge, experience and achievements since its beginnings.

"... In effect," the Brother went on, unable to hide the wonder and excitement he was feeling, "each man and woman have available the memories, that is the total knowledge and experience, of their ancestors or the people of the same sex with whom their ancestors came into contact as far back as prehistoric times. But these memories are not passed from male parent to male offspring, or female to female as the case may be, because the dream material made available during cold-sleep comprises complete lifetimes, and if the racial memories were inherited from the parents they would begin at conception but no memory belonging to a parent would be available after the birth of the final offspring.

"Obviously there is a sex link," he continued, "otherwise why couldn't males experience female dreams, and vice versa. But according to the Doctor, another and much more important process is at work—the release of information recorded and stored in the large unused portion of the human brain, which is the mental component of the human seedling. Since the brain is the only organ in the human body which grows without regenerating itself, this explains why complete lifetimes can be remembered.

"The reason for dreaming about people who could not possibly be ancestors is more difficult to explain, but Dr. Martin has covered even that ..."

One of the psychologist's pet theories when he was a young man had been about ghosts and similar non-material sense manifestations. He had been convinced that there was no such thing as a ghost, but he did believe that when an event occurred that involved a considerable amount of pain or pleasure or fear, or any other strong emotion, the associated mental radiation was absorbed by material in the area—the area that would later become the scene of the so-called hauntings—and would be made available to anyone who visited the place later and who was sufficiently sensitive to be a receiver for the playback.

When the Brother had reported on his dream lives experienced during a century of cold-sleep, Dr. Martin had extended and modified his theory.

According to the psychologist, mental radiation was absorbed and recorded by all forms of organic life, and the recording equipment increased its sensitivity and efficiency as the organic life in question developed intelligence. No thought or sensory impression, no matter how faint or distant in time, was ever completely lost. They were stored, not in the crude, electrochemical fashion used by the conscious mind, but on a sub-molecular level which enabled the accommodation of the vast quantity of material necessary for the retention of a racial memory.

And the reason that all this data was available was that any given person was composed of atoms or molecules—the organic building blocks—which in the recent or distant past had belonged to the structure of another person, or had been briefly in contact with another person's organic material through ingestion or assimilation into the tissues. The transfer of information to the hypersensitive recorder in the brain might even have occurred by inhaling impurities while sharing public transport, possibly even by occupancy of the same town.

Dr. Martin had been unable to establish either the degree of sensitivity or the range of the racial memory recording units in Brother Howard's brain, but it was not limitless . . .

"To express it as simply as possible," the Brother concluded, "no single person is carrying all of mankind's history in his after-brain. But the ship will contain two hundred long-term cold-sleepers, and the Doctor is convinced that half that number, considering the present-day mixing of racial types, would among them take away a record of every thought, emotion or sensation ever experienced by thinking creatures on this planet."

There was a long, uneasy silence after the Brother finished speaking. Devlin felt excited and impressed by the scope of the psychologist's concept, but he still thought it incredible. Patricia must have been thinking along the same lines.

"I can't believe ... all that," she said, apologetically but firmly.

"Not now, naturally," said the Brother. There was a strong tinge of compassion, rather than irritation, in his tone and he went on, "After your third or fourth awakening you will believe, except that our conditioning will keep you from remembering this particular session, so that I will not be able to say a retroactice 'I told you so.' By now you are realizing that if you were allowed to remember this session you, and all the other colonists who run the risk of going insane, would resign from the project."

Devlin laughed politely. He said, "In a project as important as this, one with so many philosophical implications, I still don't know how you can be sure that you're picking the right seeds for your pod."

"The simple answer," replied the Brother, "is that we are *not* sure."

"Oh," said Devlin.

The other shook his head and said, "It really isn't fair to us. We are caterpillars trying to think like butterflies. The process of seeding a planetwide intelligent race may be as natural an event as the Sun coming up, but it is still an event which requires the combined knowledge of all the hard and soft sciences. Dr. Martin and myself are responsible for selecting the seed, we *think*, while the others have to prepare and launch the seedpod. A lot of time and effort has gone into the design and construction of your ship, and we know it will work, but the business of seed selection is scaring us sick.

"A seed should be capable of survival," he went on. "Fine. But do we select our most aggressive, adaptable seedlings who will establish a bridgehead and hold it against all comers? Or will we export our philosopher and artist seeds who between them may be incapable of growing a potato? Or a mixture of both which might result in the seeds destroying each other? All this is an oversimplification, you realize, but you can appreciate our dilemma. Finally we decided to take the easy, and perhaps cowardly, way out.

"We decided that if the approaching racial seedling phase was a natural event like childbearing or like the Sun coming up," he continued, "then the seeds themselves should be aware of the process. So we began to look around for personality types who were trying to expel themselves or who wanted to be expelled. We found that the strong-minded, aggressive, highly intelligent and resourceful types, the kind which to our minds would have made the best colonists, had adapted to present-day society and, under deep probing, were not really interested in going.

"The group who really hated Earth and who desperately wanted to escape comprised more than ninety percent of the world's population," he concluded. "That's right, the sheep! We didn't even have to go outside the city to find enough candidates."

There was a long silence, then Patricia said quietly, "You seem to have made the right choice. Ordinary, average, peace-loving people are in the majority. They always have been."

"Yes," replied the Brother. "The highly intelligent and aggressive types are responsible for a lot of advances, but it has been progress without stability. The sheep can grow more slowly and gently, so long as they don't land among wolves."

"I see," said Devlin, then added, "Don't worry, I think you made the right choice, too."

"Kind of you to say so," said the Brother dryly, "But another worry was how you people as individuals will react to becoming the repositories of this store of racial experience. From first-hand knowledge I can assure you that the process is anything but pleasant at first, and we have tried to devise ways of cushioning the psychic shock which is involved.

"Perhaps," he said, going off on a tangent, "a voyage

on a generation-ship, with the original personnel and their descendants living out their lives naturally during the trip, and sleeping normally instead of going cold, would be easier on all concerned, Maybe that is the way it is supposed to happen, But we can't be sure— and anyway, we haven't the technical ability or the psychological control capability to produce that kind of seedpod. All we can do is try and make the cold-dreams a little easier to take.

"During the training sessions which you will be allowed to remember," he continued, "we have told you lies, half-truths and generally given impressions which are nothing but red herrings. Periodic awakenings to reinforce and exercise the mind and body, for instance. Remembering will never be a problem where you are concerned. Hints dropped about the necessity of dreaming, when you will not be able to stop doing it, and oblique references to the use of new psychodrugs which will make you suspect that the whole business is simply an elaborate simulation. All this lying and misdirection was to enable you to assimilate the sharp and intense and extremely confusing race memory data without it driving you insane."

Devlin nodded. He no longer thought the Brother a religious fanatic, but neither did he feel particularly reassured. He said, "Surely there are psychodrugs available which would cushion these shocks. They could be injected immediately preceding the awakening, and they would dull the initial sensations so that—"

"No!" said the Brother sharply. "The seedpod is a product of the race's technological achievements, but the seeds themselves we are afraid to touch in case we adversely affect them. The psychodrugs might deteriorate over such a lengthy period or, if injected before launch, have a damaging effect on the recall process. So you are going out untouched, medically speaking. The conditioning process, which we will begin shortly, is psychological and aimed at controlling your dream recall by non-material means. It is being done so that you will remember, or dream, the earliest episodes first and so that the racial memory material will be presented more slowly and in chronological order. We hope that the conditioning will prevent all of your recall memories being made available during your first cooldown and that it will enable you to retain your sanity after the later awakenings. But we can't, of course, be sure of that."

There was another long silence, broken again by Patricia, who said, "We both know that there would be risks."

"Yes," said Devlin, wishing that he could be as confident as she sounded. "But you had us worried for a while—we thought we'd fallen among religious fanatics. I realize that this project has all sorts of philosophical implications, but it has nothing to do with religion, surely, or the afterlife."

"No?"

"Well, no," replied Devlin. "Of course, I may not have thought deeply enough about it."

"You haven't," said the Brother, "and I'll admit that in the objective sense I may not have undergone a religious experience. That reaction depends on your own point of view, or on how your parents brought you up to regard such things; I found that my after-brain recorder had been switched on and its return to Earth's gravity and temperature did not seem to be switching it off; I kept assimilating impressions from everyone around me. This was material which, if I could spare the time to dream about it, gave me their whole life experience up to that point—providing they were men, of course. So I became very understanding even though my basic feelings and beliefs did not change very much.

"Mostly I kept remembering the lives of people who died long ago. They were a pretty varied bunch, with good qualities and bad qualities in combinations which made their lives very recallable. They are all here, complete in every thought and feeling."

He tapped the side of his head, then added seriously, "Everybody suffers, but nobody dies."

"But surely," protested Devlin, "they are only the memories of people, not the people themselves."

The Brother shook his head. He said, "Think of it in this way. When you go to sleep at night your life is switched off, you die. I'm discounting, for the purposes of this argument, the dreaming which some people do and remember and which doesn't really count. When you awaken in the morning you may clearly remember your life of yesterday, but it is only a memory. You will better understand what I'm talking about when you have experienced your first few cold-sleep memories. My point is that everyone who was ever alive is still living in the minds of you colonists, and as for the religious implications ..."

He paused for a moment as the door opened and the incredibly old psychologist rolled in; then he went on, "I have a purely personal view regarding the meaning of my racial memories, you understand, and one which Dr. Martin does not agree with. The vast majority of these lives are recallable because, even in the most simple and mundane lifetimes, there is so much in them that is interesting and valuable and demanding to be recalled. But there are other lives which are so twisted, so violent and unpleasant in one respect or another, that nobody would want to recall them even in part. So there is this mass of material which will rarely, if ever, be recalled. It belongs to people condemned—by their own acts, you will say, and not by any higher authority—to the outer darkness of the forgotten, to Limbo. So far as I am concerned the religious implications are clear."

Dr. Martin rolled his chair behind the desk, and the Brother stood up and solemnly shook hands with Patricia and Devlin. He smiled and said, "The Doctor here describes me as a lapsed atheist, whatever that means. However, now I have to tell you that, following this conditioning session, you will be cooled and stored awaiting transfer to the ship. We will not meet again, and I want to wish both of you good luck and a safe landing."

As he turned to leave, Devlin said, "Wait, Brother. I'm still too confused and frightened by all this to say thank you and really mean it. But I still think it unfair that you people, who have done all the real work, have no chance of getting away. Surely we could make room, or do something to . . ."

Brother Howard held up his hand.

"With the problems you are shortly going to face, Doctor," he said drily, "trust you to worry about us. But there is one thing, just one, that you can do.

"Remember us in your dreams."

21

THERE WERE NO colonist or crew awakenings while the ship killed its tremendous cruising velocity and began to return to Target Nine, so there was plenty of time to remember and dream. The dreams were as vivid and complete as before, but now Devlin was aware of what was happening and was able to integrate his dreams with his own memories, and he no longer felt helplessly imprisoned by them, as in a nightmare.

He became more and more unselective regarding the material available to him. He learned that pain as well as pleasure was a part of every life that was great or worthwhile, and he recalled people who were truly great to everyone but themselves, and others whose greatness was known only to a few close friends, or perhaps to only one other person. He also learned that there were very few lives that were uninteresting or unworthy of recalling, and even fewer that were completely valueless.

To understand all was to forgive almost all, and Devlin's understanding—or his education, as the Brother had described it at a time when he did not know what was involved—was complete.

He recalled the people he had met in his own lifetime: colleagues at Sanator Five, young Tommy Bennett and his father, Patricia's father, Dr. Martin and Brother Howard. He had met them briefly or for extended periods of time, but everything they had thought and felt up until that point in their lifetimes had made an impression on his after-brain and was available for replay. Each of them lived again in his memory, their lives so sharp and vivid and utterly complete that they lived, period.

He could understand the Brother's point of view about an afterlife, as well as many other things.

Devlin was Brother Howard as an infant, a toddler, a young man rebelling against the constraints of highly moral parents who in their turn were overreacting against the increasing permissiveness of their society, as a test pilot and an astronaut under training, as he had walked the awful emptiness of Mars, as a helpless cold-sleeper reliving, in savage and confusing detail, some of the lives that made up their race's memory.

He was Brother Howard when they had first met in the house of Bennett, a project worker, and when he had met Patricia and Devlin for the first time and decided that they would qualify he had decided that all of the others would qualify, because he alone on Earth had the ability to know a man completely. He had been responsible for the selection of all the male project personnel and colonists while Dr. Martin, using more mundane methods, had been responsible for screening the women.

As Brother Howard, Devlin was aware of seeing himself as another had seen him, and of the peculiar mental double-image that was his own recollection of his past life superimposed on the one detected by the Brother.

But the subjects for recall included contacts on the project, men who knew the workings of the ship inside-out and from preliminary design sketch to finished and tested hardware. Devlin knew he was only a seed in a fantastically sophisticated metal pod, and that the pod was beginning to deteriorate seriously. He thought that it should be possible for the seeds to help sustain their own ageing and withering pod ...

He was still investigating that possibility when he was awakened.

GOOD MORNING DEVLIN. SHIP STATUS ONE THOUSAND AND THREE YEARS INTO MISSION. SYSTEMS AND/OR BACK-UP SYSTEMS FUNCTIONING AT LEVELS ADEQUATE FOR INSERTION INTO PRE-LANDING ORBIT. SHIP PERSONNEL CURRENTLY AWAKE—TWO. IDENTITIES PATRICIA MORLEY AND JOHN DEVLIN.

No further messages were on the display, Devlin noted as he began exercising. Patricia had said that she would erase the useless reminders about exercising and remembering as a means of saving ship's power. But the single message had told him enough, and his impatience made him complete the exercises while on the way to the control center. Patricia, who must have been fractionally less impatient, arrived there a few seconds later.

With fast, expert movements, they called for the situation report and read that the ship was closing on the target plane and estimating just under five days to pre-landing orbit insertion. All four of the mission termination probes, the most highly sensitive and complex that the ship had available, had already been launched. One had taken up a surveillance orbit and was transmitting data on all channels, another had developed a control malfunction while attempting a soft landing which wasn't, and the other two had been too sick to leave the launching tubes.

The ship itself was not sick, just very, very tired. Even so it declared itself capable of landing them safely on their new home.

"Not an ideal home," said Patricia, following his train of thought, "even if we don't fall into a clump of thorns." She gestured toward the surveillance probe's display and asked, "Shall I look for a few less thorny spots?"

Devlin shook his head. "Not yet, if you don't mind. Will you help me with the ship's personnel status board?" There were twenty-three cold-sleepers in malfunctioning cubicles which, while capable of preserving them, were no longer able to complete resuscitation procedure. "I've been thinking about that problem, and dreaming some of the people who might have been able to solve it."

"Me, too," said Patricia. "Some of the engineers were brilliant women, but they would have needed a lot of skilled help, special equipment and a lot longer than five days to put it right . . ."

She broke off as the display announced that seventy-eight of the two hundred-odd remaining sleepers were likely to stay in that condition permanently.

Devlin stared at the figures disbelievingly, his mind reacting to the disaster they represented. Pleadingly, he said, "Is there no chance of repairing the faulty resuscitation equipment? No chance at all?"

"We know what to do," said Patricia gently, "and perhaps if we resuscitated enough of the other sleepers, they might have dreamed enough about the project personnel to recall what must be done. But they were not aware of the problem, remember, and would only dream about the project by sheer luck. As well, we do not have the time or the special equipment needed for the job. You know that, don't you?"

"I know it," said Devlin. "It was just that I was hoping you would come up with an idea . . ."

He broke off, thinking about the people who would die as soon as the ship landed and the slow, uncontrolled warmth of the planetary atmosphere began seeping into the space-cold metal of the ship's interior. At present they were in cold-sleep, not technically alive but still dreaming lifetimes and experiences not their own, so neither were they dead. Was it right that he should condemn them to death, and lose so much of his race's memory and experience, by landing on this world? Would it not be better to use the last of the ship's propulsive power to shoot it out again into interstellar space, where the cold would ultimately allow everyone to dream forever about all the people who individually had made up the race of Man?

Would it not be better to be a seed which was complete and perfect and which never fell to ground, than one which was weakened, incomplete and probably destined to die before germination?

"No," said Patricia firmly. "Before you could make that decision you would have to resuscitate everyone and ask for a vote. You would *have* to do that."

Devlin had not been aware that he had been thinking aloud. He said angrily, "We won't be able to count seventy-eight of the votes, remember. What would you have me do about that?"

"I don't *know*," she replied furiously, "any better than you do. But you could put two of them in the cubicles belonging to Caldwell and Purdy. Those cubicles were switched off to conserve power, remember. They weren't malfunctions ..."

She broke off to stare at him while he stared just as wildly at her.

They had the answer.

Cautiously, Devlin said, "Do you think we can manage it in just five days? There are seventy-eight of them, after all."

"But we'll have help," Patricia replied excitedly. "If necessary we can warm as many of the others as we need to help with the transfers. We will be very congested towards the end, and the voyage-only consumables will probably run out, but it should work."

"Yes," said Devlin.

He watched her excitement fade as she, too, realized that they had solved just one, the least important one of their two problems. With the exception of Yvonne Caldwell and Thomas Purdy, their metal pod would arrive with its full complement of seedlings. But they had still to decide on a landing site, on which particular area was least densely overgrown with thorns.

The picture from the surveillance probe, which was capable of virtually unlimited magnification, filled the main display screen.

"Let's deal with one problem at a time," he said. Then seeing her disapproving expression, he added apologetically, "Despite my extensive education and everything, I haven't changed very much—I still try to put off things."

"Yes," she said, and smiled. "And I still seem to be a nag."

For the next two days they were kept very busy resuscitating cold-sleepers, explaining the situation to them and helping them move the people in malfunctioning caskets into those that were still working and lately vacated by other colonists. The solution had been simple and perhaps obvious.

By warming up the occupants of functioning caskets, then initiating a cooldown with the casket empty, the people who had been cooled with no hope of resuscitation could then be moved to functioning caskets and warmed in the ordinary way. Care had to be taken to make sure that a partial, and lethal, warm-up did not take place during the transfer, and even more care was needed to avoid injury to their ultra-frigid and brittle bodies. But once the steadily increasing number of helpers understood what was required, Patricia and Devlin had little to do except stay in the control center and prepare for the landing.

"The latest estimate is that everyone will be warm at re-entry minus six hours," said Patricia. "The drain on consumables will be considerable, so we can all expect to be very hungry—but not enough to weaken us physically. All ship's personnel, except Devlin and me, will take landing deceleration in their caskets, and their displays will keep them informed of what is going on here. People in malfunctioning cubicles will be in the dark, in both senses of the word, and very cold. They will have to borrow a couple of sets of coveralls each if the cubicle heaters are also out. The post-landing food supply and food synthesizers, seeds, livestock breeders, agricultural and construction machinery have been checked. The automatic unlocking systems are functioning and will open these supplies to us as soon as we touch down.

"I wonder," she ended worriedly, "if we will be given the chance to eat a hearty meal before—"

"Several, I should think," said Devlin reassuringly. "Especially if we land in the middle of nowhere."

Patricia smiled and said, "Let's try to find nowhere."

The post-landing food supply and equipment, designed to enable them to survive for at least two months while they established a base and set up the tissue and plant synthesizers, that would further extend their reserves until the first crops came in, had been locked away during the voyage for obvious reasons. He wondered, remembering his first experience with the pallid, pear-shaped, spindly and highly aggressive aliens, whether a self-guiding nuclear weed-killer would put an abrupt stop to their first celebration dinner on the new world.

They were here first, he thought despairingly, *and we would not trespass if we had any other choice. But could the aliens believe that? Was there any chance of communicating with them and of making them understand?*

There was not enough time to do it from orbit, and by the time they were down the natives would already have made their decision. There was nothing to do but set down in one of the least densely populated areas and hope that they would not be noticed until they were able to work out some method of communication or, he thought bitterly, until a few of the sheep grew fangs.

He was remembering Hawn and the young king and the millions of others who had learned how to survive amid violence and whose knowledge was instantly available should the colonists need it. But were they capable of using such knowledge? And if they did use it, would they ever again be able to think of themselves as sheep?

Would the meek, he wondered bitterly, ever inherit anything?

In silence they called up the recordings of their original fly-by, comparing them with current views of the same planetary area. Obviously the world had an awful lot of usable empty space; there had been no major building or expansion programs and the colony had suffered something less than a population explosion. Radiation sensor data comparisons still showed minor emissions, chiefly on the communication frequencies, from the widely scattered housing and unmistakable evidence of nuclear technology in the towns, which were obviously the manufacturing centers for the colony world.

"It isn't exactly an expanding colony," said Devlin, rubbing his eyes. They had been staring at displays for nearly three hours. He added, "I wonder if the planet is only marginally suited to their form of life, as it is to ours. Maybe there are trace elements in the atmosphere which are toxic to them, or the heavier gravity makes it difficult to have children . . ."

"Then we must look for parks and schools," she broke in quickly. "Anywhere likely to contain children. Even with a totally strange life form you should be able to tell if the children are healthy."

"Yes, indeed," said Devlin, and tapped for maximum magnification from the probe's visual sensors. Together they concentrated on holding the images steady, swearing when heat eddies distorted the pictures or the guidance went slightly off to leave them staring at an uninteresting expanse of roofing. They saw many natives, foreshortened except when they were lying down, of all sizes. They were unable to find any structures remotely resembling a school—at least, they could not recognize it as such if they did see one. There were children in the parks, in the streets with parents, playing on the beaches. All of them appeared to be healthy and very active.

"There isn't anything wrong with that lot," said Patricia, frowning. "But I wouldn't say the same for their parents—they are, well, negligent! Some of those children are very small, little more than infants, and they are playing unattended on a dangerous stretch of beach. There should be an adult there to tell them that . . ."

"Maybe," said Devlin, laughing suddenly, "they don't need to be told."

All at once he was feeling great, better than he could ever remember feeling in his life, better than he could remember feeling in any of his lives. He was sure everything was going to be all right.

"What's the matter with you?" began Patricia, giving him a frightened look. Before he could reassure her regarding his sanity, a red light began winking for attention, and the image they had been studying blanked out and was replaced by a printed message.

FLY-BY NINE ORIGINAL SOFT-LANDED PROBE
MALFUNCTION CORRECTED, PROBE SENSORS
REACTIVATED. TRANSMITTING.

Devlin said quietly, "They found the first damaged probe and repaired it. I thought that it would be impossible to communicate with them from space, considering the difficulty of matching frequencies and the other technical problems. But they took the easy way out. They studied, repaired and used our own equipment, and I'm betting that they were able to build a receiver as well as repairing our transmitter.

"But now we need a fix on their incoming signal," he added, "if we're going to send as well as receive."

Patricia nodded and began tapping instructions, still looking confused and worried. Devlin called up the data which was arriving from the repaired probe and angled a vision pickup to cover both their couches.

The picture showed a large room with two windows. It was dark outside. The walls of the room were covered with large charts and simple line drawings, display screens and associated equipment at least as sophisticated as that in the control center. Three adult aliens were watching the probe's vision pickup and the displays, and two of the screens lit suddenly with a picture of Patricia and himself lying on their control couches. The excitement in the room was plain to see.

This is the first time they have seen human beings, thought Devlin. He had seen their species during the near-catastrophic fly-by of System Five, but at that time the progenitors of the beings on this world must already have left their home system.

"The transmission is coming from an area on the night side," said Patricia, who had been dividing her attention between the main and a side display. "I've called up the visuals recorded during a daylight pass and magnified them. The area is several hundred miles from the nearest town, a clearing in a well-wooded valley, with a few small buildings and a large, steerable dish antenna in it. The interior of the dish is highly reflective. There are surface power lines, apparently, raidating from the installation, and one of them goes to a similar dish about twelve miles distant ..."

"Look at this," said Devlin.

The vision pickup on the surface was being directed toward a large and simplified drawing of Five's solar system, with a smaller drawing of an alien place above their home planet. The pickup lingered for a few minutes on that drawing before moving to another which showed a spherical ship, also with a picture of an alien close to it, leaving the home system and passing several representations of stars before arriving at system Nine.

"Those charts, that whole installation," said Patricia worriedly, "was not put together overnight. They have been expecting us. At least, they must have decided that there was a strong chance that we would be back and . . . and . . ."

"Yes," said Devlin, readying the white plastic boards and stylus which were available for just this contingency. "But they don't know anything about us. I wish I could draw."

Nevertheless he produced a recognizable if crudely executed sketch of the Earth's solar system with a stylized man above the third planet and presented the picture to the control-center pickup. On the surface there were more signs of excitement, and he followed with a sketch of the ship leaving the solar system and coming to Nine, the only difference between their drawing and the aliens' being the human figure above the ship and the number of intervening stars. The excitement below became intense, then suddenly they all became very still as the surface pickup was directed at another drawing.

It showed a stylized alien lying recumbent and slightly off-center on an otherwise blank sheet.

Eagerly Devlin began to sketch again. He copied as best he could the picture of the recumbent and off-center alien, then added a stylized and recumbent man beside it and presented the drawing for viewing.

Their reaction beggared description. It was just possible that the aliens were waving their double-handed arms at him in anger, but he did not think so.

He said, "I think that was the right answer."

"But what was it?" asked Patricia. "A representation of the lion lying down with the lamb?"

"You're half right," said Devlin seriously. "What they are asking, and what I hope I told them, was that we, too, experienced a lot while we were on our way here. That we are not afraid to lie down unprotected beside them and exchange, if such a process is possible, our respective racial memories while we are asleep. Most of all I think I was telling them that we, too, are sheep ..."

During the fly-by of Five, the aliens' reaction had frightened him so much that he had not been able to use his brain properly. They had been so aggressive, so wildly and violently antagonistic, that he had only briefly considered the possibility that there might have been people on that world like Brother Howard, Dr. Martin and the other dedicated members of the project. Perhaps an alien vessel passing too close to Sol a few decades after the colonists had left would have found the humans degenerated even further than in his own day, become even more violent, and reacting in exactly the same fashion as had the people on Five's planet. But now he had begun to think.

He thought about the absence of schools and of what it would be like to have children educated, from a very early age, by dreams which stretched beyond their race's earliest recorded history. He thought of a non-human race sharing a world with his own people, perhaps sharing their racial dreams, and of what they might ultimately achieve together. They were unlikely to do anything violently or in a hurry, because the evidence was that the aliens had made no attempt to grab territory or cover the planet with their offspring. But sometime in the distant future it would be seeding time again, and he was thinking like a caterpillar. Instead he should be thinking like a sheep or, more accurately, a shepherd.

"Any time now," he said confidently, "they should produce another sketch or make some kind of signal that they understand and are—"

"They have," said Patricia, pointing to the other display.

On the half of the world that was in darkness there was a tiny brilliant circle of lights which burned